I.D. RUSSELL

Rock 'N' Roll Nightmare: River City Hell Book 1

First published by Ringo Jones Productions 2023

Copyright © 2023 by I.D. Russell

All rights reserved. No part of this publication may be reproduced, stored or transmitted in any form or by any means, electronic, mechanical, photocopying, recording, scanning, or otherwise without written permission from the publisher. It is illegal to copy this book, post it to a website, or distribute it by any other means without permission.

This novel is entirely a work of fiction. The names, characters and incidents portrayed in it are the work of the author's imagination. Any resemblance to actual persons, living or dead, events or localities is entirely coincidental.

First edition

ISBN: 978-1-988383-32-3

This book was professionally typeset on Reedsy. Find out more at reedsy.com

PROLOGUE

He turned the greyish pink piece of brain over in his gloved hand, admiring the intricate patterns cut in cross section.

"Strange that this is the source of all that we know of ourselves, is it not?"

"Indeed, sir," the man in the lab coat said.

They stood leaning over a prone body laying on a stainless-steel operating table.

"And how little the potential of this crucial part is truly understood."

The scientist looked at him with eager anticipation. The body, with its cavernous skull cavity delicately carved and open to the air, was waiting for that piece of grey matter.

"And you're sure this will work?" he said to the waiting man in the lab coat.

"Not sure. Hopeful."

He shot the man a glare that would have put the fear of God in anyone. He didn't like to hear answers like that.

"You've poured over the late doctor's research?"

"Absolutely. And that of the others that you brought to me."

"Then what is the concern?"

"The concern is that this is a realm of what used to be termed pseudoscience. I was not even aware that these theories existed until recently, let alone that they were so advanced as to allow for–"

"Spare me, doctor. You were hired for your surgical skill, not your previous beliefs. I just need to know if you are fully prepared to follow through on what we're attempting here."

"Of course I am. I'm as desperate to find out if this is possible as you are. Why, just think of the possibilities! What this could mean for the world of medicine and–"

"I don't care what it could mean for anyone else, doctor, I care about what it will mean for me and those that I work for."

"Yes, of course. I understand."

"I wonder sometimes."

The lights in the immaculately clean lab had been dimmed. A lone floodlight over the operating table was all that lit up the space. Every machine and tool was here. Every precaution had been taken. There was the best team that money could buy working with all of their energy to perfect this process, and yet so much could go wrong. They could be left with just another corpse, as with all the previous times.

"I promise you, we've done all we can. If you'll just hand over the brain wedge, I can–"

"Here," he said, handing the soft mound to the eager doctor, not letting him finish.

"Thank you, sir. I assure you that I want this to work as much as you do."

"Let's hope so."

The doctor moved to the open skulled body and began his work. He called out for surgical tools. His delicate hands worked with precision. The man was focused, as he should be.

"If this works, sir–" the doctor's assistant said.

"When this works," the doctor corrected him.

As the men worked, he turned to face the wall of brains in jars, each one ready to be unleashed, each one offering so much potential. But all things must begin somewhere.

He turned back to eagerly watch the team, waiting for the moment when they could pull the switch and find out if what the research said was true. If not, they would simply try again.

It was only a matter of time before it worked.

CHAPTER ONE

"Ladies and gentlemen, this year's graduating class!"
Pomp and Circumstance blared over the speakers as lights flashed all around her. Happy parents snapped away behind cameras and phones. Their faces beamed with Cheshire smiles, knowing they had at least managed to not screw up their kids enough to turn them into dropouts. Hands waved, names were shouted, miniature starbursts erupted all around her. A sea of intermittently blinking red lights, the telltale sign of everything being recorded for posterity, stretched from a hundred different angles. It was all too much, leaving her disoriented and confused. She focused on the person in front of her leading the procession of blue-clad graduates.

"Ashley Aaronson!" Principal Pascal called out over the microphone.

She knew where she was going.

"Samantha Abraham!"

She ascended the steps to polite applause. She approached the smiling little man and took the diploma as he handed it to her.

"Congratulations, Samantha," he said. He gently turned her to face the event photographer, who snapped away a picture that would hang on her parents' wall until the end of time.

Then it was back down the stairs, following Ashley Aaronson to the designated seating area, three hundred and sixty chairs at the front of the massive super church that John A. MacDonald High had rented for the occasion.

She almost didn't come. Empty ceremony was of no interest to her. She wanted to stay at home in her room with something dark and industrial pounding in her ears, but her parents would have none of that. She was dolled up, tossed into her grad gown, and had her dark hair brushed over the birthmark above her left eye. She was dumped in line with the rest of this year's exhausted eighteen-year-olds about to take that first big step into the real world.

She didn't pay any attention to the others getting their degrees. She didn't look up when hockey star Rick Hansen was called and didn't budge when valedictorian Debbie Peterson strode forward in her high heels to the thunderous applause of an admiring crowd. Bruce, Eddie, Vicky, Nan, none of their names could shake her.

She could have stewed in her own world the entire day. She was prepared for that, but then they threw her a curve ball; a memorial service for students lost during the year with honorary degrees given to their parents. Duckie/Trevor and Joshua. Duckie's mom wore black, taking the framed diploma from a sympathetic looking Principal Pascal. The hockey team coach Mr. Lepine, who'd been Joshua's guardian, did the same in his honour. A few words of remembrance were spoken and all eyes dropped in prayer. She should have been steel. She should have been able to disassociate herself from these emotions, but something inside broke. Her best friend, her boyfriend, everything she had known, gone forever.

She remembered Duckie's last words to her, "Sam, I'm sorry. All I ever did was love you…" as he died in her arms from a gunshot wound. A last minute rescue by the police had saved her from his twisted plot to turn her into a golem. "I just… lost control," he'd said, pleading with her for her forgiveness. She'd granted him that peace, but it had come at the end of a life never realized.

The tears came pouring out, ruining her mascara. Her body was wracked with sobs. Ashley Aaronson patted her on the back kindly, but there was nothing she could offer to soothe this ache.

Then there was Joshua, the strongest man she'd ever known. He'd been a confidant, a star hockey player, a fighter, a protector and a lover. He'd been so many things despite the fact that he was a golem, a lab-created monster controlled by a mysterious gemstone called a heartstone. He was supposed to be nothing more than a mindless slave, but somehow, someway, she'd helped awaken him to so much more. After all they'd gone through fighting to free him from the control of his creator, the Professor, then from the machinations of Markham and the Necromancers guild, it hadn't been enough. The process that had created him had a short lifecycle and he'd begun to deteriorate. The pain had been too much and he'd begged her to end his suffering as his body disintegrated. The only way out for him was to free his trapped soul from its ruby prison. She'd shattered the stone, broken the spell and ended his life. He'd withered away to his component parts, leaving her alone.

People were looking at her now; Duckie's mom on stage, Mr. Lepine, the principal. Ashley embraced her. It didn't help, nothing could.

CHAPTER ONE

The whole service was a blur. There were speeches from teachers and principal Pascal, a lot of empty promises about hope for the future. Becky Vanton sang her own composition called "Falling into the Future." She clearly mistook the event for *Canada's Got Talent*. Students read poems, the brass band played their final song together. The yearbook committee presented a slide show of the year's events. It was enough to make her sick, knowing how little all these people knew of what actually went on out there, stuck in their safe and secure world. John A. MacDonald High, River City, both were a world away from the real horrors of this sick planet.

When it was all over, they mingled in the lobby, sampled dainties from catered trays, posed for photos with friends. Not Sam.

High school had been hell for Samantha Abraham. There were no happy endings for her at John A. MacDonald High, only painful memories and broken dreams. Perpetually an outcast, Sam had ended her school career the same way she'd started.

Duckie's mom approached her, looking shell-shocked in the middle of the crowd of smiling parents and happy grads. "Samantha," she said, "how are you holding up?"

"I'm OK," Sam replied.

"It was a lovely service. I think Trevor would have enjoyed it."

"I think so, too."

They tiptoed around the truth, neither one wanting to bring up the fact that Duckie had been shot by the police. He'd been found with dead bodies, stolen goods and chemicals living in the house of a teacher from St. Mark's private school who'd mysteriously gone missing months before. The story was too crazy to make sense and Duckie would forever be remembered as a "troubled teen" who'd met a sad end.

That's what they called her now, too. "Troubled." She'd seen so much death during the past three years at John A. MacDonald High, been hurt by and hurt so many that she wasn't the same Samantha Abraham anymore. The simple things that she used to find joy in left her feeling empty. Her mousy demeanour had disappeared. There would be no more insults hurled by the cool kids, no more harassment by the popular girls. Her hands had tasted the blood of golems. There was nothing that anyone could say or do to her that would put things back the way they were. She was stunned by her own emotional numbness.

Her reputation spread through the school like wildfire in those final few months. A ring of death surrounded her in hushed whispers as she walked down the halls, scaring away the masses, leaving her in her own company.

"Are you going to prom?" Duckie's mom asked.

There were no suitors lining up to take her just like how she'd had no admirers asking her out on Saturday nights. No anonymous text messages or notes sent asking if she liked so and so. She was a social pariah. Had life turned out differently, she could have gone to grad with Rick. They almost seemed destined to be together after all that had gone on these past three years, but destiny has a sick sense of humour and Rick a fragile ego. It only took Sam ditching him twice for Joshua to finally crush whatever love he held in his heart for her.

There was no sense in apologizing, she could only say so many words of regret over what she had done in a misguided love of her own. Eventually, she had given up and watched him drift away to his hockey team buddies and out of her life again.

Rick was across the lobby, laughing, posing for pictures with Chuck, Bruce, all the rest.

"Maybe," Sam said to Duckie's mom, but she had no intention of putting herself through all that.

Duckie's mom patted Sam on the arm, then decided instead to lean in and hug her tightly. The smell of shampoo and tears was thick on her. "You take care of yourself, Sam. Trevor would've wanted that."

"I will."

She watched Duckie's mom weave her way through the crowd and walk out into the parking lot, putting the event and all the horrible memories behind her. That's what Sam had wanted to do, too. She'd tried to stay in the shadows, out of the public eye as best she could. She'd suffered through those final few months of school stoically. She'd planned on going to a university out of province to start fresh, away from all the pain, but she'd been in for a rude awakening at the end of the year when her final grades came through. Apparently, devoting all your waking thoughts to the golem love of your life did hell to your GPA. Once a straight A student, Sam dropped smack dab into the middle of the pack; big fat C's across the board. For some, this was fine, an average mark and an average life, but Sam always expected more. She'd been saving up her money for years, dreamed of a real Ivy League big city education, but her fantasies of a cosmopolitan coming of age were dashed by her River City, bush league life.

Love will do that to you.

She was stuck going to River City University after all the real schools rejected her in letters barely containing their thinly veiled disdain. It was enough to break someone's spirit, but

Sam had survived worse. From the twisted necromancer's guild convention where'd they'd tried to dissect Joshua, to Debbie and her friends trying to destroy her chances at having a relationship with the man before he died. She'd had to deal with assassins trying to kill the rogue golem who'd broken free from his creator, and even the subtle sway of the ruby's whispering control, pushing her and anyone who held it to darker thoughts. If she could get through all of that, then she could soldier on through this setback, go to River City U, get her degree and then get the hell out of this city.

She found her parents in the mass of people, left the mega church for the safety of home. With the ceremony over, Sam had assumed that she could get back to being alone and depressed in her room, but her mother had other ideas.

"You're going to prom, Sam, there's no discussion," she yelled at her from behind her locked door over the blaring tunes.

"You'll regret it later if you miss it, trust me." Her dad tried to sound positive.

She heard them arguing downstairs, didn't care enough to try to make out what they were saying.

"Sam, just let your mother in and she'll help you get ready – this isn't something you can just get out of."

She sighed, unlocking the door, knowing they wouldn't give up, resigning herself to the suffering the night would bring. She had already been through so much, what was one more night of hell?

Her mother unleashed every trick in her former beauty queen bag to turn Sam from blackened zombie into prim, puckered, and cheery prom princess. It was all just a pretty candy shell on top of dark chocolate. The Sam she saw in the mirror was not how she felt inside. Her curled hair, her perfect make-up, long eyelashes, painted nails, pale blue dress; none of it was the truth. Who knew how long her mother had waited to do her up like this? What faded dreams of her own was she was trying to live through? It was as amazing a paint job as Sam had ever thought possible.

"Look at you," her mother said, beaming. "There's the beautiful Sam we all know. See how much better you feel when you get out of all that black?"

Sam just frowned.

"You should smile, let the world see how great you can look." She stood behind her, looking in the mirror above her dresser, admiring her daughter. "You've got a lot going for you, Sam, great smile, great hair, great figure. Any guy would be lucky to go to the dance with you."

"Even for those superficial reasons no one asked me, Mom," she spat back.

It didn't even register. "Let the others lock their dance partners in for the whole night, you can pick and choose. Play the field, find the handsomest guy for every song."

There was no point in arguing. She let herself be swept up in her mother's enthusiasm and the next thing she knew, she was standing in a hotel ballroom surrounded by her classmates dressed in suits and frilly dresses as blaring top forty pop music shattered her eardrums. A bartender served drinks as long as you had an over-eighteen wristband, there was a table of appetizers, some casino games in a room adjacent to the main hall. The place reeked of sweat and perfume, cologne and beer, nerves and pent-up sexual energy. Everyone seemed to be having a good time, but she wasn't feeling it. There was some kind of bubble around her that pushed everyone away three feet at all times. Nervous glances and shuffled feet followed her to the bar, to the food, and to the poker table.

It was agony; long and drawn out. Each slow song left her a wallflower in the dark, watching as the dolled up teens fumbled through sloppy make out sessions, hands down low, mouths meeting in the middle. She spotted Rick dancing with Debbie Peterson, the two of them looking like a magazine cover. She wasn't at all surprised when they were voted king and queen of the dance. Sam went home at two am feeling just as miserable and alone as she had felt before coming.

* * *

Now, months later, Sam was going to put everything behind her, shove all the shit from high school into a drawer and start fresh. Wasn't that what university was all about? No more drama, no more captive audiences now that you were with people who wanted to be there and were paying good money to attend. There would be students who came from other places, older boys, men even, girls who cared about more than just make-up and pretty shoes. This would be as close to a metropolitan world as she was going to get in River City.

The summer had been full of anticipation, signing up for classes, touring the campus, dreaming of a better life. Working in her dad's restaurant passed the time and she could almost feel the cloud of despair lifting.

A new year, a new school, a new her.

She took a crash course in culture to get ready for the big day, to become a whole new Sam. She read the classics, *The Iliad, Gravity's Rainbow, Moby Dick.* She watched the classics, *Citizen Kane, An Affair to Remember, A Face in the Crowd.* She studied

CHAPTER ONE

Monet, listened to Debussy. She wanted to be interesting, to have something to say, to be a completely different person. Then it finally came. She took the bus downtown, held her breath, and stepped out onto the River City University campus and the beginning of her new life.

CHAPTER TWO

"They may have put me out to pasture, but I can still put the boots to crime," Frank said, smiling at the client sitting across from him at the tiny desk in his cramped office above a barber shop.

"Mrs. Winkler said you did good work for her."

The dame at his desk was a real stone cold fox, a classic all the way. She was built how a woman should be, firm and round, an inch and a mile all rolled into one. No toothpick, she was a Rubenesque picture of God's beauty. It didn't matter that she was pushing eighty, Frank could look past that. He could see the way she'd looked after the war in her eyes and loved every bit of it.

"Well," he said, "she had a tough nut to crack, that's for sure. A series of daring nighttime robberies, no clues, no entry marks, nothing. It took every hemisphere of my cop's brain to figure out that one, but I busted the perp."

The grey-haired beauty smiled. "Yes, Velma was ever so happy that you found the squirrel taking her nuts, she was nearly at her wit's end."

"One less felonious furry out flaunting the city's peace."

Mrs. Feldstein nodded, and Frank felt good.

CHAPTER TWO

"You know, ma'am, I'm glad you're here. I was lost when the police force made me retire. They gave me the gold watch and nothing more than a 'thank you for the years of your life dedicated to the preservation of truth, justice, and the Canadian way.'"

"A watch?"

"Yeah, and a 'don't let the door hit you on your way out' cake and coffee party to seal the deal."

"I like cake."

"Me too. But this was a cake of confusion. See, I wandered aimlessly after that, still getting up at the crack of dawn, pounding back a coffee and dragging my ass downtown to the precinct. It took weeks to get that habit out of my system. Weeks more to stop jumping every time I heard the sound of a siren off in the distance."

"I always wonder if those sirens are coming for me," the woman said softly.

Somehow the RCPD had learned Frank's real age. The clerical error he'd shoved through years back had finally been discovered and just like that, his career was over. After a long adjustment, he started to resign himself to the fact that his days as a beat cop were done, that he wasn't wanted anymore; he was just too damn old.

"I was all set to end it all, tie one on so bad that I never woke up, jump into the river with a pair of cement shoes, and put myself out of my misery," he said. "But then it hit me, right smack dab in the side of the head like a block of cheese. I'm not useless, it's the job that is."

"What job was that?"

"I can still fight crime, only now I don't need a punch clock and a chief breathing down my neck to do it. I can be my own brand of justice out here in no man's land. Crime still happens. The city still needs a saviour. It's not content to let fresh-faced protein shake rookies stumble through reams of legislation and civil liberty rights, making sure perps are being treated above board. The city needs someone on the inside, someone with years of experience treating the wounds left by crime. It needs former Detective Inspector Sargent Frank Malone. And by god, it's got him."

The woman looked in awe of him. Or confused. It was hard to tell through the cloudy eyes behind her coke bottle glasses.

"So do you think you can find him for me, detective?" she said hopefully.

"Absolutely, Mrs. Feldstein. If your boy is out there dead or alive, I'll sniff him out."

"Oh, I hope he's not dead," she gasped.

Frank shrugged. "It wouldn't be the first time I've seen it, doll. It's an age-old story. Mother dotes on son, does her best to bring him up right, then suffers when he starts to run with the wrong crowd. He gets into things he shouldn't, goes places the honest fear to tread. Next thing you know, it's drugs and whores, guns and stick ups. If he's lucky, someone like me brings him in and puts him on the right path, if not, some piece of gutter trash out there sticks a shiv in his back and ends it all in some back alley. His lifeblood pouring out, mixing with the urine and beer of the seedier parts of this little piece of hell we call River City."

All the colour in Mrs. Feldstein's face drained out. Her skin went as pale as her hair.

"But don't you worry your pretty little head one bit – old Frank is here to make sure that doesn't happen. I've busted more heads than a salad bar jockey. The jails are full of more of my collars than a Chinese laundromat. Nothing to fear, I'm your man."

He ushered Mrs. Feldstein out of his office and shut the door behind her. He could hear the buzzing of razors from the barber shop beneath him as he admired his little piece of heaven, the Frank Malone Detective Agency. This was how he could stay useful and make a difference in a world that was done with him. This was how he could rage against that dying of the light. The agency was his world and he made the rules.

It was a spartan office, with nothing to distract him from the business at hand. A filing cabinet with write ups of his past cases, a few framed photographs on the wall from his days on the force, and a picture of Al Capone, his inspiration.

"Just like back in your day, eh, Al?"

Looking at that guy's smiling mug everyday reminded him of why he did all this, why he put his neck on the line for the people.

"Look at you. Criminal scum. Living the high life, never getting caught until old Uncle Sam finds a loophole to bust you. Too bad I wasn't born yet, buddy. You wouldn't be smiling so big. Sure, I'd probably be dead by now, but then I wouldn't be looking at your face and wondering what I could have brought you in for, would I?"

Frank had never tolerated people like Capone. He'd dealt with more than a few in his years. He made sure that he'd been the guy to finally bust them. The jails used to be full of their greedy mitts and bitter tears, but at least they were locked away from the public peace. There'd been no tax evasion collars on his watch. He took 'em down for murder one if they swiped a purse.

He sat in his chair and put his hands behind his head, proud.

Frank had only been in business a few months, but it was booming. Word had gotten out that he was a real cleaner, someone you went to when the law couldn't or wouldn't help you. The top drawer of his filing cabinet was starting to fill up nicely with what amounted to a damn decent little resume for a private dick. There was, of course, the Mrs. Winkler snatch and grab, the case of the strange tasting apples in old lady Jones's prized apple pies, the mystery of the disappearing trash cans, Mr. Ulster's missing trailer, and that most heinous of all crimes, the ghost writing on the walls of the Hill's House. Each and every case was marked down with a big green checkmark on the file, solved and done. He was batting a thousand so far and there was no way that Mrs. Feldstein's boy was going to ruin his perfect record.

"OK, kid, I've got your description and I know all your regular haunts. You won't stay missing for long."

Armed with a photo, he would ask around, see if anyone had seen the boy.

"This could get a little rough."

He grabbed his .45. You just never knew these days, packing heat was only prudent. He rose up and slipped on his long coat and hat, admiring himself in the mirror. He certainly cut the image of a real dick, right out of Spillane or Chandler. Maybe he had a few too many wrinkles on his face, maybe his hair was a little thin, white, out of place. Maybe he even had that slight stoop that people got when they hit those big digits. Hell, his bones creaked and cracked when he moved, but those were all just roadblocks, nothing he couldn't blast through with a little will and determination. And Frank Malone was nothing if not wilful and determined, even his kindergarten teacher said that.

CHAPTER TWO

He stuffed the picture of the boy in his pocket and headed downstairs, passing through the barber shop on the way out. He waved to Gino as he did a number two on some oblivious hockey dad.

"Frankie," Gino said affably, "off on another adventure?"

"Damn straight, Gino, missing person, could get ugly."

"You be careful, old man, I don't want to lose my favourite neighbour." Gino was good people; a hard working immigrant making good the old-fashioned way. He was as round as he was tall, balding and hairy.

"It'll take more than this to put the licks on Frank Malone, Gino. I'm all twisted steel and sex appeal."

Gino laughed. "You crazy, Frankie, you crazy. That's why I like you, you know." His great belly jiggled as he talked.

"It's the crazy ones that catch the real bad guys."

Frank was all set to leave, his hand on the door, when he stopped and fished in his pocket for the picture of Mrs. Feldstein's missing boy. He walked over to Gino and his customer, holding it out for them to look at. "Might as well start here. Either of you seen this boy? His mother's real worried that something might have happened. He's been gone for days now."

Gino shook his head as the customer stared wide-eyed. "Sorry, Frankie, can't say as I've seen him. You could try Tommy down at The Grove, he sees a lot of cats come through for a drink now and then."

"Thanks, Gino. What about you, mumbles?" Frank held the picture lower so the man getting the trim could get a better look.

"No, sorry. Haven't seen him."

"Well, alright, but if anything comes up, something you may

have forgotten, anything useful, you give old Frank a call." He handed the man a business card and stuffed the picture back in his pocket. He left the barber shop with a jingle of the doorbell.

Gino laughed a little and went back to cutting his charge's hair.

The man cleared his throat. "Um, Gino, he knows that's a picture of a cat, right?"

Gino just smiled as the clippers worked their magic. "I wonder sometimes, Ronny, I really do."

CHAPTER THREE

"I guess I'm just really looking to write a script about a guy who wants to express himself, but you know, like, he doesn't know how. I mean, he's got so much inside that he just wants to, um, express, like about the world and life and stuff, but he just doesn't know where to start or how to do it, so it'd be about this guy and his life and how he tries to find a way to express all that he wants to… express."

Sam rolled her eyes as the hipster sitting in front of her rambled on in her intro to screenwriting class. He was a walking cliché; tiny little Castro hat, thin moustache that looked painted on, dark green army style jacket over skinny jeans and a red shirt with "LD40" written on it. He was exactly the kind of person she dreaded would be in this class and here he was, in the flesh, telling the world about his million-dollar idea. She dubbed him Francois, purposely forgetting his name after he introduced himself.

Professor Jarrett nodded as the student spoke. "Thank you, Andrew. You seem to have an idea of the conflict in your story, but what are the stakes? A screenplay needs stakes for the character if they can't reach their goals. Like if you don't find the kidnapped girl, she dies, that sort of thing." Professor

Jarrett was a local filmmaker teaching the course, someone with real world experience rather than academic credentials. She was a mousy brunette with large circular glasses and a nasal voice who told them all that she valued class interaction more than textbooks. Too bad she hadn't said that before Sam had bought the $199.99 book.

"So, stakes? Anyone think of stakes for Andrew's idea here? The man who can't express himself."

The room full of wannabe Barton Finks stayed quiet. Sam raised her hand. "How about the guy works for a mad doctor who operates on the homeless and he's next, so if he doesn't express himself to the cops soon, he'll be a zombie?"

Professor Jarrett pointed excitedly at Sam. "I think there's a lot of drama in that scenario. What do you think, Andrew?"

"No... I think... um, I meant more like this guy wants to talk about his feelings more, not that he's a zombie or something."

"OK, well, we'll work on that," Jarrett said. "Who's next?" She scanned the room, settling on Sam. "How about you, Samantha, what's your screenplay idea?"

Sam drew a blank, so she just repeated a quote she'd heard once. "A film like a battleground. Love, hate, action, violence, death, in one word, emotion."

The teacher nodded enthusiastically. "Nice, I like that."

I must have gotten through.

Professor Jarret moved on. "Kyle? What's your idea?"

"Uhhh. Maybe like Pulp Fiction meets Reservoir Dogs."

"Tarantino meets Tarantino?"

"Sure! The best of both worlds!"

The bell rang on Professor Jarrett's phone. "Oh, that's all for today, class. Everyone work on your idea and come back next class with a through-line."

CHAPTER THREE

Sam gathered up her things amidst the clamour of everyone else doing the same. She heard a little cough from her right. Francois was staring at her.

"Yeah?" she asked.

"What's the greatest zombie movie of all time?"

He stared at her, unblinking, waiting.

"Uh, what do you mean?"

"You seem really into zombies. So I was just wondering what you think the best one is."

"I don't know, Dawn of the Dead?"

"Remake or original?"

"Does it really matter?"

She headed to the door, not waiting for his answer.

"Hey, wait!" He followed her out into the busy hallway. "Do you want to bounce ideas off each other? For the screenplays, I mean."

She stopped and looked at the timid guy, who was so pale she wondered if he even knew there was a sun and instantly pictured how exciting that conversation would be.

"Sorry, I've got a lot of coursework and I don't really have time."

"Oh…"

"But think about the zombie and the doctor idea, OK?"

"I—"

She didn't let him finish, leaving him at the door as she moved through the crowds in the hallway of the C building of River City U.

It was looking like this was going to be a crazy term. She'd signed up for a wide variety of classes, hoping that something would pique her interest and call to her as a major. But after a week of course outlines and reading lists, she was no closer to figuring out her path than she was in high school.

You wanted this, Sam. It's only been a week.

At least living at home, she didn't have to worry about how much money she was wasting trying to divine what the heck she was going to do with her life. This term, she had English, screenwriting, biology, intro to calculus, and computer science. Next term had philosophy, physics, history, and theatre classes lined up. That felt like she'd covered all bases when she picked them. There had to be something that she would click with.

Her stomach rumbled. It was noon and she hadn't had time to eat more than a banana for breakfast. She joined the march of students towards the cafeteria.

So far, River City University wasn't at all what she was expecting. It was way busier than John A. MacDonald High. There were people of all ages. The guys had beards, the girls dressed like hippies. The floors were carpeted instead of linoleum covered. The walls were plastered with posters advertising seminars, movies, panels, clubs, bands, and protest marches. There were people everywhere. No matter what building she was in, there were throngs of students milling about at all times.

A sign above pointed to the A building; the main building on campus where the cafeteria and bookstore met. It was the Grand Central of the entire place, with wall-to-wall bodies. She practically needed a bulldozer to make her way through, but at least she could be anonymous here.

Lunch time.

She stood in line for the hot foods behind two girls with dreadlocks.

"You going to the battle of the bands at the Burt?" one asked the other.

"Who's playing?"

"Who cares? There's bound to be someone hot in at least one of the groups."

"Geez-us," the other said. "What is it with you and guys in bands?"

Sam lost the rest of their conversation when it was her time to order.

"What'll it be?" the bored looking server asked.

"Uh, fries, I guess," she said, looking at the menu that seemed to consist of the same kinds of things John A. MacDonald High served, only double the price.

A plate of dark brown French fries was slid onto her tray.

She went to the cashier and paid. She tried to find a place to sit in the cafeteria, but it looked futile. Cliques of people already took up all the tables, talking amongst themselves, smiling and laughing in their happy group dynamics.

Is there seriously nowhere to sit in here?

Her plate of steaming French fries was getting cold. There were no waves, no invitations to join a table and make new friends, no welcoming smiles, nothing but a general lack of interest in the lost looking girl and her deep-fried food. She *was* anonymous.

Fuck it. There's no rule that says I have to eat in here.

Sam carried her plate out into the hall, descending a flight of stairs to the quiet study area in the basement. There didn't seem to be too many people here – maybe it was some kind of secret. It was a large square room surrounding a central column area of offices. The signs on the doors were of the various student run clubs and groups: the model UN, the LGBT alliance, the women's centre, the communist union, the anime club. Large futons were spaced out along the walls with small tables and comfortable looking chairs opposite them. She guessed this was supposed to be a secluded place to read or study, a place to get away from the hustle and bustle of the campus above. The noise from upstairs was muffled down here. She didn't see why this couldn't be her own personal lunch room.

There were a few small groups of people already down here, but mostly it was a room of empty seats. Sam took one in the centre, a soft plushy futon couch, the cushion a candy-striped pink and white. She set her bag down and put her feet up to eat her lukewarm fries in peace.

Voices from the group closest to her carried. "No, I'm telling you, there were four Doinks in the WWF, Matt Borne, Steve Keirn, Steve Lombardi, and Ray Apollo, although Steve Keirn only really did one appearance outside of a few house shows."

"Dude, the fact that you know that is scary... scary and sad."

"It is not!"

She looked over as she ate, curious. It was a group of four clearly long-term friends, two guys and two girls. The girls were both good looking, dressed to the nines, sporting long, dark hair, one curly, the other straightened. The one with the curly hair had a slightly pronounced nose and round eyes, while the other had large, full lips and thick eyebrows. The guys were polar opposites, one heavyset sporting a vintage Monday Night RAW shirt, the other trim and chiseled, with short, cropped blond hair, blue eyes, and a large smile that seemed to span his entire face. He was giving the larger guy a hard time.

"If you only devoted half the time you spend memorizing useless pro-wrestling trivia on girls instead, you'd be a real player!"

The heavy guy reacted as if he was offended. "If I only devoted half as much time memorizing useless pro-wrestling trivia, I wouldn't know half as much useless pro-wrestling trivia."

The girl with the straight hair scoffed, her voice an octave higher than everyone else's. "Can we have one lunch without you two talking about wrestling, please?"

"Erin's right, can't we talk about something else?"

"I don't know. Marlon? Can we talk about something else?" the blond guy asked the heavy one.

"Let me think on that one, Everett…" He held his hand up to his chin comically and made a loud "hmm" sound. "No, sir, I don't think so."

The two of them laughed conspiratorially.

The curly-haired girl noticed Sam sitting nearby alone and smiled at her. "Hey, do you know anything else to talk about besides WWF wrestling?"

"It's WWE now, Avital," Marlon said, rolling his eyes.

"Whatever, man, let me talk to the new girl for a second. Sorry about them," she said. "They love to talk about oiled up men in their underwear pretending to fight. We don't. You want to join us?"

Sam was taken aback and nearly inhaled a fry. She coughed. This had never happened before. She was being invited to join a circle of friends, seemingly on a whim. She didn't know what to say. "Sure," she croaked out, grabbing her bag and standing up. As she stood, she dumped the rest of her plate of fries all over the floor. *Oh, shit.* Now she'd done it, total social death.

"Yeah, I wouldn't eat those either," Everett said, laughing.

"Ahh, man, I would've," Marlon said, disappointed.

"Ten second rule." Everett reached for the nearest fry on the floor and popped it into his mouth.

The girls laughed, putting Sam at ease. "Yeah, I was done anyway, that's how I roll." She took her bag over to where they were sitting and sat down in between Avital and Everett. "I'm Samantha, but everyone calls me Sam."

"Hey, Sam, I'm Avital, that's Erin, that's Everett, and that's Marlon." The curly-haired Avital pointed out each of them in turn, confirming their names to Sam's assumptions.

"Hey." She waved.

"You can call us the Hue Crew," Erin nearly shouted.

"Hue Crew?"

"Hebrew United Education. It's where we all went to school. And before you ask, yes, we're all Jews."

Sam blanched – was this some kind of joke? A test? Her confusion and fear must have been written on her face for all to see.

"No, seriously," Marlon reassured her. "That's what we call ourselves. Hue Crew because we're all Jews from Hebrew United."

"Where'd you go, Sam?"

"Wait, so that's not a bad word to use?" Sam asked timidly.

"What?"

"Uh…"

"Hebrew? No, it's a language."

"She means Jew, Marlon," Avital said.

"Oh."

"Yeah. Isn't it? I've never been sure about that one," Sam said.

"Nah." Everett shook his head. "Of course not, it's just

CHAPTER THREE

shorthand. Instead of saying Jewish, like when people say ELO instead of Electric Light Orchestra."

"ELO? What is this, 1979?" Sam said sarcastically.

"Oh, burn. New girl shoots down Everett's disco fetish," Avital said.

"ELO are not disco, they're prog rock, like Rush or Emerson, Lake and Palmer."

"Or Tangerine Dream?" Sam asked.

Everett's eyes grew three sizes. "Whoa, I'm impressed. New girl knows her stuff."

Sam shrugged. "My dad has a lot of old LPs kicking around."

"So, you a first year-er like us?" Erin shouted, her voice seemingly just operating on a higher decibel level than the rest of them.

"Yup, I tried to find a place to sit upstairs, but man, it's a zoo in there."

"Yeah, I know what you mean," Marlon said, as he picked up the rest of the fries on the floor and piled them on Sam's discarded plate. "I had to eat all my food standing up while I waited for these guys to order."

"Oh, come on, F-O, you're always done before we order."

Everyone laughed, but Sam was confused again. "F-O? What's that mean?"

"Oh, right, duh us," Avital said, rolling her eyes. "You don't know the accros. Like he's F-O" – she pointed to Marlon – "for fat one. Erin is L-O for loud one."

"Avital is H-O for hot one, and Everett is S-O for slutty one."

Sam smelled something fishy. "And you guys came up with those names yourselves?"

"Heck, no," Everett said. "Everyone at Hue had one. It was like a badge of honour. If you're gonna hang with us, you should have one, too."

"Yeah, totally," Avital said. "Hmm, let's see. I guess the first thing we need to do is figure out what your deal is. How about you be D-O for dark one?" Avital said.

"Dark one?"

"You know, cos you're all in black. Seems to fit."

"I don't know," Erin said. "Isn't D-O some kind of singer or something?"

"Yeah, heavy metal," Everett said.

"I've never heard of him," Avital said.

"Everyone has," Marlon said. "He's the guy who invented the devil horns thing at concerts."

"You heard of this D-O guy Sam?" Avital asked.

"I've had the occasion to play some his stuff in Rock Band. Back in high school."

"Okay fine, D-O is out, how about M-O?" Avital offered. "You know, for mysterious one, cos we don't know much about her yet."

"That doesn't work," Erin replied. "M-O means modus operendi, that's already a thing."

"Shit, you're right."

"How about we hold off giving her a nickname until we know more about her?" Everett said calmly. "Instead of rushing in and putting something on that doesn't fit, you know?"

"Good idea."

"Then it's settled: Sam must show us her inner self before she gets a nickname."

"Fine by me," Sam said.

And just like that, Sam had friends. Maybe this whole university thing would pay off after all.

CHAPTER FOUR

The music blared in her ears. A pounding bass beat, repeating keyboard section and an auto-tuned voice robotically singing about love and dancing. It was all noise to her, but the club was hopping. Everyone was dancing and having a good time.

"What a great song!" Avital shouted, barely audible over the music.

"It's totally, uh, great!"

"I don't see him?" Avital shouted back.

Sam didn't bother repeating herself. She just kept moving her head to the music.

You're out, Sam, really out. Look at all these people doing normal things. And you're right in the middle of it.

How had this all happened? Her new friends had spontaneously invited her to go clubbing with them and here she was, a part of it all. It was a whole new world; line ups outside, coat check, handing over of ID, and finally entry into a crazy world of hedonism and alcohol. Everyone had a beer bottle or precariously titled cocktail in their hands, as far as the eye could see. It was a maelstrom of guys and girls of all shapes and sizes, every one dolled up like a magazine cover. She felt massively overdressed in her black button up shirt and black pants, the only skin showing on her arms.

Avital darted away from them to the dance floor. In a flash she was grinding up against a dark-haired stud in a tight sweater. Everett was tongue deep in something blonde in the seat next to her while Marlon nursed a coke, looking completely uncomfortable. Erin bounced with nervous energy as she sipped something purple.

"I love this song," she shouted.

"That's what Avital said, too," Sam shouted back.

"She's over there," Erin said, pointing to Avital on the dance floor.

"Yeah, I know!"

"I'm not done with this one yet," Erin said, holding up her half-empty cocktail. In a flash, she sucked the rest up and grinned at Sam. "Now we can get another drink!"

She pulled her by the arm towards the bar. They moved through the crowd, brushing up against strangers as they weaved their way to the huge circular centre of the far wall. A swelling throng crushed up against the wood, fighting for one of the six bartenders' attention.

Sam soaked it all in, still trying to process what was going on.

Seriously, how did you get here?

How did Samantha Abraham, who'd spent most Friday nights at home alone with a William Gibson novel, end up surrounded by party-goers smelling of hormones, sweat, and spilled beer? A week ago, she would have never seen this coming, but lo and behold, here she was.

It had all started so innocently, an invite out on Friday night, pre-gaming at Avital's place while the girls did each other's hair and make up before the boys picked them up. She'd rung the doorbell to Avital's parents' house, a massive modern brick mansion on Park Avenue. Her dad was an orthodontist and obviously loaded. The place even smelled like money, making her feel poor just by walking up the driveway. Erin was already there, the two of them squealing with glee when they opened the door.

"This is gonna be so awesome, Sam!" Avital shouted.

"We're gonna make you look so hot!"

"Um, thanks?"

They never once denigrated her wardrobe, hair, or make-up. They were already one up on every girl from John A. MacDonald High School.

Sam was led inside on a quick tour of how the upper class of River City lived; modern art on the walls, leather furniture, white carpeting, dark tiles, chandeliers, and wine glasses behind glass doors. There was an air of 'don't touch anything' in the place.

"My room is in the basement," Avital had said.

A twisting staircase led them downstairs. Whereas Sam had primarily known either unfinished basements, or wood panelled anachronisms that had escaped from the 1970s, Avital lived in the lap of luxury. Her basement was a massive open space of beige plush carpeting, mahogany wood walls, and a flat screen TV bigger than anything Sam had seen outside of a Jumbo-tron. There was a huge stone bar with a completely stocked cabinet fronting a mirrored back wall next to blinking neon art prints.

"What do you think?"

"Screw going out, this place is awesome."

"Pre-drink?"

Avital had taken a bottle of Red Sour Puss from the shelf and lined up three shot glasses on the marble-topped bar. She deftly poured each one and raised hers up in the air. "Party time!"

Erin grabbed hers. "All night!"

Sam took the remaining glass and raised it up to join them. "Every night?" she said hesitatingly.

"Right on!" the girls cheered and downed the drinks.

The shot was warm and most definitely sour, instantly coating her stomach in a fuzzy feeling. Before she had even processed the taste, another was poured and downed, then another.

"Alright, let's get ready!"

Sam was ushered into Avital's room, a huge bedroom just off the main basement sitting area. It was a mess of expensive looking clothes strewn about the floor and piles and piles of make-up on a huge dark wooden dresser. The bed was at least a king, with dark red satin sheets in a rumpled pile at the foot. A couple of ratty looking old stuffed animals sat next to two huge pillows. The closet was stacked with shoe boxes, threatening to spill out of the confined area, with more outfits hanging from a rack just above. Sam had never seen so many clothes outside of the Gap.

"OK, so I'll do Sam's make-up and Erin, you do mine. Then Sam can do yours!" Avital had been nearly beside herself with glee.

"I'd better not," Sam said hesitatingly. "I'm no good at that stuff."

"It's not hard," Avital said. "We'll teach you!"

She was put onto a bar stool in front of the large mirror in the bathroom that attached to both Avital's room and the main sitting room.

"I've giving you the full Hollywood treatment."

The girl knew her way around mascara and lipstick, that's for sure. By the time she was finished, Sam was a work of painted art. She almost didn't recognize herself: her eyes highlighted, her lips full and red.

"So?"

"I'm impressed."

"You could totally be on the cover of Vogue."

"Your turn!" Erin said to Avital.

She went to work on Avital and the results were equally as stunning, but when working on someone as naturally pretty as Avital, it didn't take much. Her curly hair framed her face perfectly, the dark blue, glittering eyeliner minimized her slightly prominent nose and her tanned skin only needed the smallest of touch ups to look perfectly smooth and chiseled from marble.

"OK, Sam, your go," Erin said, taking the seat as Avital got up.

Sam froze.

"It's not that hard," Avital said. "Here, use this on the eyes." She handed Sam a dark eye pen and Erin closed her eyes, smiling in anticipation.

"Alright, but I'm not responsible for what comes out of this." Sam called on any latent drawing skills she may have had and carefully traced around Erin's eyes, darkening lines around them.

"Now this."

Avital then handed her a brush and Sam painted faint pink on the eyelids.

"I'm still not convinced you want me doing your face."

"I'm sure you're doing fine," Erin said.

Erin seemed completely at ease and trusting of what Sam was doing and for that, at least, she was grateful. A few pats, powders, and pencils later and the ordeal was over. Sam took a step back to judge her handiwork, sure that it would all look terrible, but to her surprise, it had somehow come together; Erin looked fine.

"See, it's just that simple!" Avital said, clapping her hands.

They all looked at themselves in the mirror.

"Check out these three hot young girls dolled up like movie stars," Avital said. "Ready to party and get drunk."

"Clothes time!"

Avital and Erin ran to the closet to go over outfits. Sam sat on the bed as they tossed off their shirts and tried on endless combinations of tops and skirts, settling on their favourites, pulling them on over dark bras.

"You want to try something, Sam?" Avital asked.

"I'm good," she said. "Besides, I'm not so sure that anything of yours would fit."

"Of course they will. If anything, they'll just accentuate your boobs. You're packing more than me upstairs, so you'll have some really awesome cleavage."

"Thanks, but I'm not feeling the massive cleavage look today."

"Suit yourself." Avital checked her watch. "The boys won't be here for a few more minutes, so you know what that means."

"More shots," Erin shouted.

There were at least three more rounds of Sour Puss before Everett rang the doorbell and they all piled into his dark green Elantra with Marlon in the front seat. Kraftwerk blared on the stereo and Sam found herself bopping to the beat as they

CHAPTER FOUR

drove downtown.

"Where're we going?" she asked.

"Only the hottest place in town," Everett said.

"Look at that line," Erin said.

Sam stared out the window at the people standing patiently behind velvet ropes, waiting for their chance to go in. They circled around the club and drove down side streets until they found a good parking spot.

She was feeling pretty great as they walked in the brisk fall night air to the massive downtown dance club. The bright neon sign out front told her it was called Mystique, and it was built in the old remains of a massive turn of the century bank. The line moved briskly and the next thing she knew, they were inside and drinking. The music sucked away any concept of time.

"Ohhhh, this is my jam, let's go!" Erin grabbed her arm, jerking her out of her thoughts. She pulled her to the dance floor. They squeezed in between bodies, working their way to the middle, right under the flashing lights in the centre of the maelstrom.

Erin started swaying, her arms moving up and down as she turned her head, hair flying back and forth. Sam wasn't a dancer; she had no real idea what she should be doing, but somehow that didn't matter right now – something inside her told her inhibitions to shove off and she just let go. She jumped and swayed to the beat and felt her spirits rising. She bumped up into a blond guy in a button-up shirt and mouthed an apology. He reached out with both hands with an inviting look on his face.

What the heck, why not? Sam thought.

She took his hands, and he pulled her in close, his hands

falling to her hips, moving along with the music. She nearly jumped as he clamped down centimetres from her butt. They were soon so close that she could smell his body spray and the breath mints he was chewing on. They touched foreheads briefly, moving in unison.

Song after song passed and they were stuck together like glue.

What are you doing? Oh, who cares.

Maybe it was some energy in the air, or maybe it was the alcohol in her stomach, but she was really feeling a pull from him, as if she was being reeled in on some kind of invisible wire. Erin brought her a drink, but she was lost in this unnamed blond guy's dark eyes and open collar.

The next thing she knew, he was pulling her by the hand towards the door. What was going on? Where were they going? She wasn't about to leave with this guy, she wasn't that kind of girl.

They were in the small parking lot behind the club, moving to a shiny black car parked in between a couple of beaters. The door was open, she was in the passenger seat. His lips were on hers and her hands were on him. He had muscles underneath that button-up shirt, hard and packed from trips to the gym. He tasted of peppermint and beer. Their tongues engaged in a session of wrestling in their mouths.

No one said anything, there was no need, their bodies were doing all the talking. He pulled her hand down to his waist. She felt something warm and smooth. She looked down as they kissed and saw that his pants were open and he had pulled out his manhood. She recoiled at first, but he pulled her hand back and she found herself exploring the flagpole quickly rising to full mast. He shuddered as she moved up and down, caressing with her fingers.

What are you doing? This isn't you. You don't do these kinds of things with people you don't even know.

But her hand moved faster and faster. He stopped kissing her and bit his lip. Something warm and sticky poured out on her fingers. He still hadn't said a word. When the spasms stopped, he kissed her again and moved to close up his pants. She didn't know what to do, her hands were covered in slime.

He opened the door and got out.

"Hey, where are–"

He shut the door.

She couldn't stay in the car alone, so she followed him out. She held her dirty hand aloft as she tried to figure out what to do with it.

He didn't even look back at her, just headed inside the club.

What the fuck? She moved to catch up, stopping at the doorway.

You can't go inside like this.

She looked around the parking lot, spotting a clump of weeds next to the building. She bolted over and wiped the warm and sticky remnants of their meeting off on the unsuspecting greenery. She got her hand as clean as she could get as another couple exited the building and moved to one of the cars.

"Which one's yours?" the girl asked.

"The Volvo," the guy replied.

"I've never been in an Italian car before."

They ducked inside, shutting the door, disappearing behind tinted windows.

"Is this some kind of hookup spot?" Sam said to herself.

The blond was gone. He'd led her out here and just…

"What a prick."

She was angry. She felt used. Her buzz was wearing off. Her friends were still inside. She gathered up her dignity and rejoined the party.

CHAPTER FIVE

"You did what?"

"Yeah, in what I'm hoping was his car."

Erin looked impressed. "Just like that? I didn't have you pegged for a party girl."

Sam shrugged. "I don't know, it just sort of happened. I've never done anything like that before."

"Was it consensual?"

"I guess? I don't remember him asking, just sort of taking it out."

"But did you actually want him to do that?"

"I was too shocked," Sam said. "It was just there and then… well, yeah."

It was late. They walked back to the car on quiet streets. The sounds of shouting drunks serenaded them as they looked for the Elantra. They'd partied all the way until close.

"What a night, eh, crew?" Avital said.

"How many guys did you give your number to?" Erin asked.

Avital had stormed through a progression of different dance partners, laughing off advances from all of them.

"Zero. What about you two? You spent most of the night dancing with each other."

"Hey," Sam said. "I was doing my best to avoid contact with any other dick wavers, OK? I wanted to put the car incident out of my mind."

"Shots do the trick better than anything," Avital said.

"Yeah, that's why it's the end of the night and I'm back on a massive high."

They found the car. Marlon helped Everett into the front seat. Lipstick was smeared all over his neck. "At least we know you had fun," Marlon said, grumbling with the drunk.

"Party!" he slurred.

Everyone crammed inside.

"Where am I driving exactly?" Marlon asked.

"I don't want to go home yet," Avital said.

"Sounds like food is in order," Erin added.

"There's an all-night diner down on Smith Street," Everett said.

"What's it called?" Marlon asked.

The answer was snoring. Everett was so wasted, he'd instantly passed out.

"Oh, great."

"Relax," Avital said. "There can't be that many diners on Smith Street, right?"

Erin checked her phone. "Google isn't showing anything. UrbanSpoon's giving me a list of twenty-three downtown restaurants, but none on Smith Street."

"How about I just drive around until we find something?" Marlon offered.

"You're the only sober one left," Erin said.

"As long as it's not McDonald's."

"Or Burger King."

"Or Perkins."

CHAPTER FIVE

"You guys are just lucky I don't mind the alcohol fuelled whims of three drunk women."

He pulled out and started driving. Everett dozed, passed out in the front seat, oblivious as a world of neon and streetlights painted abstract art on his face. They moved through the silent downtown as the late-night hip hop station played songs they'd just danced to in the club.

Sam stewed in silence for a moment before sighing. "I still can't believe I let that guy do that."

"Ahh, don't worry Sam, we've all been there before," Avital said.

"Really?"

"Was he hot at least?" Erin asked.

"Yeah." Sam thought back on those dark eyes and that mysterious silence. "I guess if I think more about it, the whole experience was kind of hot, in a sleazy kind of way."

"Then consider it notch one on the old belt."

"You know, this one time, I gave a guy a blow job and he farted, like, right in my face," Avital blurted out.

Sam saw Marlon's eyes bug out in the rear-view mirror as Erin squealed.

"Ewwwwwwwww. When was this, at the bar?"

"No, of course not. It was at his place. I went down and then *pfffft*. The way he was sitting, it shot right up my nose. I almost gagged. And not from his dick, either – he was pretty lacking down there if you get my drift."

Sam and Erin laughed. She knew she was blushing, but it was dark, so who'd notice?

"Who was this?" Erin asked. "Anyone I know?"

"Tom."

"TOM?! OMG, girl, why didn't you tell me right away?"

Avital scoffed. "We only went out a couple of times – there wasn't really a spark, you know. And besides, after having the smell of a dude's dinner shot in your face, you're pretty much done with him."

"After fucking him?" Erin asked.

"No." Avital looked aghast. "Farting in my face is no way to get in my pants. That was it right there."

"Did you finish?" Sam asked timidly.

Avital snorted. "Whatever, it's just a blow job. You only had to give that asshole a handy."

Sam's head was spinning as she looked out of the side window, watching the lights go by. She was covered in the smell of sweat and spilt drinks, but felt warm and alive inside. Her regret was drifting away behind her with the downtown. She was having more fun then she'd ever had in her life before. This is what it must feel like to be a normal girl.

"What about you, Sam, any crazy sex stories?"

They were all looking at her. Avital's shirt was ruffled, Erin's skirt rode high up her legs. Their hair was out of whack, their skin glowed in the light. Sam had never had anyone to talk to like this before, free and open. Duckie had been even nerdier than she was and would never dream of talking about sex. Any inhibitions or sense of privacy slipped away on an alcohol fuelled train. She found herself wanting to talk to them. "This one time, this guy I was with, his dick fell off in my hands."

Blank stares. Then all of a sudden Erin and Avital burst out laughing. Sam found herself joining in, tears falling from her eyes. When she said it out loud like that, it all seemed so ridiculous. She found herself even wondering if it had ever happened in the first place.

"That's hilarious, Sam. I've had a guy go soft on me, too, but

I've never heard anyone call it that before." Avital laughed in fits.

"Look! There's one!" Erin shouted, pointing out the window to a small neon sign above a square building next to an old apartment.

Marlon hit the brakes and they were all flung forward into the seats. Everett stirred awake. "We there yet?"

"Yup," Marlon replied. He swung the car around and parked in front. The girls filed out of the back seat. Marlon locked the doors behind them.

They were one short.

"What about him?" Sam asked, pointing to the newly passed out Everett still inside.

Marlon barely stopped. "As long as he doesn't puke in there I don't care."

The girls were already at the door, so they hurried to catch up. The place was small, but open and at two thirty in the morning, that was enough. There were a couple of custard yellow booths alongside the window wall, and a long seating area next to the kitchen. It was a diner from the movies; dingy, old fashioned, and nearly empty. A couple of late nighters sat nursing coffees near the cook who eyed the group suspiciously as they filed inside. Erin and Sam took one side of a booth, Avital and Marlon the other.

The burly cook shuffled over, his stained apron and three am shadow not the most welcoming of sights. "You kids pay before you eat or no service. You make a mess, you're out. I ain't got time to put up with any shit from a bunch a drunks, capiche?"

"No problems here, sir," Marlon replied.

"We don't want a bunch a shit, mister, we want FOOD!"

Erin cackled. Avital laughed. Sam blushed.

"I take it you all want coffee?" he grunted.

"Good idea," Marlon said. "Food, ladies?"

"Ohhhh, pancakes!" Avital said. "I want pancakes!"

"Yes!" Erin agreed. "Pancakes! Gimme some, too!"

"And you, kid?" He turned to Sam.

"Stack 'em up, Chef Ramsey!"

The girls laughed loudly as the man glared at her. His leathery face folded into itself, unimpressed. "That's eighteen-fifty, up front."

Marlon pulled out a twenty and handed it to him. The man grumbled and stuffed it in a grease-covered pocket on his apron and stormed away to cook their food.

"Stack 'em and rack 'em, too funny, Sam."

Avital pulled out her phone and started cycling through text messages. "This guy's a loser. Who texts a girl right when they get home? Delete."

"From tonight?" Sam asked. "I thought you didn't give your number to anyone."

She rolled her eyes. "Nobody important. Sure, I gave digits to a couple of guys to get them off my back, but they were nothing serious."

"No one even asked me," Erin said.

"Me either," Sam replied.

"Yeah, they probably thought you were lesbians. Also, you had a bunch of cum on your hands," Avital said.

The two girls cackled in glee and Sam could see the cook scowling at them. The other two patrons in the diner hadn't moved an inch. If Sam didn't know any better, she would have assumed that they were just part of the decor.

"Ah, I'm just teasing, girl, don't get upset."

"That's OK, no one forced me to jack that guy off."

"If they try, you come to me. My brother knows kung fu," Erin said, scowling.

"Don't worry about me, I can take care of myself," Sam said, smirking.

"Here ya go, hot pancakes all round." The cook dumped four plates of steaming hot pancakes in front of them, pulling out a bottle of syrup from inside his apron and dropping it in the middle of the table with a thud.

"Oh, hey," Marlon started, "I actually was fine with just the coffee."

"Growing kid like you? No fucking way. Eat." He stormed off.

"Yeah, Marlon, those pancakes aren't going to eat themselves," Erin said, giggling.

"Ohhh, but what if they could?" Avital chimed in.

The entry bell dinged, and another large group walked in. Five guys in leather, flannel, and tight jeans. Three had long hair, the other two short and spiky. There were five girls hanging off their arms and they all carried beer bottles. Sam could just pick up the tail end of their conversation: "...fucking awesome gig."

"...so hungry I could eat a horse."

The cook noticed them and shouted across the room, "Not you punks again. I told you before, you pay upfront. You make a fucking mess, you're out."

"No problem, pops," one of the guys called. "Here's a down payment." He tossed a couple of bills at the man and the group went to sit down at the booth at the far end of the tiny diner.

"Must be a band," Avital said, "a couple of real hotties, too."

Sam took a closer look at who had just walked in. They

definitely looked the part of a rock band, real bohemian, clothes a mishmash of tight and stylish. Or they could have been lumberjacks, who knows? But there was something different about them, an air of confidence that only someone who performs on stage for a living has.

"You recognize them?"

"Nope."

Sam could tell right away that this wasn't just a bunch of guys fooling around, they were serious. Their five companions all looked wasted, falling over themselves drunk. One slumped forward and her breast popped out of her tiny top. One of the guys nudged another and pointed to the scene and they both laughed.

"Bacon and eggs and keep 'em coming, grease monkey!" the guy with long dark hair shouted. His group all laughed and talked over each other.

"Check out the leader." Erin nudged her. "He's a babe."

She was right. The one that must be the singer was a total babe. Long dark hair, deep mysterious pools of amber for eyes, small scratchy beard outlining angular features. He had on a black shirt, open halfway down, showing a smooth chest of tight skin glistening with sweat. There were at least a dozen chains around his neck and twice as many wristbands on his arms. He just seemed to radiate confidence. Sam found herself unable to look away. She was drawn to him as if by magnetism. She had to meet this guy, had to know him.

"Whoa, drool much there, Sam?"

Erin's words snapped her back to reality, but before she could look away, the mysterious man caught her staring, shot her a butter melting glance and smirked at her. Sam spun back around and felt herself tingling inside.

CHAPTER FIVE

Who was he?

CHAPTER SIX

"Sir, I believe you'll be interested in seeing the progress we've made extrapolating from the recovered Necromancer files."

"Indeed. I would very much like to see where all of our research funds are going. I'm being asked questions about timetables almost weekly."

The man in the lab coat led him through a steel doorway into an observation room. A large one-way mirror window looked into a waiting room where two young women flipped through magazines while sitting on plain red-backed chairs. The table between them was piled high with even more magazines. A water cooler bubbled calmly in the corner. A potted plant in the opposite corner helped to maintain the image that they were in an everyday common office waiting room.

"Where do they think they are?" he asked the scientist.

"A staffing recruitment office. They each answered an ad that has since been scrubbed from the internet. No one could ever find it, let alone trace it here."

"Just what is it that you plan on showing me?"

"This." The man in the lab coat pressed a button on a console. The two women put down their magazines and looked up towards the corner of the ceiling.

"What did you do?"

"Just observe their reactions."

The first woman, a dark haired, tanned woman in dark pants and a sweater began breathing heavily. Her eyes darted back and forth. She gritted her teeth and grabbed the chair handles so hard her hands went white.

The other woman, a blonde in a blue dress, was sweating profusely, hyperventilating, moving back and forth around the room like she was desperate to escape.

"What's happening?" he asked, but the scientist held up a finger to silence him.

The pacing blonde finally seemed to notice that she wasn't alone. The brunette, rocking in place in her chair, was oblivious to the focused gaze of the other. The blonde's face turned feral. As if all humanity had been drained from it in an instant. She lunged at the brunette, pushing her off the chair to the floor. She grabbed her hair and rammed her forehead into the ground.

There was no noise on this side of the glass. It was as if they were watching an old silent movie playing out before their eyes. The brunette's face was bloody, her nose flattened and mangled. She reached a hand behind her and grabbed the blonde's face, digging her thumb into her eye socket. The blonde let go and shouted silently.

He watched in horror as the brunette scrambled free, then flipped over the blonde and rammed her other thumb into her eye socket. Blood dripped from her, on to the face of the blonde as the brunette squeezed and pressed in harder. Her thumbs crushed through the softness of the eyes. Blood bubbled up from the pierced sockets. The brunette seemed to howl, then leaned down and licked up a huge mouthful of blood.

"Good God," he said, watching the spectacle from the safety of the other side of the glass.

"This goes beyond God," the scientist said. "This is something else."

The brunette, thinking she'd won, rose to her feet and stared at her bloody hands. She started sucking on her fingers, cleaning them, devouring the bits of gore with her tongue as if her digits were popsicles.

He watched, fascinated. Then the woman was thrust forward, her face slammed into the glass so hard he jumped back, worried the window was going to shatter. Instead, her face was slammed again and again, splattering bloody circles in a sick pattern all over the once clean mirrored side. Over and over, until the skull gave way and caved in like a cantaloupe. The brunette went limp and the blonde, eyeless and bleeding, began smearing the wreckage of the dead woman's face all over the glass, painting the whole thing red.

He didn't dare look away. Whatever the scientist had done had turned these two seemingly normal women into animals.

The blonde dropped the body. Then she crouched down. He couldn't see what she was doing so he stepped closer. Through the crimson blood smears, he watched as she peeled away pieces of the ruined head of the brunette and began eating them.

He recoiled.

"Good God, man, we don't want them eating each other. What good would that do?"

"But, sir, this proves that with the right control vector, we can–"

"Create cannibals? We're not looking to create killers, we want slaves."

"But with more tweaking we can and will be able to change the reactions to the control vector."

"Then get on it. I can't go to the board with this. I need something we can use."

"But–"

"But nothing. You've shown good progress, of course, but this path is a dead end. Get back to work. And next time don't turn them into flesh-eating monsters, OK?"

"Yes, sir, right away, sir."

CHAPTER SEVEN

"I swear, man, I've never seen that pussy!"

Frank slammed his forearm into the shorter man's chest, pushing him back against the wall with a force that was greater than his years would seem to allow. The man was nervous. His eyes shifted. Beads of sweat poured down his wrinkled, tanned face.

"Are you really calling Mrs. Feldstein's little angel a pussy? You, a no-good stoolie from cockroach city?" Frank leaned in close, spit flying from his mouth into the face of the squirming man who tried desperately to avoid the food shrapnel. He shoved the picture in close. "You take a good look at that face, scum. That's the face of a boy with more potential in his little finger than you've got in your whole body. The face of a kid that's going places. Uptown, maybe sit in a fancy chair in Parliament down in Ottawa, maybe head up the next moon mission, who knows? What I do know is that a nothing doing twerp like you has no right to call him a pussy without any evidence to back it up."

Frank looked deep into his eyes, looking for that tiny slice of truth he was hiding. It would be in there, burning with a fire to get out. Even the worst of them had it, they just denied it, buried it so far that a miner couldn't find it. But Frank had dug for a lot more than gold in his day; he knew how to get the precious cargo out and it wasn't with a few kind words.

"Are you going to tell me where he is, or do I have to get angry?"

He reached into his pocket and took out a two-dollar coin, silver and gold, the best of both worlds. "Now, my little friend, Whitey the polar bear here says you've seen the kid." Frank slid the coin into the man's front shirt pocket, waiting.

The rest of the bar had gone quiet. The pool games had all stopped. The winos looked up from their musty glasses of what passed for beer here at the Shattered Cue. This was one of those places where people who knew things congregated. Numbers runners, pimps, junkies, fences, people who kept their ear to the ground. Only things had changed a little since Frank's last visit. Instead of an old jukebox filled with Johnny Mathis and Al Martino, there was some kind of touch screen thing playing people he'd never heard of. Instead of the dank aroma and sawdust covered floors he remembered, there were revarnished hardwoods that looked a day old. Instead of a bunch of men with more lines in their face than the parched earth of the great salt flats, there was a bunch of pony-tailed dorks in flannel.

Maybe stoolies had a new look that he wasn't up with. It had been months since he'd been on the force after all. No matter, if this bearded Mexican kid wasn't going to spill the beans, then someone else would.

"What about you, Marley?" Frank spun and pointed at a skinny white guy with his hair all bunched up in rope knots, stuffed under a knitted hat. "You seen Mrs. Feldstein's kid, or you too busy smoking that reefer to notice when a good egg goes missing?"

The man, holding a bottle of golden beer with a lime inside, looked on either side of him, then back to Frank, confused.

"Yeah, you. I'm talking to you," Frank said, marching up to him. He shoved the photo in his face and snatched the beer away. He took a sniff. "Fruit? In beer? What's this world coming to?"

"Hey, man, I ain't seen no fur-balls around here."

"Spare me your beatnik rhymes, Jimmy Cliff. I need answers, not smooth dub."

"I swear, I know nothing!"

"So you really are Jamaican then."

"Huh?"

"You're Ja-makin-me crazy." He slapped the man on the side of the head, but only managed to dislodge the wool hat, spilling a mountain of hair all over the place.

Frank spun around the room, eyeing everyone, looking for that weak link, the guy with the low breaking point who would squeal. Short skirts, glasses, little curled moustaches. Shit, these twerps couldn't even do dive bar right.

"Alright then, I'll let you hippies off the hook. This time. But I find out any one of you had something to do with this kid going missing, I come back here and bust the place up. I shave those sideburns and ram those pool cues so far up your asses that you'll be brushing your teeth with chalk. Capiche?"

No one said a word. But the message was loud and clear, so Frank left.

When the old man was gone, Karlos, the man at the bar, turned to the bartender. "Who let the geezer in here?"

"Must've thought it was seniors' night or something," the man said as he picked up a glass to clean.

CHAPTER EIGHT

"So then I thought, if those pants were two for sixty then I might as well get four pairs, you know, since they looked so good on me and all," Avital said.

"The black ones? With the lines on the leg?" Erin asked.

"You know it."

"Damn, those did look hot. How long is the sale on for?"

"It ended Monday," Avital said.

"How much were they regular?" Erin asked.

"I think $39.99."

Sam held out her hands to stop the two girls walking beside her in the busy mall walkway. "Not to worry you two, but there seems to be a clearance sale on at *Heels and Flats*."

They all shared a glance and dashed over the tiled floor into the shoe store across the mall.

"Holy shit, that place never has sales," Erin said.

"Is it a cliché for us to go crazy for this?" Sam asked as they entered the store.

"Girl, we're from River City. A sale is like our bat signal."

"I can't believe I'm doing this," Sam said, picking up a pair of black sandals. "I already own ten pairs of shoes and I don't care!"

"You've become one of us," Avital said.

"One of us!"

Sam had jumped into her new life with both feet. The girls had taken her to the mall, hitting all the major stores and a few hidden away ones she didn't know existed.

"What do you think of these guys?" Avital asked, holding up a pair of tiger-print heels.

"Awesome," Erin said, "those would go great with that top you got at Parisienne."

Avital beamed. "You're right, they would!"

Saturday afternoons were mall time. They'd trolled the stores for three hours already. Avital had three boxes slung in bags over her arms while Erin looked at a pair of something pointy and dangerous. Sam examined a pair of crimson pumps.

"I need something flashy to go with the new dress," she said, holding them up for the others to examine. "Thoughts?"

"You don't clash colours, Sam," Avital said. "You want darker."

"Oh, right."

They were having so much fun buying things. Avital and Erin had helped her pick out new clothes that showed skin, in colours other than black. She'd been tucked, prodded, poked, dressed up and dressed down, but was walking out with a new wardrobe that was going to make her look like an entirely new girl. Dresses, blouses, halter tops, expensive bras, lace underwear. She had it all now. It was too bad that she had to dip into next year's tuition money to afford it.

She'd spent almost as much as she had on her Computer Science class at the make-up store. The girls had seemed delighted to give her a crash course in the finer arts of make-up application. They'd schooled her in all the essentials a girl like her should have had for years. What, when, how, and how much.

She'd worry about the bill later.

University was quickly becoming just the time between Friday and Saturday night partying. Her project to make herself more interesting no longer seemed necessary. *Citizen Kane* gave way to *Cosmo,* Vivaldi to *Vogue,* Stravinsky to *Style.* With her new friends' help, she'd gone from pondering the nature of mankind to pondering the three hows. How to catch a man, how to keep a man, and how to tell what a man was thinking.

Appletinis, Margaritas, wine, tapas, shots, top forty hits, blinged cellphone cases, high heels, flowing hair, dancing, reality shows, nights at every club in town. She'd tossed her old Cure albums under the bed, boxed up the science fiction paperbacks, and put a lid on old Sam. New Sam was here to stay.

They were a team – her, Avital and Erin. Parties, girls' nights, dining in expensive restaurants; living like the hot young things they were. Finally, Sam had real friends. Sure, she rarely saw her parents, her bedroom was only used for sleeping it off, the kitchen for quick refuels, her coursework was blurring together... but who cared when she was having this much fun?

"What do you think of these?" Avital asked, holding up another pair of heels. "They'd go with that shirt, too."

"Didn't you already buy shoes for that top?" Sam asked.

Avital rolled her eyes. "Sam, those were Friday shoes, these would be Saturday ones."

"Duh, me!" Sam said, not really understanding the difference.

"Ohmygodholyshitbirds," Erin shouted. Half the store turned to look at her.

"What?"

She tossed the shoes in her hands aside and darted out of the store.

"Umm, Erin?" Sam called after her.

She ran across the mall and stood hopping up and down in front of the HMV. Sam and Avital left their potential purchases and joined her.

"What is it?"

She was pointing, vibrating in place. "Ohmyfuckinggod, LOOK AT THAT!"

Sam noticed now. In the window of the HMV was a massive cardboard cut out of five amazingly hot, clean-cut guys standing with pensive looks in shirts of various levels of openness. She knew those faces like the back of her hand. They might be a little older now, with a few more lines around the eyes, but it was still them. How could she forget the object of her deepest schoolgirl crushes?

"Factor 5ive is back together and coming here?!" Avital said in shock.

"Why did we not know this?" Sam asked.

"Because it was just announced," someone said from behind them.

Sam spun around to see Rick Hansen and Debbie Peterson standing a few feet away. Debbie was attached to Rick's arm like a cast.

"Hi, Sam," Rick said.

"Oh, hi, Rick."

"Sam," Debbie replied coldly.

Rick carried multiple shopping bags over his shoulder.

CHAPTER EIGHT

Debbie looked the same as ever, a stunningly beautiful icy blonde, stacked and fit, like something out of a magazine. Her clothes were immaculate, clearly expensive and in style. The only blemish on her was the air of complete bitchiness she exuded.

With the way Rick looked, a well built, dark-haired, athletic Adonis, they were a Hollywood couple here in the mall. He'd changed since Sam had last seen him at Convocation. He'd let his hair grow out to borderline rock star level now. It was pulled back behind his head in a ponytail. Sam didn't know if she liked that look on him or not. He'd always read jock, not mysterious artiste. Still, there was something different about him that she couldn't put her finger on.

"Debbie," she said curtly. "You guys are–"

"Shopping, obviously," Debbie said. "That is what you do in a mall after all."

"I–"

"It says tickets on sale inside! Holy shit, we have to go," Erin screamed and disappeared into the store.

"Wait for me," Avital called after her. "Sam, you coming?"

"Yeah, just gimme a second here."

Avital bolted off to join Erin getting in line for tickets.

"They know you can get them online, too, right?" Debbie asked.

Sam just shrugged. "We just heard about it now."

"It was announced four days ago, but hey, whatever."

"So, how've you been doing, Sam?" Rick asked while a quickly bored Debbie took out her phone and scrolled through text messages.

"You know how it goes, coursework, reading lists, all that stuff."

"Yeah, I get that," Rick said. "What're you taking?"

"This and that, a piece here and a piece there."

"I'm pretty much locked in to engineering. Dad wouldn't hear of anything else."

"How's hockey going?"

"Things looked a little iffy there when I didn't get drafted out of high school, but my agent figured it was because I hadn't quite hit that last growth spurt yet. He thinks that as long as I have a good year on the U team, put on a few pounds, I'll be a shoe-in next year. Or someone could offer me an entry level deal earlier, too."

That's what it is. He's put on at least ten pounds of solid muscle.

Now Sam knew why he looked different. He'd started filling out, looking more and more like the elite athlete he was. She couldn't help but flash back to when she'd seen him outside of that jacket and jean ensemble he wore so well. They'd gotten to know each other pretty intimately before it had all gone sour. But that was the past. He was clearly back with Debbie.

"I always knew you'd make it."

"I'm not there yet, but I think I have a shot. I'm told the scouts are all impressed as hell with my game. I'm working hard, and it'll happen, but..." He trailed off. "If not, well, that's why I'm in engineering."

There was an awkward silence for a moment as the two of them danced around bringing up their past.

Debbie looked up from her phone. "Hey, Sam, isn't this the store where Joshua fought that guy and broke the window?"

A flood of emotions surged over her as Sam remembered the glass-breaking mall brawl in which Joshua had protected her from the mysterious golem assassin. It had been almost three years ago, but the mall never changed. The HMV soldiered on

CHAPTER EIGHT

and all she had were the painful memories. She wasn't going to let Debbie have the satisfaction of hurting her. "Yeah, you know, I guess it is. I'd forgotten."

"You forgot your dead boyfriend already?"

"Debbie," Rick said, annoyed.

"Hey, I'm just saying," she said haltingly, "that seems a bit cold."

"Sorry, Sam," Rick apologized.

Sam wanted to smack the bitch, but she had to let it slide. "No, it's OK."

"Now that you have friends, I can see why you don't want anyone to know where you came from, but you can't erase it, Sam. It'll come back to haunt you someday." Debbie was on some kind of mission to press her.

That broke through her wall. "Is that a threat, Debbie?" Her blood was boiling.

Debbie rolled her eyes. "If you think people finding out what a loser you were is a threat, then take it for what it's worth."

"Debbie, enough." Rick stopped her. "We should get going. It was nice to see you, Sam. Maybe we'll run in to each other again." He led Debbie away, taking none of Sam's boiling anger with him.

Sam went into the store and joined Avital and Erin in line for the cashier.

"You OK, Sam?"

"Yeah, I'm fine."

"You never introduced us to your other friends," Avital said.

"That was just an ex and his queen bitch girlfriend."

"Is that jealousy I hear?" Avital asked, grinning.

"That's old news. You guys are–"

"Holy shit, can you really believe Factor 5ive are back together and coming here!" Erin spoke over her. She could hardly contain herself.

"I had the biggest crush on Joey in junior high," Sam admitted.

"Ewww, Joey? No way. Freddy was the hottest one." Avital swooned.

"You're both wrong, it's clearly Theo. He's so tall, and those glasses... hawt!"

They giggled conspiratorially together, three girls tossed back to their younger days crushing over the hottest boy band in the world. Back then Sam had no one to share her love of their carefully orchestrated pop hits with; Duckie certainly had no interest in talking about boy bands. She'd been left dreaming over *Seventeen* magazine stories, cutting out pictures to stick to her wall, fantasizing about seeing them in person.

"Let me guess, tickets?" the bored looking woman at the cashier said.

"Hell, yeah!" Erin said. "What's the best you have?"

"Row two, right in the middle," the woman said.

"Those are gonna be awesome seats!" Erin said.

"Uh, how much?" Sam asked.

"Sam, you can't put a price on seeing Factor 5ive IN CONCERT!" Erin said.

Unfortunately, you could. And it was more than any of her textbooks.

"You only live once, right?" Sam said, smiling as she dug for her credit card.

"I can't believe this is happening," Erin said. "If they'd come when I was a kid I would have just died!"

CHAPTER EIGHT

With a few swipes they were handed the printed blue tickets.

"It's really real, guys," Erin said, holding hers like a precious gem. "We're gonna see Factor 5ive LIVE!"

Sam looked back into the mall for any sign of Rick. He and Debbie were long gone.

CHAPTER NINE

"And where are you off to looking like that?"

Sam jumped in shock to see that her mom was in the kitchen. She was drinking a protein shake, decked out head to toe in her yoga gear, more pastel than human.

"I thought you'd left for yoga class already."

"You assumed you had the house to yourself, is that it?"

"I just came downstairs for a quick snack."

"In your underwear?"

"I'm just getting ready, Mom."

Sam couldn't even remember the last time she'd even spoken to her mom. Her life had been so busy lately and their schedules never lined up. Not that she wanted them to. Their relationship was complicated at the best of times. Sam never felt like her mom thought much of how she'd turned out.

She took out a pot of Greek yogurt from the fridge.

"And here I thought it was some new trend I'd missed," her mom said as she licked the remnants of the thick shake from her lips.

"Like you'd miss anything trendy," Sam countered. She took a spoon from the drawer and started wolfing down the honey

CHAPTER NINE

flavoured yogurt.

"So you are going out? Again?"

"Commerce social, it's only the biggest party of the year."

"I remember. I went to my share back in the day."

Sam tossed the spoon in the dishwasher and threw away the empty yogurt container. "Well, good for you then. But I've got to finish getting dressed. My friends will be here any minute." She started for the stairs but her mom made a plaintive throat clearing sound. It was clear she wanted to talk. Why now? Couldn't this wait? "Yeah?"

"Sam, I get it, I do."

"Get what?" She furrowed her brow.

"I get the whole rebellion thing, staying out late, partying. I was there when I was your age, too."

"I don't know what you're talking about."

Her mom stood up and paced the kitchen. She was desperately looking for anything to focus on but her daughter's eyes. "It's completely natural to do that when parents are fighting. Kids run away, find something to distract them. Avoid the issues at home. Trevor's mom said he did the exact same thing when she and Ted got divorced."

Well, that was a bombshell she hadn't been expecting. "Wait, you're getting divorced? When the hell did this happen?"

Her mom turned to the sink and washed her hands under the spray faucet. "Not divorced, at least not yet. Maybe not ever, I don't know. Just... separated for now. Maybe it'll be good for us, maybe not. It could be that all we need is just a little space, to reconnect. I don't know."

"Space? What do you mean, space? Dad travels all the time. He's never home and you're always out. What could be more spacious than that?"

"You don't understand. Despite graduating, you're still just a kid."

"Eighteen! Almost nineteen."

The numbers rolled off her as if they didn't matter. "We just have some stuff to work out. Your father and I decided that the best way to do it would be apart."

"What the fuck am I supposed to do?" Sam was in shock – this was the last thing she had expected to hear tonight.

"Language," her mother said scoldingly. "Of course you can stay here with me. Your father is getting an apartment downtown."

Now there was an idea. Downtown, closer to all the action, closer to school. No more bus rides, no more carpools. Sam formed a quick plan, based on necessity, desire, and spite. "Why can't I go live with him?"

Sam saw the hurt written all over her mom's face. She clearly hadn't expected her to suggest this, and it crushed her. She wasn't disappointed in that fact.

"You want to live with your father?"

"You think I want to live with you?"

"Sam!"

"It's closer to school. It'll be better for me."

It looked like her mom accepted that answer, like she was putting the briefest thought that Sam didn't like her out of her head, that being too much to bear right now. "Well, talk to him about it then."

Her mom just looked at her, waiting. But for what? Sam didn't have time for this. "We done? I have to get ready, or I'll be late."

Her mother clearly had more to say, but remained silent. She was obviously pained. Sam saw the beginnings of tears in her eyes. This was a moment where the mother/daughter divide could be bridged, she knew that. But she was supposed to be going to the biggest party of the year in a few minutes. There wasn't time.

Sam's mom nodded, defeated.

Sam turned and bolted upstairs to her room, even more excited than she had been a moment earlier.

My own place!

While not technically hers, her dad was always out, so she'd have the apartment to herself most of the time. It would be just like living on her own but without having to pay rent.

This could be amazing.

There were so many possibilities running through her head that she nearly tripped over the stairs. She couldn't wait to tell her friends all about it.

* * *

"How the mighty have fallen."

Frank stared at his weathered face in the reflection of a faded photograph of he and the mayor from years ago, when he'd been given the Order of the Raging Beaver award.

"Look at you, Malone," he said. "You were the pride of the River City police force for decades and now you're reduced to working security at a teenybopper sock hop."

He turned to the bottle of Jack on his desk and poured himself a small finger. Only a taste for now. He had to work.

"It's all your fault, Feldstein."

A folder rested on his desk, the photograph of the missing kid peeking out. His first big time failure.

"It's always the way, isn't it? The spicier the dame, the deeper the shit she brings."

It shouldn't have been this way; his business was going great. He had clients lining up at his door. He was cracking cases wide open, earning heavy lettuce, but then that damn Mrs. Feldstein had to drop her missing son in his lap.

"Missing, ha," Frank spat.

He'd really looked for the kid, turned over every stone in town. He shaken down every two-bit thug he could find, called in favours, ruffled feathers on Broadway, but all for nothing. The kid was a lost cause.

Another photo peeked out from the bottom of the folder. Reds and pinks and blacks and whites all mixed together.

"One hell of a crime scene, Feldstein."

It turns out that mothers didn't like having their babies handed to them in a box, but that was what happened. By the time Frank finally caught up with the kid, he'd been run down, turned into pavement pancake by some rowdies out cruising late. There was no saving that little boy. His guts were smeared halfway down the road, pouring out of his mouth like rubbery vomit. The best he could do was shovel him up and dump what was left in an old shoebox.

"Women don't like to see their son's insides on the outside, it's just a simple fact."

Mrs. Feldstein didn't take the news well. She'd screamed at Frank for not finding him sooner, blamed him for how he turned out. It didn't matter how much he explained to her that it was just a sorry result of the kind of shit he was into: drugs, robbery, assaults, rape. Her good egg had gone bad, but all she saw was the shining baby boy she'd shot out of her womb all those years ago.

"You can't reason with a mother's rage."

CHAPTER NINE

He took another sip. That was all he could allow himself. He had to leave soon.

"Answering a classified ad," he said. "Could there be anything worse?"

Mrs. Feldstein liked to talk. She'd scared away all of his clients, turned him into a pariah, crushed his burgeoning detective business. He'd gone from cock of the walk, to a stain on someone's shoe.

He picked up the rumpled newspaper ad with the big red circle around the caption "WANTED: SECURITY GUARDS."

"At least I can still do this."

Security, the poor man's cop; no badge, no gun, no real crime. Just a bunch of drunks and rowdies out to cause a ruckus. He remembered those days; a few shots of gin and the next thing you know old Charlie was trying to put a potato sack over your head. Nothing he couldn't handle. He'd been a shoe-in for the job, too. With all his police experience, the manager hadn't even bothered to interview him, just told him over the phone to show up at the convention centre at seven o'clock for a jacket and a headset.

"Get ready, boys, hells a-comin.'"

A quick walk from his apartment downtown and he was there, waiting in a room with the other charges, men as wide as they were tall, covered in tattoos and hair. Some looked more animal than human. They were all younger than his underwear.

Fucking rookies.

Nobody talked. They all just sat scrolling through their phones, reading magazines, or staring off into space. He doubted a few even had the ability to form complex thoughts.

After a couple minutes the site manager came into the room

with a clipboard and a box of headsets.

"You all know the drill here. Twenty an hour paid at the end of the night. No unnecessary fighting. Call for backup at all times. Report any unruly drunks so we can toss 'em out before shit happens." He was reading them the riot act but it was all old news.

"Blah, blah, blah. Tell us something we don't know," Frank mumbled.

The weasely looking guy started reading names off the clipboard and various brutes in the crowd called out "here" or "present" or "yo" or "'sup" when they heard theirs.

"Frank Malone," the man read out.

"Right here, chief," he replied.

The man looked up and his eyes grew three sizes. "Jesus Christ, you're old."

"Keep religion out of it, kid, we've got a job to do."

"Who the hell hired you?" he asked.

"Someone named Hinkle," Frank said. "He told me to show up here to keep the peace at your little ice cream social."

"But you're so old?"

"Crime doesn't retire. It just sits around and waits until you piss in a bag and drink from a straw."

"Wait, what?"

"Ex-cop. I've probably busted half of these idiots' dads in my day."

The site manager held up his hands, exasperated. "OK, fine, whatever, I don't have time to call anyone else, just take a headset and keep your eye out for any trouble."

Frank took the plastic headset from the man. "Ten four, chief, but trouble seems to find me."

The man shook his head and read the next name on the list.

CHAPTER NINE

"Anton Nixon?"

Frank looked over the tiny earpiece and attached headset – it looked like a fucking hearing aid. He slipped it inside his right ear and heard the faint sound of radio silence. It would have to do; he'd left his gun at home.

* * *

"Partying one, that's your nickname."

The girls had been so excited when Sam told them she was going to move in with her dad, the prospect of their own place to party erasing any and all thoughts of her parents' potential divorce.

"Yeah, but P-O?" Marlon offered from the front seat. "Isn't that like pissed off?"

"Eh, who cares? This just fits," Avital countered.

"P-O, partying one. I guess I can tolerate that."

"Then it's settled."

None of them seemed to care that she wasn't exactly Jewish; with the nickname, she was finally, truly one of the group – accepted.

The darkening city flew by in the windows of Marlon's car as he drove them downtown to the Convention Centre. The anticipation was killing Sam, both for tonight's social and the potential of living on her own.

"Seriously, though. Your own place. Downtown. Yours! That's so freakin' awesome!" Avital said.

"Let's not get too exited. I haven't actually talked to my dad about it."

"But your mom said it was OK, right?" Erin asked.

"I don't think she wanted to, but she did, so it's done. I'll ask him as soon as he gets back from his business trip."

"And he wouldn't say no, right? You're his only daughter, right?"

"As far as I know. And no, there's no way he'd say no."

"Then it's totally happening, Sam. Your own place!"

"I guess so," she said.

"That is gonna be so..." Erin started.

"Awesome!" Avital finished for her.

* * *

"The world sure has changed."

"Repeat, Geezer One. What was that?" the voice in his headset crackled.

"I said the world sure has changed," Frank repeated.

"Keep the line free for official calls, Geezer One."

Frank stared out over the room, a thick haze obscuring his vision. He'd never seen anything like this before. It was disorienting; lights flashing, something that must be music blaring, fog, kids wearing next to nothing, odd movements, jerking arms and legs, shouting, throbbing pain in his head, heat, strange smells, and alcohol as far as the eye could see. Red plastic cups, filled, emptied, poured, drank, flying through the air, kicked along the floor. Noise.

The noise.

"The fucking noise."

The commerce social. A massive party for the university crowd. It took place in the River City Convention Centre, a massive football field sized show floor. The whole space was taken up with multiple dance areas. There were theme bars set around the centre, a stage at one end, food kiosks, and a

CHAPTER NINE

section of tables where the drunks went to eat. There were thousands of people here, some half in the bag, a few having moved well beyond bags at all.

The few shots of whiskey he'd taken sloshed around in his empty stomach as he wandered around in a confused haze, the strange noise messing with his equilibrium. Something was off. His head felt too light for his body. His eyes went in and out of focus. For half a moment he wondered if he'd accidentally consumed one of those tainted bottles he'd saved from the old Van Lundgren case.

"No, I used all those up. Didn't I?"

There was another explanation that he'd missed. None of this was real. He was hallucinating. No. It was something else. Not the River City Convention Centre, there was no way. This was hell.

"That's it, you've died and gone to hell."

He'd seen visions like this before. Those weren't drunk college kids, they were all demons writhing in the flames of Lucifer. They weren't dancing, they were suffering through torments beyond imagination. That certainly wasn't music, it was the cries of the damned, begging for salvation.

Frank said a quick "Hail Mary."

He suddenly regretted skipping church every Sunday for the past sixty odd years.

"When did I die?"

Nothing rang a bell. "Dying. I think I'd remember that. It must have happened in my sleep."

That was it. The only explanation. Only in a cop's worst nightmares would he be reduced to working security at regular pay.

"There's a way out of hell. I know it. I've seen it."

He couldn't let it end like this. There still had to be a way to save his soul. A demon jumped up in his face, shiny red skin and tribal arm tattoos, hair spiked with blood. It shouted something in its twisted demon language that could have been, "Party time, dude!"

"Back, hell spawn," Frank shouted and pushed the thing off to the side, launching it into the throngs of its brethren with a righteous shove.

The crowds of the unclean massed all around him, throngs of pressed together bodies and limbs, a twisted sea of unimaginable bodily horror. He had to cross through to escape. *Exit!* He saw light at the other end of the room, a huge white glow from the heavens. It must be an angel, here to redeem the good and just. "I'm here, Gabriel, don't blow that fucking horn yet!"

He forced his way into the morass, the sounds of hell louder as he struggled through the maelstrom. A force pushed him back, but he wouldn't give in. It wasn't his time. He couldn't be dead. Not now. Not yet. He still had work to do, there was still so much he had to accomplish. He still hadn't finished the crossword in yesterday's Free Press. He had to get out of here. He had to save his soul.

* * *

"Now this is a party."

"Let's go!"

Sam, Avital, and Erin pushed their way into the centre of the dance floor to the accompaniment of a pounding electronic beat. There were bodies everywhere. The flashing lights and fog machines created an otherworldly atmosphere.

CHAPTER NINE

"Where's Everett and Marlon?" Sam asked.

"They were right behind us," Avital said.

"Not anymore."

"I'm sure they'll turn up."

Sam looked around the room at the mass of humanity and wasn't so sure. She could barely make out anyone's face in the vast expanse of gelled hair and short skirts.

"But they're our ride home," she shouted as they moved deeper into the crowd.

"Chill, Sam," Avital said. "Marlon has his cell."

Avital found their spot and started dancing. Sam took one more look over the mob and decided to forget about the guys for now. She could smell weed. They'd split a bottle of coconut rum in the car on the way here and the few drinks they'd pregamed earlier had started her off with a nice buzz.

"This is great!" Erin shouted.

Sam bumped up against foreign bodies, tossed her hair, bounced with her arm around Erin and lost herself in the moment and the music. The smell of sweat overpowered all of the body spray and cologne. The floor was sticky with spilled booze. Her new shoes were already killing her ankles, but somehow none of that mattered, there was only the music. Erin shouted something unintelligible over the noise.

Sam just shook her head. "What?"

Erin leaned in closer and screamed again, "I have to go pee."

Avital started grinding with a huge guy in tight pants.

"She has to go pee," Sam said but the girl was clearly in no hurry to leave. "OK, don't go anywhere. We'll be right back."

Erin and Sam forced their way back through the mob, suffering grabs and pokes along the way. The great maw of the crowd chewed at them, spitting them out at the edge, dishevelled, but still in one piece. They headed to the far corner of the hall where the bathrooms were.

"Holy shit, it's nuts in there!" Erin said. "Some guy grabbed my ass."

"Me too," Sam shouted, "but I think I got him back. At least I hope it was him. I sure kneed someone in the balls."

Erin giggled as they reached the edge of the party. Along the far back wall of the hall hung a huge black curtain, dotted with twinkling stars. It covered the entire massive north side of the room. Peeking out from behind it was the cream coloured brick wall, not exactly party decor. The curtain served to keep the atmosphere in check. Sam spotted something strange – there were about half a dozen guys standing at the curtain along the whole span. She had to squint to make sure that what she was seeing was what she thought she was seeing.

"Umm, what are those guys doing?" She poked Erin to draw her attention to them.

Erin screamed. "Eewww. They're pissing on the walls!"

So she had seen what she thought she'd seen.

"That's what I thought..."

Each of the guys held their Johnsons in their hands, letting loose a stream of urine all over the black curtain. Clearly drunk, they were having trouble staying upright, spraying their shoes as much as the wall hanging.

"That's fucking gross," Sam said, aghast.

"I'm not doing that," Erin said. "The ladies' room is through there."

A large, illuminated sign marked the washrooms, hidden past a set of open doors. They passed through into a massive corridor that diverged in two, one aisle for the men's and the other for the women's. There were a couple of bored looking security guards standing watch to make sure that no one tried anything funny.

The men's washroom was closer to the doorway and Sam could see inside as they walked past. Complete chaos. There were guys peeing in the sink, on the floor, everywhere. That shortest of looks in there that she took was enough to disgust her forever.

"How are we going to find Avital again?"

"You worry too much, Sam."

"Oh shit, look at that line."

There were about forty women waiting in a queue outside the entrance to the ladies' washroom. They took their place at the end.

Erin held her phone up for a selfie and leaned in next to Sam.

"Say best party ever!" she said.

"How about worst line ever?"

Erin took the picture and instantly started typing in a caption to post it.

They waited for almost ten minutes before they reached the doors and from the looks of the washroom, it wasn't much better than the men's. Getting in confirmed it. Each stall was covered in urine, empty makeup, spent roaches, empty baggies, used paper, and rags.

"Gross. There's no way I'm sitting on anything in there."

"Unless you're going to squat over the sink, I don't think we have any other options," Erin said.

Sam did her best to squat over the seat and took care of business while angry drunks pounded on the door.

"Hurry up, bitch."

"Chill out."

Whoever it was outside finally just said, "Fuck it." Pee slowly seeped under the stall door.

"What the fuck?"

They'd gone on the floor anyway.

Sam finished, righted her clothes, and carefully stepped around puddles to get to the sink. Someone had plugged it. It overflowed all over the ground. She ran her hands under the stream that wouldn't stop and shuffled clear as more people pushed into the empty space.

"I'm getting the hell out of here."

"Good idea."

Neither bothered to check over their make-up, they just fled, passing the never-ending line inside.

"That was horrible."

"New rule, no more peeing tonight."

They stepped back out on to the party floor just in time to hear the DJ announce, "Over on the main stage we have a special treat, a live performance by Radiant Cyanide."

"Is that a band?" Erin asked.

They weren't too far from the stage. Sam could see a group of guys setting up their instruments. "Let's check it out," she said and pulled Erin along. They joined a line of people heading over to the stage. The spotlights came on and the band fired up with blaring guitars. Sam and Erin made it near the front of the stage as more people rushed over, pressing them in tight.

The band looked familiar, but Sam couldn't place them. Then the lead singer turned around and she saw the truth; it was the band from the diner. The singer scowled under his dark hair and light beard.

"He's hot," Erin said.

CHAPTER NINE

She was right. His tight pants were painted on, his loose shirt billowing as he moved. He screamed into the mic as the music kicked in faster and the crowd started hopping up and down.

The music was loud, guitar heavy, pounding the floor like an anvil. It was nothing at all like the electronica the DJ had just been playing. It got the crowd moving wildly.

"Holy shit!"

Sam and Erin were pushed along in a sudden mosh pit and quickly separated.

"Erin!"

Bodies flew all around her, some hoisted up above on hands raised to the heavens. The god of a singer wailed away, but she couldn't really make out what he was saying as she struggled to stay close. Whatever it was, she knew it must be deep.

A couple of huge guys in black thrashed around like mad ping pong balls, slam dancing like it was 1979. One smashed into a couple of Asian guys with thin tattoos peeking out beneath white dress shirts loose at the neck. The slam dancer smacked one on the head and waved for the Asian guy to retaliate and join in, but he just looked at him with a death glare. Someone from behind shoved him forward and he crashed into the mosher. He swung around and slugged who he thought did it right in the nose.

The recipient's face exploded in blood. His friend shouted something unintelligible against the music, then rushed the Asian in a fury. Someone bumped into Sam on their way to the melee, and she was knocked into the fray, just ducking a punch from one of the Asians. She slid to her knees, throwing her hands up in a cross block, only serving to deflect the blow into someone else's ribs.

Then it was total chaos, hands and feet flying, knees and elbows all around her. A hurricane of craziness. Sam tried to crawl away, but she was swarmed.

Someone crashed into her, a massive man covered in tattoos and piercings wearing a security guard shirt. He had some kind of small stick in his hand, swinging it wildly at anyone within reach. The slick looking Asians taunted him as he tried to control the brawl. Another Asian came up beside her, reaching into his pocket. He took out something small and black. He twirled it in his hands and Sam could see that it was a switch blade straight out of the movies.

"He's going to stab someone!" she shouted, but she knew that nobody would hear her.

Everything seemed to be happen in slow motion. Without even thinking about it, her dormant Hapkido skills took over. She reached out and grabbed the guy's wrist. He turned in shock at her action, but before he could react, she torqued his wrist inward, stepping into his body, sending him spiralling over as he shouted in pain. She pressed down on his elbow with her knee and his fingers opened up, dropping the knife. There was another flash behind her. Knife? She spun around, letting go of the man on the ground. Then all hell broke loose.

* * *

"Almost there, Lord!"

Frank had finally made it to the light, a beacon from the heavens shining on the trim figure of the King of Kings standing on stage. He had to be Jesus, he had the long hair and beard. He was dressed weirdly, but he held his arms out and wailed something loud and incoherent. Was that Aramaic?

CHAPTER NINE

Or had Frank fallen so far that the word of the Lord no longer reached him?

Frank pushed his way closer, fighting through crowds of the damned trying to keep him from basking in the good word.

"Get out of the way," he shouted through parched lips.

There were too many demons. They surrounded him, forming an impenetrable wall. He could see other like-minded souls searching for salvation in their midst. He saw something flash in the light, and a voice in his ear called out, "Situation." Was that the voice of God? At least it was English.

"Situation," he cried. "I heard you. Situation. Situation."

He had no idea where he was anymore or what was going on. The drums of hell pounded in his brain. Beelzebub screeched in harsh feedback. A small silver light caught his eye. Frank reached out and grabbed for it, finding a demon's wrist. Did demons have wrists?

Instinctively he pulled it in around his back. The creature stopped in shock, shouting something in tongues.

"You won't poison me," Frank said.

There was no time for ceremony – Frank shoved the demon down and pinned it with his knees. He pulled out the pair of handcuffs he always carried, locking the vile thing up. They weren't silver, but they seemed to be doing the trick. He caught a small glimmer of light on the concrete floor. A knife. Frank picked it up and folded it back into the handle.

Another massive creature of hell, face covered in the words of the devil, pushed in closer, intercepting the demon's partner with hands the size of cement blocks. He and Frank caught glances and the thing nodded at him.

"Good job," it said in English.

What was going on? Was he a part of all this? Frank looked

down at the squirming thing under him, leathery, sporting shiny black scales, weird symbols on his skin. It certainly wasn't human. The voice in his head spoke again: "Back-up at stage, situation under control, need escort."

The fog rolled in. The damned sped away from the scene. Three more huge brutes came to help Frank with the squirming thing on the ground. They led him and his friend away. Where were they going? Did they know how to get out?

Frank looked around, spotting nothing but expressionless faces staring back at him. He had to get away from this place.

"Hey, wait for me!"

He ran after his helpers, away from the light.

* * *

It all happened so fast. Sam saw the second knife, then the oldest security guard she had ever seen stepped out of the crowd to take the Asian man down. More back-up came in a flash and the two attackers were escorted away. It must have been something gang related. In a crowd this big, it was bound to happen.

Why had she gotten involved?

She got a closer look at the old man guard. She blanched as a sea of memories came flashing back. It was the cop who had shot Duckie. What was his name again? It was on the tip of her tongue.

He looked right at her, but he didn't seem to recognize her. His eyes were wild and bloodshot.

Why is he here?

Her questions were dissolving in a cocktail of adrenaline

CHAPTER NINE

and alcohol. She was shaking as the two attackers were escorted away. She couldn't see Erin anywhere, but the dance floor quickly filled up again as the crowd returned to jumping in time to the band. Sam briefly wondered if the whole scene had really just happened, or if it was some trick of the light.

The singer shouted something too distorted to understand. The crowd cheered.

It didn't matter what he said, it pulled her attention. She quickly lost herself in the man. There was something about him she couldn't put her finger on, some kind of hidden energy, an aura that radiated from his scruffy appearance. He pranced around the stage like he owned it, a serpentine Mick Jagger in his prime. He moved fluidly, in control of his body, in control of the crowd. She couldn't look away. The more she watched, the more she focused on his painted-on pants. She could see the danger in his walk, and it made her tingle.

He sang words that she couldn't make out, but they still spoke to her. It was something about love and loss that she just knew was deep and meaningful. She needed these songs, they had to go in her iTunes. Did these guys have an album? A website? Did they do local shows? She knew so little about them.

Drawn by some invisible thread, she pushed her way closer to the stage, shoving through the mosh pit. Someone shouted at her as she elbowed her way up front. She was so close now. The guy was every bit as gorgeous as he looked from way back, equally as cryptic as that night in the diner. He radiated an animal magnetism. She couldn't stop herself from screaming and reaching out to touch him. He looked down in mid verse, saw her, smiled and winked. She nearly fainted. He spun in place and strutted back down the stage. He wasn't looking at anyone else like that, that was special.

He noticed me.

Someone tapped her on the shoulder. She turned to see Erin. They screamed in unison. Erin slung her arm over Sam's shoulders and they both started weaving to the music, rocking back and forth, bobbing their heads. The energy was intense, a force from behind them pushing them in, rushing to the front. Sam braced against the hard black bottom of the stage – it was all she could do to keep from getting squished against the base like bugs on a windshield. The crowd surged forward like the tide, each wave threatening to pancake them, but she held out. Arms, legs, and elbows bashed against her, but she held out.

She had no idea how many songs he sang, or how long the set was. Her time was measured in his glances to her. There were at least four. Eventually, the band broke into a big finish, bowing to the appreciative audience. The singer took the mic and shouted, "Thank you, River City! We are Radiant Cyanide. Check us out online and come see us down at The Big A every Friday night at ten."

Sam and Erin's shouts merged with the other screaming girls as the band left, disappearing behind a curtain. Show over, the crowd quickly dissipated. The DJ took back the sound system and an electronic beat pumped up, the trance of the rhythm taking over.

Sam turned to Erin, who looked like she'd been through a war. Her clothes were disheveled, her hair was all out of place. She was looking at a massive bruise on her arm. She wondered what she looked like.

"Holy shit," Sam panted, her voice hoarse, "that was intense."

CHAPTER NINE

"They ripped my shirt," Erin said, upset.

"My back is killing me," Sam said, turning to try to see the source of the pain.

Erin pointed. "There's a big ass footprint all over you."

"You ever heard of that band before?"

"No," Erin said, "you?"

"That singer was awesome."

"Hot, too," Erin said, grinning.

"We have to go to The Big A next week."

"There you are," a voice called from behind them. They both turned to see Marlon. He was glistening in sweat and looked half panicked. There were huge wet stains under his arms, and he was panting in exhaustion. "I've been looking everywhere for you. I lost Avital."

"Lost, what do you mean lost?"

"I was keeping tabs on her, but we got separated on the dance floor. I've been walking around and around all night looking for her or you guys."

"What about Everett?"

"The last time I saw him, he had his tongue down some girl's throat at the tables."

It hurt to move. Sam wanted to lay down in a pool of ice.

"We have to find her," Marlon pleaded again.

Who knew what craziness she could get up to here? "Alright, let's go find her," Sam said. Her buzz was slipping away with the prospect of responsibility.

* * *

They looked for hours as the night faded and the crowd slowly shrank. They found Everett first. He sat at a table alone, looking lost. As they got closer, Sam saw something going on at his feet. The low hanging tablecloth that covered the table was over his legs, rising in a rhythmic pace. She caught sight of a foot underneath as Erin tapped her on the shoulder. "You see that?" She pointed to the scene Sam had already become entranced in.

"Is that what I think it is?"

People walked by oblivious, the crowd stumbling around in a haze. Everett moved suddenly and hunched over the table. A few seconds later the cloth lifted, and a girl crawled out, wiping her mouth. She wore a strapless shirt that sparkled, while her short skirt had ridden up high, revealing the faintest impression of underwear beneath.

"It sure is," Sam said.

"Ewwwww, gross," Erin spat as Everett reached down and put himself back inside his pants, confirming beyond a shadow of a doubt what had just gone on. The girl walked away, and Everett's head rolled.

"Hey, Jews," he slurred as they approached the table. He was gone, totally wasted, sweating, and covered in the smell of sex and booze. He looked at them with glassed over eyes. Did people really do what she'd just seen them do? In public like that?

"We need to get you home," Sam said.

"Guys, I still can't find her," Marlon panted. "I've looked everywhere!"

"Can't find who?" It was Avital, still looking as fresh as a daisy despite the late hour.

"Where the hell have you been? I've walked all over this place!" Marlon tried to catch his breath.

"Aww, Fat One was worried. He likes you!" Everett slurred.

CHAPTER NINE

"Shut up, you're shit-faced," Marlon said, scowling.

"I've been looking for you guys. When we got separated, I started going around and around, but I only just saw you now," Avital said.

"That's what we've been doing. We must have been walking on opposite sides of the room or something."

"Uh oh," Everett slurred and leaned forward, "this is not gonna be good."

He waved his arms into a plate of food around him, half-eaten hot dogs and chips splayed over the table in a mess. He started heaving.

"Oh shit, he's gonna spew," Marlon shouted. He jumped forward to help, but it was too late, Everett let loose a torrent of puke all over the floor in front of him, covering his shoes and the spot of his most recent sexual escapade in a stream of multi-coloured bile.

"Ahhh, sick," Erin screamed.

Sam's sobriety came rushing back in the grim thought that they now had to get this guy home covered in his own vomit.

CHAPTER TEN

"Do you really think *that* is the best way to defend yourself against multiple attackers?"

Sam, drenched in sweat, lay on the hard blue mats gasping for air, nearly crushed under her huge opponent. Andy rose from on top of her, holding out his hand. She took the large, callused mitt and he helped her to her feet like she was a child.

"They're so much bigger..." she said, panting.

Master Park just shrugged. "You think that you'll only ever confront people your own size out there on the street?"

She had nothing to say to that. She should have just kept her mouth shut. There were no excuses in Hapkido.

"Try again. This time focus on limiting the range of who can attack you; use their own numbers against them."

Easy for you to say.

She tightened her red belt around her waist. She took time fixing her uniform, trying to catch her breath. She had risen far in the ranks of Hapkido, progressing well. She had learned defences against all kinds of attacks: kicks, punches, grabs, knives and even certain gun situations. This was something new, this was a full blown fight against more than one attacker.

CHAPTER TEN

They all wore some padding – shin, elbow, forearm guards, and light gloves – but it only really served to diminish the risk of injury, rather than the pain from an attack.

OK, Sam, concentrate. You can do this.

There were three of them practicing: her, Jan, and Andy. They were both much larger males. She was the only girl who came to this gym. At least the only one who had ever stuck through it this far. The odd girl would stop in to check out what went on, a few would even join when they saw her and were given the hard sell by Master Park. None lasted past the introductory three month membership. That made Sam feel special, and it could have been partly that which helped keep her coming past all of the pain, the constant challenge, and the mental breaking points. No other girls had been able to handle it. She desperately wanted to see this whole thing through as far as it would take her, even if her attendance had been slacking lately.

They're only twice your size. No biggie.

"Are you ready to begin, Miss Abraham?" Master Park asked.

"Uh huh."

"You might not be having such a hard time if you were here a little more."

"Yes, sir," she said, picking up on his subtle dig.

"Jan? Andy? Are you two ready?"

"Yes, sir," they said in unison.

Everything was formal here at Tae Ryong Park Hapkido Academy, just another part of the routine. Master Park casually leaned on a kicking dummy and watched as Jan and Andy squared off opposite her on the large blue mat area, waiting for her signal.

Out of the corner of her eyes, she could see a handful of junior belts watching as they practiced their own moves with half of their attention. Only the three highest belts practiced this multiple attacker drill.

Twice your size and male.

Jan was six foot three, nearly two hundred pounds of Czechian beef while Andy was as wide as he was tall, five foot five in both directions, with a football player's build. He loved rushing in and using wrestling takedowns.

OK, he's maybe three times your size. Soaking wet.

They had been at this for a solid half hour. First Jan had his turn. Sam and Andy had rushed him. Jan still held back with her. He didn't force her to the mat with the same power he might use on one of the guys. She used that hesitancy to knock him a few times on the side of the head when the fight inevitably went to the floor. Still, she wasn't all that helpful as a second attacker. Andy would usually just rush in and tackle Jan, while she tried to get in a few shots through the open space between bodies. The point of this drill wasn't to hurt your opponent, but to make them figure out how to control a situation where they were outnumbered.

Andy had been second to get a turn and he mopped the floor with her and Jan, taking them down with quick rushing leg tackles. Master Park had smiled as Andy controlled the pace and left both her and Jan wheezing messes on the mats. He should have been at a disadvantage against two attackers, but he knew his strengths and played to them.

Now it was Sam's turn, and she was taking it worse than Jan. She couldn't get away from them. She didn't have an answer for Andy's bull rushing or Jan's chopping leg kicks. She tried to keep her distance, but there was only so much room on the mats. They kept getting her and she was growing frustrated.

"Just remember, Miss Abraham, keep one attacker in between the other at all times, make the fight one on one if you can."

She nodded, saving her breath for the fight.

"Now begin," Master Park said as he waved his hand.

Immediately, Andy rushed forward, diving at her knees like she was a quarterback. There was no time to think so she let instinct take over and leapt over his outstretched arms, coming down in a roll past his legs. Shocked, Jan froze in place. Sam rolled through and pushed down against his knee and calf, sending him toppling over backward. She could feel Andy coming back and rolled sideways just in time to have him pass by, soaring in the air. She rose to her feet as Andy pushed himself off Jan and came at her, this time in a boxer's stance. She sidestepped, keeping him between her and Jan. He let loose a light jab, clearly a fake to set up a takedown. She stepped in and quickly kicked him in the ribs. It felt like her leg had hit a brick wall.

He didn't even react.

She was careful to snap back her kick in a quick motion, not allowing him to grab her leg. His fingers just dusted her calf. Jan was up now. Sam kept moving, not letting him have a direct line towards her. Master Park watched in silence, showing only moderate approval in her tactics.

Andy rushed in once more, and this time his hand caught her lead leg before she could step away. He held fast and Jan took that as his cue. He reached out with both hands to grab her. She temporarily ignored Andy and blocked the grab, pushing Jan's hands out wide, striking up into his ribcage with a short palm strike.

"Oof," he huffed.

She didn't let the advantage slip. She grabbed his collar with each hand and kicked her leg in between his, swinging it back and pushing him down in one motion. Andy holding her other leg kept her balanced and she swept Jan over backwards to land with a thud.

Andy stood up with her leg still in his hand. She hopped with him, keeping him from taking her down as he swung for her free leg. She only had one real defence to keep this from going to the ground. She reached over to grab the back of his belt, positioning her leg in between his. She stepped inside his centre, then sat back, kicking up and using his weight to send him flying forward through the air. She held on and ended up on top.

Now Master Park finally smiled as she did a downward thrust at Andy's face, pulling up enough to prove that the blow would have been true. Andy let go out of acknowledgment that he would have been stopped.

Jan rose and Sam pounced, taking him down at the waist, bending him over backward. They fell to the ground in a heap and she broke her arms free, flailing down with short punches that he blocked. He pulled her in tight with his hands on her lapel. She was stuck and she knew it. Andy soon had her in a headlock and the drill was over.

Master Park clicked his lips. "You were doing well, but then you took the fight down to the ground. One on one that's fine, but when there's someone else in play, you have to be careful. If the guy on the bottom holds you, keeps you from reacting, then you're done. The other guy has easy access."

Her body pleaded for air, the split second of action having happened so fast that she had forgotten to breathe.

"Don't be in so much of a hurry to grapple – you want to be able to get away if the odds turn, right?"

She could only focus on the slow intake and outtake of breath.

"Now, try again and if the fight goes to the ground, twenty push-ups."

This was going to be a long night...

CHAPTER ELEVEN

"Standing on the precipice of despair,
  Nothing matters now, no one's gonna care."

Silence. The band didn't play a note. The singer's eyes were shut. His voice echoed. There were goosebumps on Sam's arms as she stared transfixed at his face in the lone spotlight.

"It's not too far to jump now,
  don't wanna grow old anyhow."

Then, *crash*, the drums and guitar broke in, driving forward like a locomotive. They took over the room, drowning out the conversations from the back of the bar, thundering the walls and shooting through her body like wildfire.

Friday night, The Big A. The bar was only about half full. It seemed like Radiant Cyanide wasn't packing them in yet, but they played like they were at the River City Stadium.

Oh my god.

"They're loud," Erin said.

Sam just watched. She'd been talking about this all week.

CHAPTER ELEVEN

Erin and Avital had agreed to come along, but didn't seem to share her enthusiasm for the trip. Marlon was still parking the car.

"I'm not so sure this place is going to hold up," Avital said as she looked at the decor.

The Big A was somewhere between dive bar and fallout shelter, situated on the wrong side of the tracks. Literally. It was next to a massive train yard in the industrial part of town, the part her crew would never have visited in a million years had Sam not insisted.

The sound of a train coming in rattled the walls. The lead guitarist hit a pedal at his feet and the band played even louder to drown it out.

Avital tore up a Kleenex and stuffed it in her ears. "They serve drinks here, right?"

"In clean glasses, I hope," Erin said.

Sam was oblivious to their conversation, she just watched the band.

"Do we go over to the bar or is there someone to take orders?" Avital asked.

There was a long bar on one side of the room, where a surly looking bartender cleaned glasses and scowled at the hunched over regulars taking up space on the stools in front of him.

"I'm not going over there," Erin said timidly.

A waitress who looked half ready to ride the rails to the next town and start a new life as a washed-up stripper walked over. She carried a tray that glistened with the puddles of spilled drinks. She wore something tiny and leather. She might have pulled that off ten years ago when the look was in style and she cared.

"What'll you three have?" the woman croaked.

"Appletini," Avital said.

"Bellini," Erin added.

The woman looked disgusted and scribbled something on a pad of yellow paper. "You?" she asked Sam.

"Uh, beer," Sam said off-handedly, not wanting to miss the band.

"Yeah, what kind?"

She blanked. She didn't know any.

"Um, what's on tap?"

"How about I just bring you the house special?" the woman said.

"Yeah, sure."

The waitress snorted and left them.

There were a few other young people here. Some stood in front of the stage, a few others were bobbing their heads from tables.

"So these are the guys you just had to see?" Avital asked.

"Yeah," Sam said.

"They sure pack 'em in, don't they?"

There were no crowds, no rush of bodies, no screaming fans. While it was a little disheartening to know how few people had come after the performance at the convention centre, it did bode well for Sam's master plan of talking to the lead singer after the set.

"They're up and coming," she said.

Sam focused on the rough tenor of that singer, his walk, his deep eyes, and his long dark hair. Even here, in this shithole, he commanded the place. This time she could make out the lyrics. The songs were born from something honest. It was music from the heart, not from a prefabricated machine.

"I guess everyone has to start somewhere," Avital said.

"The guy at the HMV had never heard of them," Erin added.

"They don't have any albums yet," Sam said. "I found the band's website after the commerce social. There was just a three song demo up for download."

"Was that what you've been listening to over and over again on your phone?" Erin asked.

The song ended and Sam burst out clapping, louder than everyone else in the place put together.

"Thank you," the lead singer said.

"The singer is kind of cute," Avital admitted.

"His name is Scott," Sam said.

She had pored through the band's simple webpage for any and all information on the guys that she could. There were a few photos from gigs, simple profiles on the members, lists of upcoming shows, which were all at The Big A.

"Scott?" Avital said. "And they're called Radiant Cyanide?"

"Yup."

The band counted off another song and the room vibrated.

From the limited bios of each member, she'd learned that Scott had a poet's way with words. He sang about love, heartbreak, and alienation in the modern world. He was obviously some kind of bohemian lyricist. His words cut through the excessive vernacular of the digital age with biting criticism and astute observations. Sam had been hooked from song one, "Alone on the Bridge."

"What's this song about?" Erin asked.

"The pits of loneliness and despair that everyone falls into," Sam said.

"Sounds cheery."

Scott knew where she came from. He understood her, even if he'd never met her. She just needed to meet him, and he would realize it.

"You know the other guys' names?" Avital asked. "A few of them are kind of cute."

She watched Scott with rapt attention. As far as she cared, the rest of the band were invisible.

"That's Vic on keys and guitar, Tommy on the other guitar, Jose on drums, and Ben on bass," she said.

"Radiant Cyanide, right?" Erin asked.

Sam couldn't shake the feeling that they were just humouring her here, but she didn't care. She was here for Scott, not them.

"Yes."

"What'd I miss?" Marlon asked as he joined them.

"Loud music," Erin said.

The band played for about an hour, their three demo songs interspersed with other arrangements. Some Sam knew, a couple of Velvet Underground and Clash covers, others she didn't. Near the end of the set, they broke into some kind of spoken word free association sonnet by Scott. She could tell as the show went on that Avital and Erin weren't impressed by the music or their drinks.

"Uh, guys, I'm starting to think that this place might be a biker bar," Marlon said as he played with the straw in his empty glass.

The band finished to a scattering of applause.

"Thank you and good night," Scott said into the mic. He was dripping in sweat. The band went about putting away their instruments as a radio station took over the sound system.

This is your chance.

Sam stood up from her seat.

"Where're you going?" Erin asked.

CHAPTER ELEVEN

"I'm gonna go talk to him," she said calmly and walked over to the stage area, her stomach already in a flutter.

The stage wasn't large, barely even qualifying as a stage at all. It was only raised about two feet off ground level, but it was still enough to put the band on a pedestal. Scott was sitting down, drinking from a beer bottle. A leather coat hung loosely over his shoulder. His hair dangled over his eyes as his bandmates put away their tools. Sam stopped in front of him, suddenly blanking as to what to say. She stood there in silence for a solid thirty seconds before he looked up and met her glance.

"Yeah?" he asked calmly.

"Umm, great show, I mean, awesome show. I mean, just wow. Awesome, awesome stuff."

"Thanks," he said, staring right into her eyes.

"I, uh, I saw you play at the commerce social and was blown away, just totally. I downloaded your stuff from the website."

"Cool, so you a fan?"

"Totally, the biggest."

He took another swig of his beer. His eyes looked up and down her figure, admiring what he was seeing. She had taken extra time to make sure she looked great tonight: make-up, hair, tights, skirt, button-up black shirt. She knew she was blushing, but there was nothing she could do under his melting gaze.

"Scott, you want another?" the drummer called as he left the stage to go to the bar.

"Yeah," he called back.

More silence. She could sense this chance slipping away. She was going to blow it. "So, you guys play here often?" She wanted to hit herself.

He looked away, scanning the audience. "Yeah, it's a regular gig for us. Good way to get exposure, you know, build a buzz."

There were so few people here, Sam didn't know how much of an anything they were going to build, but who cared. None of them could see into those eyes. Amber pools. She had never seen anything like them.

"You going to go on tour?"

He shrugged. "Maybe. If we can raise the capital. We just need that break, you know. Someone to see us, take us to that next level."

"Yeah, I know what you mean."

"Scott, we staying or leaving?" Tommy asked behind them.

"Just a sec," he said and turned back to Sam. "It was real nice talking to you and all, but we've got some drinking to do so…"

Her chance was slipping away, she had to let loose. "When you sing "the pit of darkness is so wide, away from the light is the only place to hide…" that really gets to me, you know? Like, I've been there, too, real dark places, seen real dark things. I just wanted to say that I totally get that, I understand where you're coming from."

He stopped and looked her over again, perhaps reappraising her. "What'd you say your name is?"

"I didn't, but it's Sam."

"Look, Sam, me and the boys are gonna party here for a bit, then head back to Jose's place. You wanna come?"

"Can I bring my friends?" She pointed over to the table where Avital, Erin, and Marlon sat looking bored.

"Sure, why not?"

Heaven.

CHAPTER ELEVEN

* * *

"Tell me again why we're driving out in the middle of shit town?" Marlon asked from the driver's seat.

"Because Sam has a crush on the lead singer," Avital said.

"You have to admit he's a hottie," Erin said.

"I'm not denying it," Avital said.

"You jealous Sam saw him first?"

"Judging by the neighbourhood he lives in… no."

They'd driven around in circles after missing the off ramp to get underneath the overpass that spanned the old manufacturing district. Now they were slowly driving up streets with the street signs missing, looking for the address he'd given.

"Even google maps wants nothing to do with this place," Erin said, staring at her phone showing her nothing but a "recalibrating" message.

"It's got to be around here somewhere," Sam said. "Scott told me it was kiddy corner to the old paint plant."

Most of the neighbourhood was long since abandoned. What remained was a collection of derelict old warehouses and houses from the turn of the century. Their decayed forms dotted the landscape like the lone teeth of a vagrant.

"Maybe if we hadn't stopped to get beer, we could have followed them," Marlon said.

"We'll find it, don't worry."

Scott had asked her to grab some beers for the party. She'd bought three cases.

"I still don't get why those guys couldn't buy their own beer," Marlon grumbled.

"Did you see how empty the bar was?" Erin said. "I doubt they can afford their tab."

"There," Sam said, spotting the house that matched the description Scott had given her. "Stop right here."

Marlon pulled up in front of a house that looked like something out of a zombie movie. A broken fence, gate hanging on one hinge, trash strewn about the grounds, peeling paint, flickering porch light.

"You sure about this place, Sam?" Marlon asked.

"It doesn't exactly look fit for human habitation," Avital said.

"Sure I'm sure," Sam said. "Scott seemed nice, I don't think we have anything to worry about. Besides, we all have phones."

Marlon shut the car off and they all got out. A cold wind blew through the dark night. The fence dangled in the breeze. From somewhere in the distance a car alarm blared. There were lights on inside. The house was one of only three on the whole street. The sound of a dog barking down the street put a chill through Sam's skin. This place reminded her a little of a smaller version of Professor Finkelstein's rundown house where he'd built Joshua.

"It's probably cheap to rent," she said cheerily as she toted a case of beer up the steps.

Avital and Erin shared a silent glance, but followed her.

She knocked on the door. It swung open, and Jose stood there. He shot Avital a lascivious glance before turning his head.

"Scott, the beer's here." He walked away and they all moved inside.

The house could only be loosely called a dump. It was a tiny white-walled space, filled with ratty couches that looked like they had been found on the side of the road. An old wooden push button monstrosity of a TV jerry-rigged to get a few channels sat in the corner. The walls were covered with band posters and photos of famous musicians, from Lou Reed, to David Bowie, to Alice Cooper, to Stevie Nicks. The band's instruments were piled in one corner.

"You made it," Scott said. He emptied the beer in his hand and rose from the couch. "And you got beer. Thanks, Pam."

"Sam," Sam said.

"Right. Here, let me help you with those." He took the cases of beer and dropped them in front of the couch. Like vultures the guys tore into them.

"Have a seat," Scott said, gesturing to the floor.

"Where?" Avital muttered.

Sam shot her a dirty look and took a beer from the case, moving to sit beside Scott.

Erin, Avital, and Marlon moved a pile of empties stacked on the floor and sat near the window. The television was playing an old black and white movie.

"Hey, Bride of the Monster," Marlon said. "I think this is Ed Wood's best movie actually."

"Is that what that is?" Tommy said, as he cut guitar strings with wire cutters. He reached over for a beer, finished it and took another one.

"I got super into Ed Wood for a while. That big guy, Lobo. That's Tor Johnson. He was played by George the Animal Steele in the Tim Burton movie and…"

He trailed off to the cold looks of a band more interested in drinking than hearing his trivia. He quickly pulled out his phone and started scrolling.

"You girls drinking?" Vic asked Avital and Erin.

"We're OK," Avital said. She and Erin formed a wall with their shoulders, avoiding the others.

Sam could sense that this wasn't going well. She turned to

Scott, who drank as he watched the movie on the television.

"So, Scott," she said haltingly. "You guys all live here or what?"

"Most of the band live here during the week. You know, crashing on couches. There's only two bedrooms. It's kind of a lottery system. Everyone's got different schedules. Tommy and Vic work in a furniture warehouse downtown. Ben's a driver for a pizza place, and Jose does landscaping."

"And Scott's unemployed," Jose said. "He–"

"Spends most of my time here writing music."

"You can tell," she said. "Your lyrics are on point. I know you only have a few songs, but I've got them all memorized."

"Really?" He seemed genuinely surprised that she knew his words by heart. Although Sam was sure that buying the beers for the band had been a good way to ingratiate herself, too.

"Where do they come from?" she asked. "I really identify with what you're saying, so I'm, you know, curious what inspires you to write like that."

She obviously hadn't said anything too stupid, because he looked like he was really thinking about his answer.

So far, so good.

"Sometimes I just go to a really dark place, you know? But that's part of life. It helps you to understand the light, right? Breakups, divorced parents, a dad who was never around in the first place, people who I thought were friends betraying me. You name it, I've been there. The only thing I have is the music. It's my escape. My bandmates are my only real family at this point."

"That's why we let you stay here for free, right?" Jose said.

"And cos I'm the lead singer."

Scott was even deeper than she thought. They shared so

many traumas. They'd both experienced pain and heartbreaks across the whole spectrum. How could one man know her so well without ever having met her?

"I totally get that," she said. "I've been there, too... still am," Sam corrected herself. "So your songs are how you deal?"

He nodded. "Music is what consumes me," he said. "I've got this need to get all the darkness out of me, to really communicate, you know? Like, tell the world and all that." He took another swig of his beer. His hair fell away from his chin alluringly.

She listened with total focus, lost in his eyes. She put her empty bottle on the floor and grabbed another. How many had she had? There were more bottles on the floor than she'd remembered drinking. Were they all hers? She'd somehow lost count.

"So, you guys have a record deal, or you just plan on playing dive bars forever?" Avital asked.

"The Big A is where Nirvana played when they were in town in 1990," Tommy said.

"Did they ever come back?" Avital asked.

"Not there," Jose said, scoffing.

Avital rolled her eyes and went back to her phone.

"You gotta start somewhere," Scott said. "But I really think we've got potential, you know, to really reach people."

"Your big break is right around the corner," Sam said. "I'm sure of it."

"We just need to stick it out."

There was a knock on the door and Jose rose to answer it. Three girls in flannel and jeans came in carrying more beer and pizza boxes. "Tommy, Vic. Sheila's here."

"The rest of the band's old ladies," Scott told Sam.

"Mandy ain't coming," one of the girls said to Scott.

"Why you telling me?" he asked.

"You gonna play that card?" She put her hands on her hips.

"Ah, fuck off, Nancy," he spat.

Sam was just about to ask him who this girl was when he interrupted her train of thought.

"Why don't I give you the tour, Sam? Show you where I do all my writing?"

"Umm, OK," she replied.

She rose to follow him into the bedroom. "I'll be right back," she said to Avital and Erin.

The band cracked open more beers with the new arrivals and ignored them and Marlon.

"Uh, Sam?" Erin said, raising an eyebrow.

"Don't worry," she assured them, "I'll be fine." She took a couple of beers as company.

* * *

"So where did the name Radiant Cyanide come from?"

She was in the inner sanctum, the room where the magic happened. Scott's writing haven was nothing more than two mattresses on the floor, a closet stuffed with clothes in piles, and a tiny desk crammed into a corner. There were posters of Bob Dylan, Kurt Cobain, and surprisingly James Taylor on the wall. Heaps of scrap paper cluttered the desk. She counted at least three leather bound notebooks.

He sat on one of the mattresses, drinking before answering. "I really wanted something that emphasized the dichotomy of all existence, you know? Like a yin yang for the modern world kind of thing. Like radiant is all bright and religious while cyanide is poison that kills you. Yin and Yang. Like the snake eating its own tail. Understand?"

"Totally," she said as she picked up one of the notebooks and flipped through it. The pages were filled with chicken scratch writing at awkward angles, like he just wrote down anything anywhere, with no rhyme or reason. Some pages had what she guessed were song titles written on top with lyrics underneath, others had notes on different bands and what he liked about them: "Bowie's glam, Cooper's stage show, Morrison's poetry, Metallica's edge, Taylor's soul..." The rest of the pages were full of strange doodles and cartoons. It was like looking at a window into his thoughts and she was determined to figure out what made him tick.

"You work everyday?"

"Mostly," he said. "When the right muse hits me."

She stopped on a page in the notebook with a song called, "Death of Childhood." There were side notes written upside down saying "Dirge," and "Riders on the Storm," whatever that was supposed to mean, but it was the lyrics that got to her. Deciphering the handwriting she read:

Losing a friend, doesn't have to be the end,
   it's a new beginning for someone.
   You have to grow up sometime,
   not everyone makes the trip,
   letting go's not letting go
   if you hold the memory in your heart

A hole opened in her gut. She wanted to break down and cry. This was exactly her life, here on paper. Everything she had gone through, losing Duckie and Joshua, her parents' separation, graduation. He really got it. Even if he didn't realize it yet, he really understood.

"Which one you reading?" he asked, scoping her out as he drank his beer.

"Death of childhood," she answered. "You lose someone close to you, too?"

"That song's really about how we all do in a way. The child we were dies when we get older. You forget all that bright-eyed innocence and then it's all about jobs and money and stuff."

She caught his eyes and hung on them for a lingering moment. She felt like she could see into his soul. He was open and honest. He was unique. She was sure of it. There was kindness there, sensitivity. She felt like she could tell him anything. "My best friend died," she said.

"Oh shit, really? That's terrible." He held out his arms then patted the bed beside him for her to come sit down next to him.

She took the book with her, her thumb inside the page, marking her place, and joined him on the makeshift bed. It sagged under her weight. The sheets looked like they hadn't been washed in a dog's age. None of that mattered, she was next to him. Her body tingled, the hairs on the back of her neck stood up. He smelled like hard work: beer, sweat, and manliness. His hair had the faintest hint of something fruity.

"So, what happened?" he asked softly.

"Long story, you probably wouldn't believe it if I told you, but it ended with a police shooting."

He looked impressed. "Damn. Now that sounds like a song. Like *Tweeter and the Monkey Man*."

"Or *Monster Mash*."

CHAPTER ELEVEN

He furrowed his brow. "Huh?"

"Don't worry about it." She tried to laugh away the awful feeling inside, drown it out with his powerful presence. She opened the book again to read some more lyrics.

"You like what you see?" he asked.

She looked up to see him intently staring at her, amber eyes dissecting her to the core. He was reading her. Taking her in for who she was. His hair hung near his chin, brushing against the stubble that he called a beard. There was a small scar near his lip, a faint line of danger marring the otherwise perfect features. Neither of them spoke, more than words being shared in that look alone.

He reached up and brushed the hair away from her eye, revealing her mole, her shame that she kept hidden as much as possible.

"I get the feeling that you get me, that we understand each other."

He looked at the mole, but not in revulsion, more like a rare book collector examining a pristine tome for the first time. Nobody did that. Her heart rose, her pulse quickening at his touch. He spoke softly, his tenor voice like music. "There's a connection here. Do you feel it, too?"

"I do," she whispered back.

"The universe is calling to us, we just need to listen."

He leaned in and kissed her softly on the lips.

Oh my God.

It was the lightest touch, but full and passionate all the same. He backed away and their eyes met. Sam was frozen, locked in place by a feeling bigger than herself.

"Was that OK?"

"Yeah," she said wistfully.

Then he kissed her again, this time with force. Their tongues met in the middle, intertwining as his hands grabbed her and pulled her in close, threatening to inhale her completely. She lost control and moved her hands over his body, exploring the tight form hidden underneath the rockstar apparel.

He pulled back. They both panted, recovering the air lost in the battle of lips.

Holy shit.

He pulled his shirt over his head, the chains jingling as they fell against his tight, firm chest. He wasn't built, but he was ripped. Skinny and wiry like a statue of marble, a body of compact muscle but little mass. He was smooth, shiny, a runway of pristine asphalt.

He pulled her hand to his body and kissed her again. Sam traced the lines of his muscles as their lips were locked in a titanic struggle. His hands moved down to her shirt, unbuttoning her blouse, lightly brushing her breasts as he pushed the fabric away to reveal her stomach and chest. The cool air on her skin and his touch stiffened her instantly. His fingers brushed her lightly.

What are you doing, Sam?

His hands moved around her chest to her back, loosening the clasp on her bra, freeing her in one quick flick of the wrist. He moved back around her front and grabbed her in each hand, squeezing her with firm grabs.

You just met this guy.

Her blood was boiling. He guided her hands slowly to his hips. He moved away from her mouth and started kissing her body, tracing the delicate, sensitive skin with his tongue. A tingle ran through her. She could feel herself getting ready.

CHAPTER ELEVEN

This feels so right.

The next thing she knew, her hands were at his belt, fumbling with the clasp, trying to figure out a way in. He took over for her, undoing it like it was nothing. He slid up and made some space, reaching inside his boxer shorts and taking out his pride. He moved back to her mouth and kissed her fiercely, grabbing her hands and moving them down to what was between his legs.

It's like deja vu.

He was quickly stiffening in her hands. The feeling was strange, not at all what she was expecting. He curved upward, a shape more like a smile than a straight line. She had so little experience that it threw her for a loop. Rounded and smooth at the top, the rest faintly hairy. She tried looking down, but he was in her face, kissing. He seemed to be responding to what she was doing.

Are we really doing this?

The heat between them was rising. She was ready. She forgot all about the others on the other side of the door.

Oh God, we are going to do this.

This wasn't like that night outside the bar. This time she wanted to keep going. He read her signals completely. He reached up and caressed her chin, his touch soft and assured. Then, he pulled her down in a slow motion, putting her face to face with his exposure. There it was, looking her right in the eye, a damaged and strange looking contraption, not at all the perfect form of shape and drive of her dreams.

What am I–

She had no time to think, he moved her right on to it. She opened her mouth. He tasted of sweat and body wash. He tickled the inside of the roof of her mouth as she closed her lips and moved up and down.

I can't believe I'm doing this.

Her tongue traced him. He started to shudder, enjoying what she was doing. A hundred Cosmo articles flew by in her mind as she did her best to remember what she'd read. This was her first time doing this. Would her total inexperience betray her?

Shit. This is real. This is—

Up and down with her tongue, tasting him. He moved her other hand down lower. She nearly jerked back when she felt the prickly skin.

Can I really do this? Should I?

Faster and faster. Was she doing this right?

There was a knocking on the door. "Sam, you OK in there?" It was Avital.

"Just a second," she tried to call, but her words were muffled.

He spasmed. She wasn't ready. Didn't know, couldn't pull away. She tried to break free, but he held her tight to him. She felt like puking. She reflexively swallowed even though she didn't want to. When he was done, he let her go. She pulled away and coughed, the taste still in her mouth. She wanted to retch.

"Sam? Marlon wants to go," Avital called again.

Scott grinned at her, like what had just happened was the most natural thing in the world. She felt dirty and used. She hadn't wanted to go so far so fast, but he hadn't stopped to ask her.

"Hey, I…"

"What?" he said, staring at her innocently.

She should be mad at him. She should slap his face and storm out of there. But God, he was so gorgeous. Shirtless

CHAPTER ELEVEN

and glistening in the soft light, exposed in the chill air.

Guys like him must think this is totally normal. I'll bet he does this all the time.

She was conflicted. Everything had happened so fast. She'd had a few drinks. She'd wanted this. She'd never really said no. But *did* she want this? Like this? Here? Now? In this filthy room. Half drunk?

He seemed completely fine with it all. Of course he would be. He was the one who pressured her.

But did he? The words in the journals. The songs. The looks. She walked in here freely.

Maybe this isn't your Me Too moment. They all saw you come in here of your own free will. Maybe you just need to loosen up.

She flashed back to the commerce social, seeing Everett and the girl under the table. A million articles, a hundred how-to threads on the internet, slumber party talks, Avital telling them about her own experiences. Movies, television, books. What was right here?

Was she trying to convince herself this was no big deal? Or was this a really big deal?

It happens all the time, Sam.

The nagging feeling of unease wouldn't go away. He said nothing.

You just need to get with the times.

She'd ask the girls. They'd know. There wasn't anything she could do here now. The unpleasant taste lingered.

Don't let him think you regret this.

"Sam?" Avital repeated. "Do we need to come in?"

"I'm coming," she said.

She grabbed a beer from the desk and took a swig. She'd have more time to sort out her feelings later. "Gotta go," she whispered, buttoning up her shirt.

He lay back on his elbows, not even bothering to cover himself up. He looked ready to fall asleep.

How can he be so casual about all of this?

"Hang out again?" he asked languidly.

"Call me," she replied as she slipped out of the room.

CHAPTER TWELVE

"Now watch the reaction after she hears the trigger sound."

The man in the lab coat pressed a button. Nothing was heard in the safety of the observation room. The group watched as the woman in the plain white room looked up from her place at the desk. She'd been writing in answers on the survey they'd prepared for her. At first, she began listening intently, bobbing her head.

"The sound is embedded subliminally?"

"Indeed. Without the covering of other musical accompaniment, the noise is too shrill and painful."

"But not underlaid with–"

"A song, yes, sir."

"And are there certain styles of music that work better as cover?"

"This we're still working on. Right now, the test is a full symphony orchestra, but we are currently engaging in an elimination process to find out which instruments expose the noise and which do not."

"Good. This concept is no good to anyone if it only works for symphonic music. Young people don't listen to classical like they did a hundred years ago."

"I understand, sir."

The group kept watching the woman on the other side of the one-way viewing mirror. As the song played, her eyes seemed to glass over. The pen fell from her grasp and rolled off the desk. She reached over to her purse and took out her phone.

"What is she doing?"

"Just watch."

He stared through the glass, curious as the woman swiped on her phone with robotic motions. She began unbuttoning the top few buttons of her blouse, watching herself in the reflected image on the phone.

"Is this–"

"There's more."

The woman slid down her blouse over her shoulders. She preened and posed in front of the phone.

"Is she recording?"

The man in the lab coat nodded.

The group watched in rapt attention as the woman ran her hands over her body suggestively. Then she cupped her breast and kissed towards the camera. She proceeded to rub her shoulders, stripping off her bra, revealing her body.

"Is this all of her own free will?" one of the others in the room asked.

"Only while under the influence of the control sound," the man in the lab coat said. "She is doing precisely what we implanted within the noise."

"But will she remember any of this?"

The man in the lab coat shook his head. "That's the beauty of the process. It creates a temporary state of amnesia wherein the subject in the controlled state does not retain conscious

CHAPTER TWELVE

control of their actions, nor will they remember doing any of them later. For the duration of the control, they are like puppets, highly suggestible to further requests by those implanted with the correct sub-frequency sound generators."

"I don't understand," one of the men said.

"Watch and I'll demonstrate," the man in the lab coat responded.

The door to the room opened and in walked a fit man in a too-small lab coat with torn sleeves. His large biceps were oiled and tanned, and his square jaw was right out of a romance novel cover. He said something they couldn't hear to the woman who playfully covered her nude torso with her hands.

"What did he say to her?"

"The script isn't important. With the surgery and implants he speaks in the right frequency to interact with the controlled state."

"Explain."

"Whatever he says she will do."

"Can anyone control those under the spell?"

"That feat is beyond our technology, I'm afraid. To have even managed this is an amazing accomplishment."

"So the controlled state mimics that of the created ones when faced with the heartstones?"

"Absolutely, sir. That is the process we are trying to duplicate. But we're aiming to have it work on those that were naturally born rather than those created from parts in the lab."

"So on regular humans rather than golems?"

"Exactly."

There was a murmur of excitement in the room. They

clearly understood now why he'd put so many resources into developing this process. The possibilities were unimaginable. They continued to watch as the woman and man on the other side of the glass man acted out a full adult movie scenario, filmed by both the woman's cellphone and two hidden cameras in the room.

"As you can see, her inhibitions are completely erased. Any self-control, unwillingness, refusal, disgust, non-commitment, gone while in the control state."

"What about him?"

"As a created one, he has no will other than what the heartstone commands."

"So they are–"

"Slaves. Temporarily, at least. We can use this footage for whatever we choose. Blackmail, profit, third party services."

"But it only works on women?"

"Right now," the man in the lab coat said. "But I'm confident that we can eventually learn to adjust the parameters to affect men as well."

"That won't be in the cards. It's too dangerous, for obvious reasons."

"So we won't be pursuing full parity?"

"You don't have to concern yourself with that. But what you've accomplished here, I can take to the board. First I suggest a field test."

"How, sir?"

"A band. We will start local, on a small scale in case anything goes wrong. Then, if we see results, we'll expand this nationally, with the intention to go global next year."

Chattering excitement among the others told him they were as behind this idea as he was. He'd proved what he wanted to and now he'd earn the accolades for this success. He grinned a serpentine grin as they all watched the man and woman perform their unaware bedroom scenario.

"Just imagine it, friends," he said. "Every woman who hears the control noise will be slaves to our chosen controllers. There won't be a girl under thirty in River City we won't own. Now we just need the right group."

FOUR WEEKS LATER

CHAPTER THIRTEEN

Thunder cracked overhead as the rain fell in sheets, drenching the grounds of the unfinished Apex Towers. Police, paramedics, and firefighters moved through the exposed girders and piles of waiting materials. Flashing lights bathed the fenced-off area in reds and blues.

"How in the world did I know I'd find you here, Frank?"

Frank looked up from the gurney they were forcing him to sit on while the paramedics cleaned his cuts and checked him for any signs of a concussion. Two detectives walked towards him, a man and a woman. One he didn't know, the other he knew a little too well. Shaved head, thick muscular physique under a brown suede jacket, olive skin, too white teeth.

"Jimmy," he said. "Don't tell me you're my ride home."

"Detective Hooper, you know this geezer?" the other detective said.

"He was my–"

"I've got underwear stains older than you, girl, so how about you show a little more respect to your elders."

"Old partner," Jimmy finished.

"Oh god, this is Frank Malone?" the woman said. She was dark-haired, with a pretty face, a sturdy build and good teeth.

Most of those things weren't going to serve her well on the force.

"The one and the same and if I wasn't getting stitched up by the field medic right now, I'd have half a mind to put you over my knee."

"He's exactly like you described," the woman with the trimmed eyebrows and crisp shirt said. She looked like she'd imported all her clothes instead of going off the rack like the regular joes. She read more middle manager than detective, exactly the kind of gal Frank had seen starting to take over the force before he was forced out.

"They making you babysit now, Hooper?" Frank asked.

"This is my new partner, Veronica Tockett. I'm showing her the ropes."

"If you teach her what I showed you then maybe, just maybe, she'll be worth her salt."

"Don't worry, Mr. Malone, he's told—"

"Veronica, how about you go and start to question the other guy here, OK? I'll handle Frank then come join you."

"Sure thing, Detective Hooper."

Veronica left to find the other guard on site, the one who was a lot worse off than Frank. That kid had seen a heck of a lot more of what had gone on down here at the Apex Towers construction site. Frank had been more of a clean-up man.

Frank watched Jimmy watching Veronica walk off. He was a little too interested in that walk. That could be bad news.

"A girl for a partner. You better watch out, kid."

Jimmy turned back around, blushing just enough for even the low light to reveal. "Why? You fall in love with one, too?"

"Hell, no. She quit to join a top-secret commando team."

"Huh?"

CHAPTER THIRTEEN

"Never mind. Just be careful with this Detective Veronica Tockett."

"Maybe she has to be careful with me."

"All done, Mr. Malone," the paramedic said. "You're lucky you only have a few scrapes and bruises. A fall like that could have really done some damage."

"I landed on the guys in the corner, ma'am," Frank said calmly. "They're the ones that you should be patching up."

"The corpses?"

"I guess I landed harder than I thought."

"What exactly went on here, Frank? We get a frantic call from some kid about ghosts, dead bodies in the walls, gangsters, then we show up and it looks like a war zone. The crane's toppled over, half the building's trashed, there's some bodies back there that'll need dental ID, handcuffed thugs, and you. Sitting here in the middle of it all with a few cuts, a rent-a-cop uniform and a flashlight, acting like it was all no big deal."

"It was all no big deal. At least it isn't now. I solved the case."

"What case!"

"The one I wrapped up. You're too late. As usual. Old Frank, the guy you all said was past his prime just put you all to shame without even a license to carry."

"Please don't tell me you shot anyone. I'd have to bring you in."

"Didn't have to. This time it was all with the old noggin," Frank said, tapping his head.

He rose from the gurney and brushed off his pants. He'd have to get another pair from the site office. These were covered in masonry, blood, and bits of whoever it was he landed on back there. He put his arm around Jimmy, the man he'd mentored his last few years on the force. The kid wasn't half bad. They'd had a few adventures in their day, but apart from him, he seemed a day late and a dollar short. Oh well. Frank could still teach him a few things.

"Since you're here to give me a ride, how about we stop in for some Danishes on the way. I'll tell you all about what I'm calling the Case of the Haunted Construction Site."

"Haunted? Really?"

"You'll have to wait to find out, now, won't you? No spoilers until I see a Danish."

He led Jimmy towards the flashing lights of the police cars that surrounded the huge tower construction site. There was going to be a lot of work to unpack all of this. A lot of paperwork, too. Some parts of the job Frank didn't miss.

"It's one hell of a story, kid. Hope you still have that notebook of yours."

CHAPTER FOURTEEN

"Guys, guys, guys. This needs to be perfect. We can't fuck up for the showcase. Try again."

Scott called out "one, two, three, four," and shot his hand out, starting the band off into a slow, driving rhythm, heavy on the bass. Jose kept time on the drums. He looked exhausted. He was shirtless and drenched in sweat. Tommy and Vic bobbed their heads as they strummed their guitars. Ben seemed off in his own world on bass. They'd been practicing for hours. Sam and the other band girls sat on the ratty couch, watching. At least Sam did. The other three, Nancy, Sheila, and Beth, were too busy with their phones to be paying much attention.

Scott, his eyes shut, silently counted down the bars until his cue. He was in the zone, totally wrapped up in what they were doing. She'd never seen him so driven. He clenched the microphone and started singing his lament to lost dreams, "Forgotten in the Morning."

"Visions of a better world,
　of time and space so far away.
　Lost in the rising light,

as nighttime turns to day."

He was completely focused, ignoring everything around him. It was still hard to believe that she was here, watching the guys work on their stuff, a part of the inner circle.

You still at rehearsal? A text came through from Avital.

Yup, she texted back.

We on for tomorrow?

Sam stared at the message from Avital, wondering what to text back. The past weeks had been a whirlwind. It had been five days before she realized that she'd never given Scott her number that night. She'd gone back to The Big A the next Friday, worried that their experience had simply been a one-night thing, but he'd greeted her with a post-set hug.

"Hey, you came back," he'd said.

"Great set," she'd said, inhaling the aroma of sweat and beer that permeated him. Her feelings had been all mixed up and his eyes didn't help matters.

"We really hit on a few of the songs, I could feel everything clicking."

She hadn't known what to say. Time had passed in awkwardness as neither said a thing about what had happened. Finally he'd broken the ice.

"Hey, you want to come back to Jose's place?"

Without thinking she'd said yes.

"Cool. Mind if we stop at the LC first for beer?"

Then it became routine. Friday night shows. Beer runs, trips to his room to hear his lyrics and fool around.

"You think he's using you for beer, Sam?" Avital had asked after the third night.

"He's not like that," Sam had insisted.

CHAPTER FOURTEEN

"Then what do you do in his room with the doors closed?"

She'd never told them what had happened that first time and the more things happened, the less she could wonder about how consensual it had all been.

"We talk."

"Right. Talk."

Avital, Erin, and Marlon didn't get her fascination with the band's music. They no longer came to the shows. Beer seemed to be her way in with the band. After a few cases they stopped looking at her like a nuisance. With her parents' car and money taken from her savings, she became transportation and alcohol supplier. But with Scott, she was much more.

"They look at you like a star-fucker," Avital had said.

"But they're not even famous," Sam had countered.

"Soon-to-be-star-fucker then."

"It's not like that."

"You ever do anything you want to do with him?"

She did lots of things with him. More than she'd ever planned to so quickly, but the chemistry was off the charts. Alone in his room, listening to him talk, his scent all around, his eyes, his voice. She'd broken her own rules.

Are we? Avital texted again.

Sam shut off the phone and put it back into her pocket, watching the band move through their practice. Scott winked at her briefly as he sang. At least she thought he did. She knew she wasn't just a lay to him. He read her his new lyrics. He asked her opinions on his works in progress. He listened to what she had to say and some of it appeared on paper later. He turned her stories into tiny microcosms of emotion wrapped up in 4/4 time.

"What do you see in the guy?" Erin had asked her during

one lunch in the basement futon room.

"I don't know. He's like Robert Smith mixed with Jim Morrison in Adam Levine's body."

"I only know one of those people."

Now she was sitting on the couch and her best friends were at Avital's place having a slumber party. They were watching old John Cusack movies and she was watching a guy on his way to being a huge superstar. It was electrifying to be in on the ground floor of something like this. She was one of the group of girls that were the band's girlfriends and things were about to blow up.

The song ended and Scott nodded his approval. "Alright, guys, I think we can move on to the new one, OK?"

"More?" Tommy groaned.

"Seriously? Can't we break for beer?" Vic asked.

"Dude, this is our big break. We have to be ready."

They'd received huge news. The band was going to perform a showcase for a big shot manager on Saturday. Word was out that the great Simon Karlsson was looking for the next big thing. Someone had given Scott his business card after a set at The Big A.

"He's a big deal," Scott had told her. "Look at how classy his business card is." He'd shown her a simple white card with a phone number and address for some office building downtown.

"Do you think he was actually there?" Tommy had asked.

Sam had never heard of Karlsson, but the guys insisted he was a massive deal, a hotshot who could turn them into stars if he liked what he saw.

Oh shit, tomorrow night? I was supposed to hang with the girls.
The unanswered text remained on the phone in her pocket.

CHAPTER FOURTEEN

She should probably say something now before it caused a fight.

"Why can't we play one of the old songs for the guy?" Jose asked.

"No. He can hear those on the website. We need to wow him with something he's never heard before," Scott said.

"The Suburb of Despair?" Sam said aloud.

Scott pointed approvingly at her. She caught the angry looks of the others. The girls weren't supposed to get involved in band matters, but she felt like she'd earned it. Scott had spent the past few weeks writing what she thought was the perfect song for them to play. It was a mid-tempo, dark song of suburban alienation. She'd given him some ideas and he'd turned them into poetry. Lines like, "Mansions dressed in white, hope sunken in the black, once you move in, you ain't never comin' back."

"You want Karlsson to be impressed then we should play Rock 'n' Roll Nightmare," Tommy said. "That's the most commercial song we have."

"I vote that, too," Vic said, putting his hands up.

They'd been practicing for hours. The band was as tight as she'd ever seen them. They knew the songs like the backs of their hands, but Scott was a perfectionist. He'd stop them playing in a flash if he thought something was wrong.

"I like the new one actually," Jose said.

The other girls had lost interest a long time ago. Nancy, her curly blonde hair hanging over her ears, restlessly tapped on her phone. "This is so boring… are we gonna go out or what?" She was barely eighteen, dressed in a dark shirt and short skirt over red and white striped leggings. She wore a green vest covered in band patches and small black gloves missing the fingers. She was Tommy's girl, a real punk stereotype, straight out of an eighties fashion magazine.

"How many times you gonna play the same songs?" Sheila asked. Sheila had taken the punk image even further than Nancy. Half her head was shaved to the skin and the other side was bleached blonde and curved down to her chin. She wore a jean jacket covered with safety pins and a black halter top over tight black leggings torn in the sides. Massive Doc Martens easily added six inches to her height. She was incredibly impatient, always complaining, but was Vic's girl.

"I think that's what practicing is supposed to be," Sam said.

Beth sat quietly at the end of the couch, looking off into space. She was a real hippie type, with long dreadlocks, a pierced nose and loose baggy clothes in all greens and browns. She kept a woven bag over her shoulder at all times and had the faint aroma of pot about her. Sam assumed she was always stoned since Beth rarely spoke. She was with Ben.

"If this is all we're going to do tonight, I'm leaving," Sheila said.

"Do the chicks' votes count?" Jose asked.

"You better hope not," Vic teased. "You're the only one flying solo."

"Drummers get no respect," he spat back in a grumble.

"Guys, guys, what song are we doing? I can't keep track," Ben said.

"Suburb of Despair."

"Rock 'n' Roll Nightmare."

"Who fucking cares? This is a dead scene," Sheila said.

"I think they're really rocking tonight," Sam said to her.

Sheila shot her a death glare, not even bothering to respond with words. It was always tense with the other girls. Appar-

CHAPTER FOURTEEN

ently they viewed Sam with something simmering just below full blown hatred. She had no idea why; she couldn't get two words out of them at the best of times. Scott told her that she was imagining it, but it was definitely there. The only thing she was sure of was that none of them were as into the music as she was – they were just here for the guys.

Scott grabbed a fresh beer. "Look, we've almost got it. We're so close to perfect. We just need a few more run throughs."

There were a few grumbles behind him. The rest of the band grabbed beers.

"We're gonna go," Nancy announced as she stood up. "I can't sit here anymore. Shit Storm is playing down at The Zoo and I don't want to miss them."

Sheila rose with her and they headed to the door. Beth made no motion of following, still staring off into space.

"Hey, babe, come on. We're almost done, just hang on," Tommy pleaded.

"Beth, yo, burn out. Come on, we're jetting," Nancy shouted, snapping her fingers to get her friend's attention.

Beth jerked upright, returning to this planet. Her clothes clinked and her hair flowed as she ran after the others.

"You come when you're done fucking around, OK, Tommy?" Nancy spat as they left, slamming the door behind her.

Sam was alone now. The rest of the band looked at her, Tommy with particular vitriol. She smiled, feeling like a cat in a house of dogs. Scott chugged what had to be his fifth beer of the past half hour.

"Aren't you going with the rest of the groupies?" Tommy asked her.

"I'm good," Sam said. "I like watching you guys play."

Groupie?

Was that what they thought of her?

I am not a fucking groupie.

She and Scott had something special. Didn't they?

"You ever do anything you want to do with him?" Avital's words rang again in her head.

"Sure we do," she'd insisted then, but a nagging voice in the back of her head wouldn't let her be fully convinced.

You drive him around. You buy him beer. You go back to his room and...

No! He cares about my opinion. He listens. He–

"It's OK, Sam, we're gonna be a while, you can take off," Scott slurred.

"What?"

Was she being kicked out? The band glared at her, and she felt on trial. They clearly wanted her gone...

"You can go. I'll talk to you later, OK?"

"Oh, OK," she said. She stood up and grabbed her bag. "Umm, alright." She headed for the door. "You guys sound great by the way."

None of them said a word.

"Scott?"

He didn't respond.

"Rock 'n' Roll Nightmare then Suburb of Despair," he said to the others. He started counting off the band. They fired up into another song.

Scott?

The music drowned her out. This time it diminished her and made her feel like she wasn't wanted. She slunk out of the house, trudging back to her car feeling three inches tall.

"It's not him," she said aloud as if she had to convince herself. "It's the others. They don't appreciate how close we are. It's just jealousy."

She drove home, listening to the demo tape on the car stereo on repeat.

No sooner had Sam parked the car in the underground parking garage of her dad's downtown condo than her phone beeped. It was a text from Scott.

"Come over?"

She texted back: "u guys done playing?"

"Y," he responded.

It was almost midnight, but it wasn't like she had anything better to do. She pulled back out, drove up the ramp and headed back out into the night.

* * *

She knocked on the door. "Scott?"

No one answered. The house looked deserted. Jose's car was nowhere to be seen. This wasn't exactly a neighbourhood that she wanted to be standing out in the dark alone for too long. She tried the doorknob. It was unlocked.

"Hello? Scott?" she called out as she pushed her way in.

The instruments were piled up against the wall. The amps were silent. Piles of empty beer bottles had been pushed over to the corner. It looked like all the cases she had brought had been polished off.

She checked the bedroom. It was empty. She heard snoring coming from the bathroom. The door was ajar. Scott was slumped down on the ground, passed out. His chest rhythmically rose and fell as he lay there with his pants around his ankles. There was a funny smell in the room. Holding her nose, she reached out and flushed the source away.

She stared at Scott on the dirty tiled floor. Even passed out he was gorgeous.

"Scott?" she said gently as she poked his compact firmness. He was unresponsive. She could see that he was very much alive and in no distress, but this was no way to sleep it off. She pulled him to an upright position and got him up on the toilet seat. He was dead weight. She tried to pull up his pants, but the damn things were so tight that she couldn't manage it. She settled on pulling up his boxers and taking the pants right off. She dragged him over to the bedroom and dropped him on the mattress, then paused to catch her breath. Who knew hauling a passed out drunk would be so hard?

"You can sleep it off here," she said.

She was about to leave when she spotted a new notebook on the desk. From the sight of it, one he'd just started that she hadn't looked through yet. She picked it up and flipped through the pages, mostly blank, a few doodles, notes, and part of a song, "My Dark-Haired Girl."

Dark-Haired Girl? That must be me!

She had to read it. The lines did not disappoint.

"My lady of the night,
   Oh, you know you treat me right.
   Loving you feels so good
   A vixen underneath a hood
   My dark-haired girl, my dark-haired girl
   Oh, she's from another world
   my dark-haired girl."

Sam swooned.

This was her proof. No matter what the others thought,

CHAPTER FOURTEEN

no matter what anyone thought. This showed that he cared, *really* cared, loved her even. It was all right there in the song. Cosmo had told her that men had a hard time expressing their feelings, but he was doing it right here on paper.

"My dark-haired girl. I like the sound of that."

The song looked like it was still a work in progress. She'd pretend that she hadn't seen it, but the whole idea made her want to scream.

"I'm his muse, that's so cool."

Scott snored contentedly on the bed, half naked. They were alone in the house. She felt so connected to him right now. She slid off her pants and shirt and lay down next to him on the bed, pulling the ratty sheet over their bodies. He was so out of it, he never even noticed. She slid her hands over his body, but he didn't react. She was about to move lower when she stopped herself.

He's totally gone. You do that and you cross a line you'd never forgive someone for if they did it to you.

There was no way she was waking him up in this state.

That's OK, I'm here with him. She slid his arm around her and lay on his chest, listening to his breathing for a long time before eventually falling asleep herself.

CHAPTER FIFTEEN

"Now, Johnny tells me you used to be a cop?" The big man looked over Frank's files, nodding at a lifetime of service summarized in a few heavily redacted pages.

"Retired, and not by choice."

"I'll bet they miss someone like you on the force."

"The whole country misses someone like me on the force."

"You were a local boy though. This resume says River City cop since, wait, is this some kind of typo? Nineteen sixty-one? You couldn't have been there that long."

"There were a few years I was working what you might call odd jobs."

Frank sat in the head of the BBS security company's office. It was nothing fancy, a small number on the fourth floor of a five-story building downtown. Waiting room with a secretary, magazines from 1997, simple, classic. Frank liked that. The boss man had sense – his workspace consisted of a desk, a computer, and a good old-fashioned filing cabinet.

"You didn't put any of those on the application, but I guess it doesn't really matter. Your cop experience was more than enough for Johnny. And me."

CHAPTER FIFTEEN

The boss was stuffed into his white shirt like cookie dough in a tube. The buttons strained at the pressure of holding in his massive girth. He had a thick beard and a receding hairline. Sweat stains already showed under his arms from the strain of remaining upright. He was a beast of a man, more bear than human.

Frank was the toast of the company. His quick thinking and deadly moves had averted disaster twice now. The big man himself, the chief of BBS, had called Frank in to his office for a little rap session.

"Malone, I don't know how you do it, but you are my hero. You've made us the hottest security company in the city. I've got contract offers coming in left and right. They all want the best. You stop a riot and you solve a murder mystery. Talk about headlines. I could kiss you!"

"Unless you got a set of knockers hiding under that stuffed shirt of yours, chief, I'd recommend you don't. These lips only touch the fairer sex."

The boss laughed. "OK, OK. I ain't actually gonna kiss you."

Frank merely nodded.

The boss leaned back, putting his arms behind his head. "I like a resourceful man, a man who can think on his feet. Someone who's not just three hundred pounds of meat and tattoos like the rest of the schlubs that work for me. The security business don't really attract the best and brightest, if you catch my drift."

"You should see some of the rookies they've got downtown."

The boss scratched his chin. "Yeah, don't I know it. The boys in blue are always on my case for this or that, hiring known felons or some bullshit." He tapped his desk. "I run a tight ship here, Malone."

"I'm six knots ahead of you."

"Then we're on the same page?"

"I've already read the book, chief."

"I like your jib, Malone, that's why I called you down here for this little tête-à-tête."

"Did we lose a war, chief?"

The boss was confused. "What?"

"I could've sworn the frogs lost on the plains of Abraham."

The boss's mouth dropped open. "You're crazy, Malone, an old fashioned, straight shooter, get what you pay for. That's why you're my new favourite. After the last two jobs, I want you for a special contract, just came in today. Big shot company downtown. No riots, no dead bodies, simple security. But they pay a lot of green for silence if you catch my meaning."

"You want me to bust them up?"

"No, no, no, no. Nothing like that. I want my best man there to make sure nothing gets fucked up. I want someone with smarts and experience who won't blow this. Lotta lettuce at stake."

"So it's a special assignment, real hush hush?" Frank loved covert ops.

"That's right. We need someone discreet, but not afraid to take out the trash. None of the galoots I got on the payroll can do more than spell their own name half the time, so I come to you for this. Make me proud, Malone, make me proud."

CHAPTER SIXTEEN

"OK, we take it from the top again."

Sam watched as Scott stood alone in the isolation booth with huge headphones over his ears. He bobbed his head, waiting for his cue to start singing. She was in the control room with the engineer, and producer / hotshot band manager, Simon Karlsson.

"We're ready, Mr. Karlsson," the engineer said.

Simon reached for the communication button again and pressed it.

"This time with more impact please."

Scott heard the words through the headphones and seemed confused, but he nodded and waited.

"Let us begin," Karlsson said.

The huge red recording light above the glass window lit up. They were live.

This is so cool.

Sam still couldn't believe she was in here. It was like something out of a movie; watching a band laying down the parts of a song that would be put together into something professional and real. She knew nothing of the recording process, so it was strange to see each member playing their part in full isolation. Simon had the whole band play together first and was then going to sift through the best takes. She guessed that it made sense, but she was no sound engineer.

Scott wanted her in the booth, which drew frowns from the engineer and producer, but neither spoke up against it.

"As long as she remains silent," was all that Karlsson had said.

"My dark-haired girl..." Scott's words washed over her as the engineer played with dials on the massive console. Simon nodded his approval as his newest charge sang his part.

You sound great, Scott.

They'd come so far so fast. The showcase had gone well. Simon had been impressed and asked the band in for a recording session to see how they sounded on tape. He'd seen something in them, which drove everyone into a frenzy of nervous anticipation. Scott became convinced that Sam was some kind of lucky charm. She slept over more and more.

Her phone vibrated in her pocket, but she ignored it as she watched the man's every move.

"She's all I need, I can guarantee..."

Drunk Scott was open with her. He told her things. "I don't know what I'll do if this falls apart, Sam," he'd said. "Without this band, what am I?"

"You're talented as hell, Scott," she'd said. "You could do anything."

"I don't want to do anything. I want to be in a band. That's who I am, that's my life."

"I'll make sure you succeed," she'd said.

Each night she would fall asleep to the sounds of his snoring contentment.

"What do you think of this one, Mr. Karlsson?" the engineer

asked.

"He is improving. He is not there yet, but he will be."

She was the only girlfriend invited to the recording session here at the Big Shiny Tunes Recording Studio. The band seemed pissed, but they'd started to accept that Scott wanted her around. They were in the waiting area, eating from the meat and cheese plate, stuffing their faces while she watched Scott sing his heart out on "My Dark-Haired Girl."

My song. About me. There is going to be a hit song about me.

It was a big, loud, pop song ode to her. Loud, beautiful, singalong worthy. Even she heard the potential commercial appeal. It didn't sound like anything they played at The Big A. With each take it was sounding less rough around the edges, a bouncy jangle-fest of emotion.

All she saw was happy Scott singing about love, singing about her.

"...my dark-haired girl."

His plaintive voice cried out for her. Karlsson pressed the intercom button. "Very nice, Scott, very nice. I think we almost have it. Now if you would like to join your fellows in the main room, we can take a quick break before we do a live on the floor recording, please."

Scott hung up the headphones on a mounted hook and opened the door to the padded room. He exited out into the main recording space. The rest of the band soon entered from the other door, still chewing on kielbasa and cheddar wedges.

She could hear what went on through the intercom speaker.

"How'd it go?" Tommy asked.

"I think great," Scott said. "Simon said the next one is live from the floor."

"Good. This whole separate parts thing is messing up my

timing," Jose said.

"Good food though," Ben said with crumbs flying from his face.

Karlsson pressed the intercom button. "Please be taking your places. We will begin in two minutes, yes?"

They all got ready. Scott grabbed the microphone, looking to the booth for his cue. Karlsson turned to the engineer who gave him the OK sign. He spoke into the intercom again. "Yes, thank you very much. Now we will do takes with the whole band. Remember, you are playing to people across the world. You are communicating beyond words. You are touching them where they do not know they can be touched. You are imparting them a message. The message of the song. You understand?"

"I think so, Mr. Karlsson," Tommy said.

"Do not think. Feel. Play the song how you wish it to be played and let me do the rest."

"Sure thing, Simon," Scott said.

"Then whenever you are ready. Wow the world please."

This is it. I can feel it.

Scott called out the count, "one, two, one, two, three, four." The band broke in, the past few hours of repetition putting them in perfect time.

"Whoa, oh, oh, my dark-haired girlfriend,
 gonna be with me till the e-e-end
 You know the way she walks and the way she talks,
 got me hanging from a thread,
 my dark-haired gi-rl-friend."

Sam grinned, despite herself. The song had changed from

those first scribbles in his notebook. It almost jumped now with childlike glee. It reminded her of old pop songs that you found yourself tapping your foot to even if you didn't know the words. She could hear this in movies, commercials, all over the music video stations. She could see it going viral.

She found herself bopping her head in time. Karlsson seemed impressed. He looked to the engineer. "I am smelling the hit. The tweens will eat this stuff up."

Sam watched Karlsson work. The guy was a mystery. Scott had told her he was a big deal, but she'd never heard of him. Although the list of band managers she *had* heard of began and ended with Brian Epstein.

"It's sounding great in here, sir," the engineer said.

"Of course it is."

Karlsson had a thick accent. She assumed it was Swedish but Scott said he came from somewhere in Eastern Europe. He was tall and thin, with sharp angular features and piercing blue eyes. His short blond hair was slicked back away from his forehead. His mouth ended in an arrow-like chin, pointed and aristocratic. He carried himself with an air of pomposity and dignity, like some kind of royalty. He enunciated his words perfectly even if he occasionally betrayed his lack of proficiency with the English language with odd phrases that he repeated like "very fine," or "yes, yes, but of course." These were punctuation marks for him, shorthand expressions that took getting used to.

"I am thinking we may not need to do another take," Karlsson said.

He bobbed his head as the band played, as invested in this take as he was with the first. The band finished the song, and Sam wanted to applaud, but thought better of it. Karlsson looked at the engineer, who gave him a thumbs up. He then spoke into the microphone, "Perfect, I think we are having it."

Inside the studio, the guys high-fived each other for a job well done. They put down their instruments and adjourned to the recording studio lobby. The original plate of sandwiches and cheese had been destroyed, but another one was being set up.

Scott ran up to Sam and hugged her, lifting her right off her feet, kissing her firmly on the mouth with a force that surprised her. "How'd it go?" he asked. He was high on adrenaline.

"That was awesome," she said, catching her breath.

"I felt it, you know. Like, I really felt the energy of the song. What Simon said. I really tried to communicate the meaning in a deeper way across the whole world. To everyone."

"Totally." Sam was confused – he was never like this, energetic and childlike. It was almost cute.

"What'd you think, Mr. Karlsson?" Scott asked.

The man looked back to the control panel for a second. Sam thought maybe he wasn't impressed, but then he turned and flashed a huge smile. "Very fine, boys, very fine. I'm thinking we have a hit in the can here."

The band cheered and high-fived each other again. Jose was in the middle of eating a ham sandwich from the catering tray.

"So, what's next?"

"Well," Simon hummed, "if we are going to make this band into the next biggest thing in the planet, then we will be needing the publicity, ja? The photos, the interviews, the radio spots, the song for download. It is very much work still to go before the fame and glory comes."

CHAPTER SIXTEEN

"Don't worry, Mr. Karlsson," Tommy said, "we'll do whatever you need."

"I'm very pleased to be hearing this, very pleased. The first step is for Scott here to come for a makeover session with a professional stylist. He is the lead singer and therefore the face of the band. He must be looking his best for all the photos and screaming girls."

Tommy and Vic looked at each other. Sam could tell that they saw a million rock band movies flash by in their heads, countless tales of lead singers hogging all the glory and fame. It was written all over their faces that they didn't like that prospect one bit, but before either one could say anything, Simon butted in.

"We won't be forgetting each of the other band members, no, of course not. You will all receive makeovers as well. There will be total image enhancement, all done in time."

"What's wrong with the way we look now?" Ben asked.

There was a gasp in the room as the engineer looked horrified that someone had dared to ask such a question of the great Simon Karlsson.

"Why, my dear bass player... what is your name again?"

"Ben."

"Ben, yes, very fine, very fine. The way you look right now is perfectly acceptable for a band playing to a half-empty bar in downtown River City. Slumming it in a rented home on the wrong side of the tracks, desperately bumming cigarettes from the four fans who follow you around."

Was he talking about her?

"But, if this band would like to live in the infamy of superstardom, then it will require a transformation. No more torn jeans and flannel shirts, I'm afraid. The public will not accept their rock gods looking like the man who changes their engine oil. They want to lose themselves in the illusion of a larger-than-life character who speaks to their dreams in a way they could only hope to."

Simon stared off into the distance, lost in his soliloquy. "I don't need to tell you that the path to fame is littered with the corpses of those who would not compromise. Countless bands play the local rodeo into their fifties, living off that shred of the dream they had as teenagers. It is only those who can make the ultimate sacrifices, those who are willing to do whatever it takes to become stars that go down in history."

Ben swallowed hard, like a child receiving a lecture from his teacher.

"Do you really think the Beatles all had the, how you say" – he made air quotes – "mop top and suits when they were discovered? No, of course not, that was a conscious decision, an image makeover. Do you really think the Rolling Stones, Led Zeppelin, Guns 'n' Roses, Coldplay, U2, and all the others did not have a guiding hand in making them palatable to the super audiences of the world? Who is the most famous rock star of all time? David Bowie? Elvis? Michael Jackson? Madonna? Lady Gaga? In all cases, image is more than half of the picture. So you can stay in your ratty second-hand thrift store apparel and continue to play in the dive shitholes I find you in, or you can listen to my team of paid professionals, wear the right clothes, say the right things and become bigger than Jesus. All religions die eventually my friends, but Rock 'n' Roll is forever." He clenched his fist as he punctuated his pronouncement. Sam was sold and she wasn't even in the band.

"Don't worry about Ben," Vic chimed in. "We're all on board

with the program, one hundred percent. Ain't that right, Ben?"

"Uh, yeah, totally. Forget I ever said anything."

Karlsson smiled, his face lizard-like, his eyes laser sight locked on Scott. He licked his lips. "Consider Scott the guinea pig for the new look of the band. The team will experiment with some ideas, then come to the rest of you with the selections. We will be making you all into a cohesive whole that will turn the rock industry on its rear. They say rock is dead, my friends, but I know that it is only sleeping. We will wake it up. Scott, and Radiant Cyanide... go to the moon!"

The band cheered. Sam couldn't help but feel ecstatic for where this was all going.

CHAPTER SEVENTEEN

"This is where you will be working," the man in the navy suit said. "These monitors on the desk show live feeds from all of the cameras in the facility. At least all of them that you will be in charge of."

A host of monitors were inlaid on the desk console, each showing nothing more than a boring hallway. Frank sat down in front of the control panel and started turning knobs and flicking switches. "How many channels can this thing pick up?"

"You have all seventy–"

"No football, no daytime movies, nothing. Just a bunch of empty halls."

"Yes, well, you see that is what we want your keen eyes to monitor."

"You want me to monitor the monitors?"

"Yes, of course."

"Then what?"

"If you see anything, uh, untoward, you can fill out your logbook and an investigation can be undertaken."

"So I'm strictly an observe and report man? Watch for trouble, fill out a form. This is what you need the best cop the city has ever seen for?"

"You used to be a policeman? How very interesting. That may explain why you brought your own handcuffs."

Frank tapped the jingling set of cuffs dangling from his belt. They were polished to a spit shine, his favourite set.

"Never leave home without 'em."

"Well, please do not feel that you must put yourself at risk trying to apprehend anyone you may see doing what you may think is against policy. We have avenues and means to deal with–"

"Flashlight, walkie-talkie, keycards, notepad; I'm a regular Batman here."

"What else do you feel you may require for this job?"

"You mean how many calibres?"

"Oh, perhaps there is some confusion. We are simply a humble corporation. Many divisions, of course, advertising, pharmacological research, medical technology, nothing involving firearms, I can assure you."

"European?"

"Eastern, why do you ask?"

"Because you sound like the kind of guy who comes from someplace else, maybe runs in circles of the highfalutin. Here in this country, we keep our falutins low to the ground, you hear me?"

"Yes, I see. I will take your suggestion into consideration. Now, are you quite clear on your work?"

"A gig is a gig is a gig."

The man called Heinrich smiled and clapped his hands happily. "Excellent. Then I will leave you to it."

They'd given Frank a uniform, none of that black shirt with yellow writing bullshit here. This one was full dress blues;

fancy dark shirt and pants, utility belt of goodies held up with a snazzy shoulder strap. It was nicer than his dad's burial suit. He was given a red armband marked 'security' and shown to the front desk in the lobby of the coldest building he had ever been in. It was downtown, one of those modern numbers you walk by a million times and never think to step into. Glass and shine, reflecting the city back at itself in all its ugliness.

Frank was alone, watching the monitors, trying to figure out what was where when some scrawny guy with a slicked back haircut and pompous air about him came in the front door. He led a rat bag kid with a painted-on beard and hippie hair. The man flashed Frank an ID badge and headed to the large doors, completely ignoring him.

The card opened them like magic, just another wonder of the modern age Frank thought was a waste of time and money. What the hell was wrong with a good old-fashioned iron key? He saw the duo walk down one of the hallways on screen and disappear into a room, out of sight of the cameras. He slumped back down in his chair. He hoped that wouldn't be the only kind of action he saw here.

"A gig is a gig is a gig, Frankie," he said, putting his feet up on the console.

Nothing else happened. He damn near could have fallen asleep were it not for the extreme cold air in the place. He shivered in his uniform, his old bones feeling the icy breeze more than they used to.

"They must have coffee here somewhere."

He looked around the room, nothing but a couple of chairs and a short table with magazines. Waiting room only, no java. He needed that black roast fix. He went over to the large double doors and peered through the glass inside. All he could see was a white hallway, stark and uninviting. There were lots of office doors on either side.

"Someone in there must have a lead on the good stuff."

He fished through his key cards until he found the one that opened the door. The faint beep of computers talking to each other tipped him off that he'd unleashed the magic. The door swung open with a faint humming sound and an even colder gust of air assaulted him. Now he was really shivering.

"They must really like their air conditioning around here."

The place reeked of antiseptic, the smell of a hospital, the smell of death. Frank walked down the hall and tried the first couple of doors. Locked, the small rectangular windows inside showed nothing more than storage rooms and empty offices. The hallway branched off, and he took the right, good old faithful right. He looked in another door and saw the strangest thing. The ratty hippie kid stood in the centre of a room, stripped to his underwear while a team of men and women in lab coats examined him. They drew lines on his body, wrote things down in clipboards. For some reason he thought of the draft board.

"Is another damn war going on?"

He watched until a face appeared in the window. Frank nearly jumped out of his skin, but his joints were so damn cold he couldn't move. The door swung open and the face asked, "Can vee help you?"

"Coffee, got any leads on where it is?"

The man smiled, his lips pulling back in a serpentine grin. "Yes, yes, but of course. You have gone down the wrong hallway. The lunchroom is the second door that way." He pointed down the opposite way that Frank had come.

"Thanks a lot, doc. Say, what's going on in there, some kind of hippie physical?"

The man never lost his smile. "Yes, yes. We are being most thorough with our evaluation. The specimen is most important."

Frank saw the hippie flinch as a dotted line was drawn on his stomach. He was starting to look like some kind of crash test dummy. There were charts on the wall, photographs that Frank couldn't make hide nor hare of and a pile of clothes laid out on a huge slab table, multiple outfits of leather, suede, and ruffles. Whatever was going on in here was beyond him – it was coffee he was after and coffee he would get.

"Say, doc, can I offer some advice? I'd say cut the hippie's hair. If the number two is good enough for the army, it's good enough for them."

"Thank you for your candour. Now, if you please, we have a great deal of work to do."

Frank headed back down the hall to the lunchroom, hearing the faint hum of the door shutting behind him.

With a fancy imported coffee warming his bones, he returned to his console and grabbed a magazine. Lost in an article about cake decorating, he almost didn't notice when the hippie kid left. It was quite a change. What had walked in as a rangy, filthy hippie was now a clean cut, sharply dressed normal. His hair was short, his so-called beard trimmed into a thin van dyke, his old clothes replaced with a tight-fitting dark suit, vest, and hat. He looked like a young Sinatra, only without the mob tie.

"You clean up nice, kid," he told him, but the kid didn't say a word, just walked out with a halfway blank stare on his face. "Same fucking hippie attitude though." Frank went back to his drink.

CHAPTER EIGHTEEN

"Scott, open up," Sam said as she knocked on the door again. There were two cases of beer at her feet and a brown-bagged bottle of Crown Royal in her hands.

"Aren't we going to the show? I'm here."

It was Friday night. She was supposed to drive Scott to The Big A.

She took out her phone and swiped it open, texting him: 'I'm here.'

There were lines of unanswered texts from the past few days. The last thing he'd told her was 'meeting Simon's image crew' and since then, nothing. She had tests to study for and reading to catch up on and figured that since the recording session the band was probably super busy with all of the attention from the record label. But this was their night. He hadn't said anything about cancelling.

She knocked again, the cold air starting to get to her as she stood on the front step. The snow fell gently as the first hints of a harsh winter approached.

"Hello? Guys? I've got beer here. Let me in!"

Still no answer. She tried the door. It swung open on its own.

Unlocked? You guys need to be more careful.

She pushed the cases of beer inside with her feet and shut the door behind her.

"Wow, you guys cleaned up," she said as she saw that the place was cleaner than she had ever seen it. Jackets were hung up in the closet, the floor was free of debris, the kitchen looked nearly immaculate.

She lifted the cases of beer onto the counter. "Hey, for once this thing is free of pizza boxes and empties."

The stove was clean, the microwave glistened, she could even see her reflection in the faucets.

"Thanks for helping by the way, guys."

She took out the Crown Royal from the bag and placed it next to the beer, then crumpled up the bag and tossed it in the empty bin underneath the sink.

I guess no one's home?

She headed to the living room.

I'll just watch TV and wait.

She screamed in shock when she saw the band sitting on the couch. "Jesus, you guys scared me. Why the hell didn't you answer when I knocked?"

No one said anything. They all just sat there staring off into space. The television wasn't on, so what were they looking at?

"That Karlsson guy does good work," she said at their new looks.

They had all been given a complete make-over: new haircuts, new clothes. They were virtually unrecognizable from their previous incarnation. They'd gone from normal looking everyday slobs to male models in a few short days.

"You guys could be on the cover of *Vogue* or *Rolling Stone*.

But then I guess that was the point of the makeover, right?"

No reply.

"Are you guys stoned?"

They sat like zombies with glazed over eyes and perfect posture, watching a black television in rapt attention.

She put her finger underneath Tommy's nose. She felt an outtake of breath. Their eyes blinked in precise motions. Their chests moved from the breathing process. She put her finger to Vic's neck and felt a pulse.

"Well, you're all alive. Are you meditating? Is this some kind of Swedish focus exercise?"

She waved her hands in front of their eyes. She held Ben's nose shut. Nothing fazed them. But there was one member missing.

"Where's Scott?" she asked.

Again, no response.

"Apparently, I'm invisible. What else is new with you jerks? Let me guess, he's in the bedroom? I'm going to check the bedroom unless someone gives me a reason not to."

Their blank faces were like masks. Every hair was in line and their skin was blemish free. Their clothes looked expensive right down to their socks. But was this silence some kind of weird game?

"Seriously. This isn't funny. Could someone just say something? Anything?"

It felt like she was talking to herself.

"OK, fuck you, too, then. I'm going in the bedroom."

Scott was sitting at the desk, writing. She snuck up behind him and gave him a huge hug.

"Hey there, handsome. The others look great, let's see what Simon did to you."

She caught a whiff of his new scent, something foreign, old world, spices she couldn't identify. It smelled expensive, not at all like the Shoppers Drug Mart discount stuff he normally wore.

"Well, you smell good at least."

Something was off. He wrote but he didn't react to her touch. It was like he hadn't heard her at all.

"You OK, Scott?"

She let go of his neck. She noticed a small cut at the base of his skull right near the hairline, held shut with stitches.

"Did you cut yourself shaving or something?"

She leaned around to get a good look at him and gasped when she saw what the image experts had done. His wild hair was tamed and shorn, a thin tracing of facial hair lined his chin. His brows were manicured, his nails, too. He wore the hippest clothes. Tight pants and a shit unbuttoned to the base of the neck.

"You don't even look like the same guy," she said. "You look great though." She almost felt bad for thinking that he was hotter this way.

His hand moved in looping arcs while he stared at a point on the wall. She followed his gaze but couldn't figure out what it was that he was looking at.

"Hello? Scott?" She waved her hand in front of his face and snapped her fingers a few times.

He just kept writing.

"What the hell is going on here? Is everyone on mushrooms? Acid? Did you guys take acid? A bunch of Ritalin?"

She sighed and sat on the bed, taking out her phone. She texted a note to Avital. "At Scott's. Think he's on something."

Three dots showed that Avital was texting her back. She

CHAPTER EIGHTEEN

watched and waited.

"He's bad news, babe. You can do better."

"I get it. You don't like him," she said as she rolled her eyes. She texted back.

"The whole band is out of it. Weird vibes."

Avital typed a response. "You should go. Come over here."

Sam was in the middle of texting a response when she looked up and Scott was gone from the desk. She hadn't heard a sound. She looked around the room, but he was gone. She shoved her phone back in her pocket and stood up.

"What the hell, Scott?"

He stood at the doorway like a statue, waiting.

"Were you in some kind of writing trance or something? I was knocking on the door, no one answered. I just walked in. I've got beer. The guys are being all weird out there, like zombies or something."

Scott stood rigid and slowly stepped out into the main room.

"Hey, wait!"

She quickly followed him. The guys were all at their instruments, standing like mannequins. Scott took his place at the microphone and looked right through her.

"If you're trying to mess with me, it's not going to work."

Tommy and Vic's amps came on, the sound of power surging through the room. She hadn't even seen them move. The drumsticks were in Jose's hands. Each member of the band was looking right at her, unblinking. It was seriously weirding her out.

"Is this a new song you want me to hear or something?"

Sam had goosebumps from the electricity in the room. Her hair seemed to flutter. A pit opened in her stomach as her feet felt glued to the floor. The band was ready, but for what? And why was no one saying anything?

She wanted to leave. She wanted to stay. She wanted to sit on the couch. She wanted to hear what they were going to play. She had to hear it. It must be important. A shiver ran up her spine.

Vic strummed once and the sound reverberated in Sam's head. It thundered in the room, seemed to shake the very foundations of this rundown, but newly clean house.

"Did you turn it up to eleven already?" she asked playfully.

Something was wrong. The words formed in her head, but they never left her mouth. It was then she realized that she couldn't talk. Her tongue felt glued to the roof of her mouth. Her eyelids were stuck in place. She felt like she was running out of air.

Help!

The purse fell from her shoulder to the ground. The phone fell out and the face showed her a text from Avital. She couldn't read it. It wasn't in letters she knew. She wasn't sure how that was possible but there it was, gibberish on the screen. Her eyes started to dry out as she stood motionless, and the band glared at her.

Jose slapped the kit a couple of times. Ben tested his bass. They were somewhere else, off the planet. Scott's eyes were the wrong colour. Or was that some trick of the light? The room seemed to dim. She felt like a spotlight was shone on her. They were each surrounded by inky darkness. The features of the house faded away. They were illuminated by their own spotlights, yet there were none in this house. How was this happening? She seemed to be floating in some kind of ether, tethered to the ground, unable to move or speak.

Then, in a split second, the song clicked in perfectly. It

CHAPTER EIGHTEEN

seemed to come from everywhere and nowhere at once. They were in perfect time, rigid like marble yet playing immaculately, a staccato pounding of noise.

The words weren't English. Yes, they were. No, they weren't. The sounds that came from Scott's throat were inhuman, guttural, a demonic keening from somewhere foreign. Had they gone death metal?

Then the scratchy rattle made sense. She could hear the words beneath it. It was simple, catchy, bubble-gum pop.

"When you want to have a good time,
 there's only one place to go,
 anything you want to
 just bring it
 P-A-R-T-Y!"

The band pounded out a wall of noise that hit her with wave after wave. Sheets of invisible energy that permeated her skin. She could feel it flowing up into her head, dancing around inside her veins. It moved with her blood, circling, questing through her entire core. She felt like she was getting an X-ray as the warmth slowly overtook her.

What's going on?

"P-A-R-T-Y, that's what I said,
 P-A-R-T-Y, never going to bed!"

What the hell kind of lyrics are these? These don't sound like anything Scott would write.

This was different. It was straightforward, simple, radio friendly. She caught herself singing along without even knowing the words. How could she?

The tingling ran through her body. She began to sweat. She could feel the beads dripping down her back but couldn't do anything about it. She lost feeling in her limbs yet didn't fall over. Only her head felt like it was a part of her.

The song was perfect. Her feet tapped of their own accord. No, they were locked to the floor. No, they were moving. Conflicting sensations bombarded her brain. She was bobbing her head, she was singing along. No, she wasn't doing any of that. She was about to pass out. The darkness around the band seemed to have eyes looking at her. Twinkling stars moving through the Stygian abyss.

"P-A-R-T-Y, that's what I said,
P-A-R-T-Y, every night till I'm dead!"

She was losing herself in the song. Forgetting her name, where she was. How she'd gotten here. What city was this? What year?

The phone at her feet seemed to exist in space outside of space. The screen lit up again with a ping and a text. The image of words made Scott's less clear. He was grunting, an orc playing at a rock star. Then, the text was gone, and this song was renewed.

This is so good.

That wasn't her voice in her head. Whose was it?

The guys were playing perfectly without any communication, no glances to each other, no hand signals, no movement. They were as locked in their own little self-contained worlds as she was. But the song. It came from them, it was them.

The music kept increasing in volume. How could the house

take this? Wouldn't the neighbours call the cops? But there was no house anywhere that she could see. They existed outside of physicality. Her ears protested, but the song wouldn't relent.

For a flash her mind shouted out a thought, piercing through the veil of the song the five statues were playing. *You've seen something like this before.*

The words fought against her mind's last desperate attempts to maintain its sanity. The weird way the band was acting, how similar they seemed to… Joshua.

Under control.

Heartstones.

How?

There was no way that could be possible…

"P-A-R-T-Y, that's what I said,
  P-A-R-T-Y, never going to bed!"

That had all ended a year ago.

The song. The words. Her mind refused to give up like her body had. Ten eyes from Radiant Cyanide glowing. Staring at her. A million from the nothingness telling her she was losing.

Not yet.

Golems. Necromancers. There'd been no trace of them since the fire in Toronto. Whatever Duckie had dug up of their research was buried with him.

But the eyes. The posture. The trance-like state. Scott. Tommy. Vic. Ben. Jose. Who were they? What were they? What had they become?

Golems?

Preposterous.

"P-A-R-T-Y, that's what I said,
P-A-R-T-Y, every night till I'm dead!"

She couldn't remember exactly how Joshua acted under the control of the gemstone.
Who's Joshua?
Other voices.
Her thoughts were murky.
They were out of it like he used to be. She tried to focus, but the song refused to let her.

"P-A-R-T-Y," her voice added to theirs.

No! Think. Resist!
Give in.
Give in.
Give in.

"P-A-R-T-Y, that's what I said!"

The band had never acted like this before… then it hit her, the manager. Who? What was his name? He did something to them. To Scott.
Scott.
Empty eyes. He was mouthing a noise that echoed in her brain. Her eyes were dimming. Her ears rang like an off-the-line phone. She couldn't hear the last of her thoughts. Her brain seared in agony. She wanted to scream, but the last note, long and deep, refused to fade away, staying in a never-ending

CHAPTER EIGHTEEN

echo behind her eyes. Her throat went dry, she lost what little resistance she had left, then it all went black.

* * *

She woke up in an unfamiliar bed. Her head was on fire, her throat felt like she had swallowed a hairball. She couldn't remember how she'd gotten here or even where here was.

She turned her head to the left and saw Scott laying next to her. The details of the room came into focus now. Scott's bed. She was with Scott. What day was it? It must be Saturday. Or Sunday.

It all made sense now. She'd slept over. Like she had been doing for weeks. She reached out and touched his hair. It was messy, sticky from whatever product he'd put in it.

Wait. Product? Scott didn't use anything in his hair. It was short, too. That wasn't right. She lifted up the blankets to see that he was naked. His nails were painted and manicured. His body had been sugared bare.

The makeover. How could she have forgotten?

Someone snored next to her. She looked over at the other side of the mattress and saw Tommy passed out naked on his stomach.

"What the fuck?"

She jerked upright. She was naked, too. A panic washed over her.

Just what in the heck happened last night?

She couldn't see her clothes anywhere. The two guys were obliviously sleeping. She frantically looked around the room for anything to cover herself up with. The ratty bed sheet was the only choice. She slid off the bed and pulled it with her.

She wrapped it around her body, leaving the two nude men uncovered.

She ran her hands through her matted hair, trying to piece together how this had happened. What even had happened?

You woke up in the same bed with two men. With no clothes on. What do you think happened, Sam?

Scott scratched his groin in his sleep. Tommy rolled over. There were two of them in her line of sight. Her eyes darted to a box of condoms on the dresser. Torn wrappers littered the floor. Empty beer bottles. Paper cups. A pile of dirty socks. The desk with Scott's notebooks. The posters on the wall staring back at her accusingly.

"You know what you did," Lou Reed said to her.

"No, I don't. That's the problem," she said frantically.

"Acid will do that to you," Kurt Cobain said.

"Acid? What are you talking about?"

"You all dropped acid."

"That might explain how you're talking to me right now," she said. "Why I'm fucking answering you, too."

Her head throbbed. She braced herself on the wall, worried she might lose her balance.

"Let me guess, you've never had a threesome before," James Taylor said.

"What did you just say?" She turned to the black and white poster of the balding man. "I mean, I must be hungover, because I'm sure you just said threesome."

"I've seen some wild chicks before, Sam, but you just about beat them all out of the running."

"You're not even real," she said.

"Of course I'm real," James Taylor said. "As real as the fire and the rain and the–"

CHAPTER EIGHTEEN

"Shut up, shut up, shut up."

Had she heard him right? Threesome?

"You heard him right all right," Kurt Cobain said. "You. Scott. Tommy. We saw it all."

"No, no, no, no, no. This isn't real. You three aren't talking to me. I'm just dreaming. That's right. I'm dreaming."

"Oh, you're not dreaming," Lou Reed said. His sunglassed visage seemed to taunt her.

"You're dead! What do you know?"

"I know you have a birthmark right near your–"

She ran out of the room.

"I need to find my clothes," she said, frantic. She couldn't focus on anything, her brain pounding a constant note in her skull. She held the stained sheet around her as she looked for some sign of her things in the mess of a house.

Wait. Mess?

Hadn't it been clean when she'd come last night? She looked around the room. There were pizza boxes and empties everywhere. A bottle of Crown Royal lay empty on the coffee table. The television was showing an old movie.

"How can I not remember anything?"

The door to the other room was propped open. She could see the sleeping forms of Vic, Ben, and Jose. Nobody stirred. They all must have really tied one on last night. That would explain the hangover.

"Could I really do something like that?"

"Of course. Acid is a hell of a drug," the voice of David Bowie said from the wall to her left.

"Oh God, now you, too?"

"Maybe you should ask the other guys what happened if you don't believe me," Bowie said.

Something was off about all of this, and it wasn't just the fact that the posters of rock stars were talking to her. A flash of a memory shot through her head. Arriving at the house. Seeing the band play a song.

"Didn't I see the guys play a new song last night?"

"I don't know. Did you?"

"You're not helping, David."

"Want me to wake up the gang? They can tell you exactly what you did."

"No, no. You keep your mouth shut, Bowie. God, why am I acting like you're real?"

"Acid flashback, maybe?"

"This is all crazy. I've got to find my clothes."

"Don't get dressed on my account, babe," David Bowie said, eyeing her covered body lasciviously.

"Stop it, you're dead too! Now help me find my clothes."

The image of David Bowie on the wall recoiled from her admonishment. "Whoa, testy little chickie."

She wanted to crawl under a rock and die. None of this made any sense. She had to get home, get away from this scene and try to piece together what had happened for herself. She certainly didn't want to face Tommy or Scott right now. She looked behind the couch, under the coffee table, under pizza boxes. She couldn't find her clothes anywhere.

"Wait till you see the video," David Bowie said.

"Video?" She froze and looked at his painted face. This was getting worse by the second.

"Cellphone camera. Real wild stuff."

"OK. I've lost my fucking mind now. What the fuck…?"

"You don't have to be ashamed. It's a whole new side of you." David Bowie looked at her in admiration.

CHAPTER EIGHTEEN

I would never do that, I would never let them do that. But acid? Could it be true?

"Oh, it's true, babe."

"None of this is happening."

"I'll get Tommy to grab his phone, maybe it'll jog your memory."

"Shut the fuck up, Bowie."

There! She spotted her clothes on the ground behind the television. She grabbed them up in a bundle and was about to pull them on when a voice rang out behind her.

"There she is," Tommy said from the bedroom. "Party girl!"

She spun in shock with her clothes and the edge of the blanket covering her body. He smirked and gave her a one-handed gun salute. He was completely naked with a tiny yogurt container in one hand. He dipped his index finger inside and licked off the creamy white substance.

She screamed and ran right through the door outside, the sheet wrapped around her blowing in the wind.

CHAPTER NINETEEN

"Then Andre the Giant was complaining that he had diarrhea all day from the food, or maybe the water, I'm not a hundred percent sure, but either way, he had the runs. You see, they couldn't just turn away all the people who'd come to the show, so they just told him to tough it out."

"Tough it out? With the runs?" Erin asked Marlon in disbelief.

"Yup, but you and I both know that never works. So picture Bad News Allen on the mat, laying flat."

"I have no idea who that is," Sam said.

"Black dude, beard, bad ass."

"Bad ass or bad news?"

"Both. He was a bad ass, but his name was Bad News."

"This story is bad news," Avital said, rolling her eyes.

"Just wait," Marlon said, holding his hand out insistently. "I'm getting to the good part. So there's Bad News on the mat and Andre sits on him, or should I say *shits* on him. Sprays his bowels all over the dude."

"Ewwww, sick," Erin said, twisting her face in revulsion.

"And this wasn't just some normal shit, this was a Mexican

CHAPTER NINETEEN

burrito, beer-filled—"

"Holy shit!" Everett interrupted.

"That wasn't what I was going to say, but that works."

"Umm… Sam?" He was holding his phone in his hand, looking from it to her repeatedly.

"What is it?" she asked.

"Is there something you're not telling us? Like about making videos? You know, of the adult persuasion."

She blanched. In an instant, her heart sank through her stomach to puddle in mush around her socks. Everett didn't have to say any more. All of the confusion and brain fog melted away and she knew that the worst possible scenario from the other night was, in fact, true. The wide-eyed look on his face told her all she needed to know.

"What is it?" Avital asked him.

"What are you looking at?" Erin asked.

"He's not looking at anything, are you?" Sam said, trying desperately to get him to stop before they all found out.

"Sure I am. It's you. You want to see?"

"No. Yes. I don't know."

She leaned over and pushed in next to him. He tilted his phone for the briefest moment.

"So David Bowie wasn't lying."

"Never in a million years…" Everett said, tilting the phone back so he could watch.

Sam sank into the futon. "You think I wanted something like this to happen?"

"Wanted what to happen?" Erin asked. "What are you two looking at?"

"I thought David Bowie was just making some kind of sick joke."

"David Bowie?" Avital asked.

"Worse case scenario it was some prank or like an acid flashback."

"Acid flashback?" Erin said, aghast.

"I mean, I know you're supposed to be Partying one, but geez, Sam. This? On video? On the internet so anyone can see it?"

"Like jerks in the middle of the day at university?"

"I mean, wow. I never knew you had it in you," Everett said, shaking his head, his eyes never leaving the phone screen.

Do you have to keep watching it?

Her head rolled backwards to stare at the tiny holes in the ceiling tiles distantly above them. The sounds of footfalls on the cafeteria floor pounded the reality into her skull that more had happened the other night than her dim recollections allowed. Jumbled images that made no coherent sense, posters talking, the band playing, beer, a clean room, waking up with two men, the splitting headache. Why would she ever have agreed to take acid? She didn't do hard drugs. Sure, she'd tried pot once, but that had been an innocent puff at a party and led nowhere. The years of anti-drug messaging had scared her straight edge.

Unless they slipped you something.

The idea was preposterous. Scott wasn't that kind of guy.

But the others? Were they?

"Could one of you tell us what the hell you're talking about?" Erin asked.

Avital was staring right through Sam with a look of disgust. Clearly, she'd pieced together what was going on even if Erin hadn't.

"At least send us the meme," Marlon said.

CHAPTER NINETEEN

"Sure," Everett said.

"The fuck you will," Sam said, shooting him a death glare.

"Sam," Avital said. "What were you thinking?"

"I can't remember what happened. Any of it."

"What did those assholes do?"

Sam had seen the tiny video proof. So had Everett. How many others? Could she contain this?

"Seriously, what are you looking at?" Marlon said.

Before either of them could reach, Erin snatched the phone away from Everett. "Gimme that," she said as looked at the action on screen. At first she was confused, but then her eyes nearly popped out of her head in shock. "Ohmygod, Sam, what is this?"

"Please, Erin, it's not–!"

"Let me see," Avital said and rose to look at the video. "Fucking hell, Sam." Her furious expression told Sam all she needed to know.

Marlon tried to make a move to join in watching, but Sam was quicker, snatching the phone away from Erin before he could see.

"What the hell are you guys looking at?" he said in a pout.

"You don't get to know," Sam said.

She looked down at the glossy screen, covered in the smudges of all their fingerprints. It was exactly as she'd thought.

"It was porn, dude," Everett said.

"Everett." Avital shot him a death glare.

"So, what's the big deal?" Marlon asked. "He was surfing porn. It's his phone."

"Sure, but in school, in public, while talking to us?"

"Seriously? That's it? It's just porn. Come on, guys, it can't be that big a deal."

"Think for a minute, Marlon," Avital said, still staring at Sam in admonishment.

"What do you mean?"

"Are you really that dense?" she asked him. "Who'd he show it to? Who acted like she'd just had a heart attack? Who am I super pissed at right now?"

He rubbed his chin, trying to put it all together but not managing to do the complicated algebra of the moment.

What she'd seen was seared on to Sam's eyeballs. Video. Blurry video. A girl. Two guys. Naked. Dark hair. The mole. Scott's unmistakable penis. Tommy's flat face. Jerky movement. Dim lights. The Kurt Cobain poster on the wall in the background. No sound, but who knew what was being said or moaned?

"Hey..." Marlon said as he started to figure it out.

A seal in a circus.

"Wait a second..." Marlon said. "Are you suggesting that–"

"Don't even say it out loud."

"Why would you do that, Sam?" Erin asked. "Just why?"

"I didn't..."

But she did. It was pixelated, but even in the poor image quality she could see the awful truth. David Bowie wasn't lying.

"So then how is there photographic evidence?" Avital asked.

Her grip on the phone tightened. If David Bowie wasn't lying about the threesome, then he probably wasn't lying about the acid.

"They slipped me something," she said.

"Who?" Erin asked.

"You know who," Avital said. "I told you those guys were no

CHAPTER NINETEEN

good."

Her confusion vanished. Replaced with embarrassment, shame, but also boiling rage. Drugs. They'd given her drugs, had taken advantage of her in an inebriated state, and then uploaded the video to whatever porn site this was on Everett's phone.

"I'm going to fucking kill those two assholes."

"Who?" Marlon asked. "Why? I'm so lost. Also, wait, kill someone? Like, for real?"

"I can't believe it," Sam said as her grip crushed the plastic case on Everett's phone. Cracks spiderwebbed the screen guard, pieces of plastic dug into her palm as she squeezed it, imagining it was Scott's face. "I can't believe they'd do this... I trusted him."

"Can I at least see what?" Marlon reached out for the phone.

"You're not going to." Sam shot him a look, freezing him in his tracks. He backed away like a hyena scared off by a lion.

"Where did you find this?" she asked Everett.

Everett shrugged. "Just online, you know, no big deal."

"No, it is a big deal."

"Don't worry, it's subscription only. German, I think."

"I don't care. It's coming down. You need to show me. I need to file a complaint or a takedown notice or whatever it is you're supposed to do."

"If this was done against your will, you need to go to the police," Avital said.

"Yeah, they have, like, a whole unit for this kind of thing, don't they?" Erin said.

"Oh shit, police?" Marlon said.

Sam looked again at the video. It was only her word that said it wasn't consensual. The visual evidence was lacking to say the least. "What would they do? They'd look at the video. Say sorry but it sure looks like you were into it. Or send some form letter to the website and hope it comes down? Meanwhile it's picked up somewhere else and somewhere else. It would be just like whack-a-mole, wouldn't it?"

"But if they drugged you then that's a whole other crime."

"And even that I can't prove. It's been days. Would there even be anything left in my system?"

"I still didn't get to see what you're talking about!" Marlon whined.

"Shut up, Marlon," Sam screamed in frustrated rage. He cowered.

"Sam, this is a Me Too thing. This isn't something you should just push aside," Avital said. "I'm not going to let you let those pieces of shit get away with this."

"I'm not going to either. But I need evidence. Their phone, some of the drugs, something to prove my story."

"Can someone please just show me? I hate being left out." Marlon asked.

"I not going to show you anything, I'm going to do something about it," Sam said.

CHAPTER TWENTY

"Another quiet night, Washington?" Frank asked.

The man flashed him a grin, his white teeth at odds with his dark skin. An open binder lay on the camera console, a thermos of coffee long cooled, a crumpled-up Subway sandwich bag. Looked like the kid was having an easy time of it here.

"You know it! I never heard a peep from the place. Nothing but blank screens and empty halls. Got loads of studying done."

"I keep telling you to stay out of those things. Ain't nothing you can learn in university that you can't learn out there in the real school of hard knocks."

Isaiah looked at him blankly.

"The streets. I mean, look at me," Frank said, waving his hand down his body. "I never paid some egghead for a fancy piece of paper and a couple of letters at the end of my name. I went out there and earned everything I had with nothing but my wits and a big fucking gun."

Isaiah shut his binder and slid it into a backpack. He rose from his seat, ready to let Frank take over. The man was on the night shift and always looked happy when Frank came to relieve him from another day of sitting on his ass all night.

The kid meant well, but starting out at a desk had him all mixed up, thinking that studying and hard work was going to pay off when he had to learn that gumption was the only quality that mattered in the real world.

"Hey, if all it took was waving a gun at somebody to get me one of them sweet human resource manager jobs, you can be sure I'd be doing that instead of working nights at this place, then going to school all day."

Frank took his place at the desk, brushed away the crumbs from the console and put his feet up on the edge. "You ever thought to try the gun angle? You never know, right?"

"Yeah, I'm trying to stay away from that life."

"Suit yourself, kid."

"Man, sometimes I wonder about you, Frank. Here you are retired and all and yet you still want to come to work? Don't you think you'd rather sit on a beach somewhere?"

"I hate sand in my underwear, Washington, and besides, just because they made me hand in my badge doesn't mean that I'm not still a cop at heart. Why, the way I look at it, this little building here is my new beat. Monitor one, that's Sargeant Avenue. Monitor two, that's Ellice. Monitor three? Young Street."

Isaiah laughed as he took out his scan card for the time clock. "Yeah, but there ain't no pimps hanging out on the corner of monitor three."

"Aren't there?" Frank raised an eyebrow.

Isaiah just looked at him, confused.

"Just because those people in there wear white, doesn't mean they don't have black hearts. Who knows what they really do in those little rooms? I've seen some fine re-education going on, but most of the time the place is Deadsville."

CHAPTER TWENTY

"You should be here overnight. No one comes in except this one dude with slicked back hair, real hoity toity walk, you know?"

"I know the type."

"Never says a word to me, just walks right on past and scans his way in. I figure he must be someone important on account of having to come in so late. But what does he do? How the hell should I know? The firm only pays me to sit and watch. I ain't about to risk this gig. It's the first safe one I've had in ages. I sure as hell don't want to have to switch again, not when I'm within spitting distance of that fine degree."

"You did your part. You kept the place standing another night. Now it's old Frank's turn. Rest easy, Washington. I've got this."

"You're crazy, man, but I like you. You take it easy, OK?"

Frank held up a finger to his lips. "Shhhhh, I'm working."

Isaiah left, but Frank's attention was locked on the screens, watching the empty halls, waiting for that first sign of crime that would kick him into action. Sure, it hadn't happened yet, but who's to say when it might? If there was one thing he'd learned from all those years on the force, it was that the bad guys popped up when you least expected them to.

"Come on, scum, try me. I'm here watching all day."

The screens hummed away silently, the soft flicker of the monitors showing nothing but white. His eyes became attuned to the refresh rate as they moved from screen to screen. His muscles were tensed, his focus complete. Frank was ready, he just needed the call.

CHAPTER TWENTY-ONE

"Open up, Scott, I know you're in there." Sam pounded on the door. "You might as well just let me in because otherwise I'm going to kick this piece of fucking shit door down."

In the debate between rationality and wrath, Sam had decided that Scott didn't deserve the benefit of the doubt. She was here on a mission. Broad daylight. An angry woman screaming at a door. If there'd been anyone around she might have ended up in a new kind of viral video, but nothing mattered beyond getting what she came here for. Satisfaction, answers, revenge. In no particular order either.

She was missing class. She'd come alone. She'd stormed off campus and driven right over, ignoring every traffic rule, too furious to think straight.

Her blood boiled. She pounded again.

"You want me to bring down this whole piece of shit house, too? I'll do it."

She knew she was an episode of *Cops* right now, but she didn't care.

"I know you two deadbeats are home."

Where else would they be? Scott was unemployed, and Tommy always seemed to have some excuse to take the day

CHAPTER TWENTY-ONE

off.

The house looked like hell, the paint was peeling, trash strewn all over the lawn, the rusted gate hanging on one hinge.

"Alright, that's it…" The door clicked and swung partway open. It was unlocked?

"OK, my bad. I should have just tried it."

She pushed the door the rest of the way open and stepped into a silent house. The room was clean, cleaner than it had ever been. The floors were polished, the empties put away, pizza boxes gone. The sink glistened, the cupboard doors were shut. She could see her reflection in the hardwood floors.

"Wow," she muttered. "You've been cleaning."

An echo in her head. She'd seen it like this before. But when? They were slobs. They never cleaned. No. They'd put everything away. Right? Wait, maybe it had always been like this? She couldn't remember. Images of the room strobed in her eyes. Clean, dirty, clean, dirty. Why was it so hard to remember?

"Hello?"

She moved as if repeating lines in a play. She turned the corner to the main room. The entire band sat at their instruments staring off into space. No one said a word, or even made any motion of recognition that she was there.

"Uh, guys, shouldn't you be at work?"

No response. She somehow knew there wouldn't be. How? She felt like she was re-enacting a scene from a movie.

"He's in his room, isn't he?"

She stepped into Scott's room. He was writing away furiously, oblivious to her presence.

"You're a dead man," she said.

She crept up behind him and reached out for his shoulder,

ready to spin him around and slug him in the nose.

She hesitated. He was writing out song lyrics, perfectly, no stopping, no second guessing, no revising, a stream of consciousness burst of creativity. She couldn't help but read over a few lines.

"My heart's turned day glo,
  bright with your love,
  oh, what you do to me,
  My G-I-R-L friend!"

"What is it with this new fascination to spell out words in your songs?"

No. He'd never done that before. Why would she think that?

Her head hurt. She rubbed her temples trying to get at a stabbing pain behind her eyes.

Scott put down the pen. He stood up from the chair, grabbing the notebook. He walked past her out of the room as if she'd been invisible.

"Hey, you don't get to…"

"Welcome back," the image of Kurt Cobain said.

"I'll be back for you in a minute."

She stormed after Scott. Found him and the rest of the band with their instruments ready to play, watching her with dead eyes.

"No, I'm here to talk to you two."

Why did this all feel so damn familiar? Like an echo in her head. They were as still as statues.

"You," she said, pointing to Tommy, "and you," she said, pointing to Scott, "are both fucking dead."

CHAPTER TWENTY-ONE

The band stared at her as if she was speaking a foreign tongue. She wondered if she'd lost her mind. "Which one of you assholes uploaded that video?"

She looked from Tommy to Scott and back to Tommy, unable to focus on either one, confused as to why they didn't even seem to be blinking right now.

"A friend of mine found it."

Silence. The ticking of the clock in the kitchen. The sound of a distant truck horn. Her breathing. Ten black eyes. She was wondering if it had been a good idea to come alone now.

Scott. She wanted to punch his pretentious face.

"I didn't consent. You put something in my drink. You undo this, or I go to the cops."

They didn't move.

She wanted to scream, to beat Scott's face into a pulp. They were mocking her, right? Treating her as if she didn't exist. She needed an outlet for her rage. A felony assault? No. She swung to her right, punching a hole clear through the wall. Her hand sank halfway to the elbow. A cloud of drywall dust and debris spilled on her shirt.

"You're not taking me seriously. That's your face if you don't fix this," she said.

Still they ignored her. She screamed again, punching the wall a second time. Tears rolled down her face. She moved to the coffee table, pulled open the drawer. There was nothing inside. She looked in the television cabinet. Empty.

"What you looking for, babe?" David Bowie asked.

She pulled open cupboards in the kitchen.

Those drugs have to be here somewhere.

She was halfway to the bedroom when the music started. She froze and turned to see them all playing, as still as before.

"You're a Yoko," Scott sang.

"A Yoko?"

*"You're a bad influence on the band.
  getting between us,
  Causing shit
  Trying to split us up,
  Go make your weird ass art,
  We're not gonna fall for that."*

"Are you seriously singing this to me?"

She tried to reach for the plug to the microphone, but her arm stopped working. She couldn't lift her hand. She shook in rage, wanted to explode, but her mouth was fused shut.

*"We made a pact when we started this band,
  no Yokos."*

"No Yokos," Tommy repeated.

"No Yokos," the rest of the band droned on over and over again.

"No Yokos?" the words repeated in her head.

She wanted to reach over and rip the guitars out of their hands, take the microphone and drum kit and punt them out the window, but all she could do was feel her heart beating faster and faster. Her jaw clenched. Her teeth were grinding upwards, feeling as if they were going to collapse into dust. Her brain pulsed with the sound of the amplifier energy in the room. The hair on her dead arms stood up.

"No Yokos," Scott said melodically.

CHAPTER TWENTY-ONE

David Bowie leered at her from the wall. The sun outside the window flared. The moving clouds seemed to stop. A bird was frozen in mid air. She could see the wings clearly. They weren't moving. The band's eyes bored into her. She was frozen in place. Scott's voice echoed in her head.

Jose hit the drums and the force sent a shockwave through her body. The guitar and the bass started in. She tried to look away, but her head refused to move.

BAM. They started into something fast and powerful.

"When you're in L-O-V-E baby,
   you can do anything."

No.

It was coming back now, in a wave. The other night. The memory was all there. The song. It was the song. It pulled at her. Wrenched her mind through her ears, bleeding out of her eyes. They played a wall that pressed her down into submission.

No. I hate their guts.

I have to leave before...

Her body wouldn't listen. Sweat poured down her face as the events of the other night played out on the television screen. She saw it all outside of her own body. It was happening to someone else.

No!

It happened to you. Against your will.

"When you're in L-O-V-E baby,
   makes you feel like a king."

It's the song. There's something in the–
Get outside.
Leave!
Her mind and body disagreed, one desperate for escape, the other refusing to budge.
Get outside.
She was pulled into the television, leaving her body. Trapped in the past. Seeing it all happen that night. Turning around on the bed and watching it again through a glass wall. She tried to run away, but she didn't know which body was hers. Disassociation. Where was she? Two places at once and yet no place at all. Her mind couldn't take it. It finally gave in and everything went black.

* * *

Pounding head. Dry mouth. Crusted eyes. An arm that wouldn't move. It took her a moment to realize where she was.
Lou Reed, Kurt Cobain. Peeling paint.
Scott's bedroom.
Her head rested on something warm. Scott. She turned to come face to face with Tommy.
She rose with a start, her arm dangling uselessly at her side.
She was naked, her hair matted, sweat drying on her body. They were both asleep, snoring obliviously, as naked as she was.
What the fuck happened?
She rubbed her temples, trying to knead out the pain in her head. The last thing she could remember was coming over here. But why? Was it Friday night? She looked for her

CHAPTER TWENTY-ONE

clothes. They were nowhere to be seen.

Why does it feel like I've been here before?

"Because you have," a voice said from the wall.

She rubbed out the crust from her eyes but didn't see anyone there. The chill air lifted goose-pimples on her body. She grabbed the bunched-up sheet from in between the wall and Scott's mattress and wrapped it around her body.

Was I drunk?

The guys were out of it. Scott's stitch marks hadn't yet healed at the base of his neck. Tommy rolled over and she saw that his hadn't either. Why did they each have them? She wondered about the rest of the band. Were they from some sort of scarification tattoo process that she hadn't heard of?

Empties lined Scott's desk. The remnants of what looked like joints faded to ash in a small bowl. It smelled like sweat, pot, and wet socks. Her throat was parched. She left the room and headed to the kitchen, opening the fridge to find only beer and more beer. The cupboards were empty. The guys didn't even have any glasses. She cracked open a beer and poured it into the sink. She filled the empty bottle with water and took a sip. She could still taste the beer, but any liquid was better than nothing.

She tried to piece together how she'd ended up here. She could remember knocking on the door. But was that last night? One of the dozen other times she'd come? Daylight. She was never here in the day. So why yesterday?

She spotted her clothes on the floor and pulled on her underwear and pants as she went over all the jumbled images that were mixed up in her mind. What day was it? What time?

"It's Wednesday morning, girlie," a British voice said from the living room.

She spun but there was no one there. The television was off, the coffee table covered in filth. The instruments were stacked in a corner, the amps quiet.

If it was Wednesday, then she should be at school. She didn't usually sleep over on weekdays. She must have come here for a reason. And why the hell was she naked in bed with the two of them?

Tommy and Scott's cellphones rested on the coffee table next to the pair of pants.

Cellphone.

Tommy.

There was something important about them, but what was the connection? She pulled on her shirt and noticed two huge holes in the wall. She didn't remember those being there before. The guys were pigs, but they hadn't trashed the structure of the house.

Her hand tingled. The blood had returned but making a fist felt awkward. There was something wrong with her knuckles, a burning sensation. She flipped her hand over and noticed cuts on the skin, faint white dust stuck inside. She walked over to the wall and held out her fist – the size matched.

She inserted her hand inside and the memories stabbed her in the cranium in a flash that knocked her to her knees. She held her breath and gritted her teeth, seeing events play out, hovering in negative space in fast forward. Everything hit her in one fell swoop. Why she'd come here, the anger she had at the two of them. Their weird behaviour. The song.

Oh fuck, the threesome video. Did it happen again?

She remembered it all now. Twice. She'd been here twice and both times woken up like this. The video. The porn site. She'd come here on a mission to get that video taken down.

CHAPTER TWENTY-ONE

Then… they played a song, called her Yoko, she couldn't move or resist. They'd…

"It's the fucking song!"

What had happened when she heard the song? She'd blacked out. Lost time. There was no acid, no drugs, just a song. It was some kind of mind control, hypnosis maybe. How? Did they know what they were doing? Who was in on this? Who was responsible? She grabbed Tommy and Scott's cellphones. The answers were inside. How to get in? She swiped Scott's on and sat on the couch.

Someone stirred from the bedroom.

Not here.

They could wake up at any moment and do it all over again. She grabbed her coat and stormed out with the phones.

You won't be putting this one up online, asshole.

CHAPTER TWENTY-TWO

"You stole his phone?"

Avital and Erin sat eating lunch on the futon. Pita wrappers were crumpled in balls on the old tables.

"I think it happened again," Sam said.

"What do you mean, it happened again?" Avital said, putting her wrap down on the plate.

Sam sat next to them on the couch. She lay Tommy and Scott's cell phones on the table. The black cases were covered in greasy stains. The screen protectors had huge cracks down the centre of them. They were the well-used phones of people who couldn't afford better ones.

"I went to ream them out."

"Alone?" Avital said. "Sam, that wasn't smart."

"I know. I was just so pissed off."

"Understandable," Erin said.

"Well, I woke up, uh, in a compromised position."

"Oh, Sam…"

"I have reason to believe they may have filmed it."

The students of the university passed by overhead. The silence of the futon lounge was broken up with the faint drifting of other groups' conversations. Both Avital and Erin

CHAPTER TWENTY-TWO

stared at her. She couldn't read their faces. Were they mad? Worried? Pitying her?

"I know it's going to sound crazy, but I was hypnotized by the song."

"Sam," Avital said. "Plenty of people are sucked in by a hot guy in a band. You weren't the first, won't be the last. But you can do something about Scott."

"Like what?" Sam said, staring at the phone.

"Report them. Take the phone to the police," Avital said. "They'll have some way to get into it. I'm pretty sure it's all kinds of illegal to make an unauthorized video of someone and post it."

"We went over this already."

"And you've got proof now."

"Yeah, I assume the video is on here. I don't actually know one hundred percent. What happens if I do this and the phones are clear?"

"There were only two of them in the video, right?"

She nodded.

"Then the chances are pretty high it was one of these two phones they used."

"So what would I tell the police? That I'd been hypnotized? Roofied? That what happened on that clip was some kind of rape?"

"It was rape, Sam, pure and simple."

"I know that, and you know that, but you have to prove it to other people. First, I'd have to submit the video for evidence, it would go into official record. Far more people would know about it than could possibly now. Word could get out. My parents could find out. Right now there's deniability. The video is grainy, poorly shot. I'd be admitting that it was me, whereas right now I could still say it isn't. Just some girl that looks a lot like me. Then there's the fact that they'd need proof that it was made under duress. My word against theirs. The evidence on screen sure made it look like I was enjoying it. They just signed with a big-time record label. Those are the kinds of people who have big-time lawyers that make these things go away."

"So, you're just going to let them get away with it?"

Sam sighed. "I'm not sure."

"You said you don't remember doing any of it," Erin said. "Right?"

"Not really. It's all blurred. David... er, they said we took acid. I googled and the internet hive mind confirmed that both loss of memory and the morning-after dry mouth were acid side effects. It also said that people experienced flashbacks and I'm getting bits and pieces of it coming in. Not the whole thing, but enough that I feel like puking thinking about it."

"So then what's your plan?" Avital asked. "You didn't steal their phones just because."

"The video existing at all is bad enough, but if I just push it away and try to forget about it, it might disappear without anyone else finding out. How many hundreds of thousands of porn clips are out there? It's just a drop in the bucket."

"That doesn't make it OK. I think you should do something about it," Erin said, crossing her arms over her chest.

"Believe me, there's nothing I want more than to go over there and kick their asses. But I have to be smart. I do that and suddenly I'm the one being charged with assault. Then I have to use the video as defence and it gets out anyway."

"You can't just keep their phones," Erin said. "They can, like, trace them or something, right?"

CHAPTER TWENTY-TWO

"She's right, Sam. If you're not going to turn them in, then you should destroy their phones as at least some small measure of revenge."

"Oh yeah! I can make a video out of it," Erin said. "Wrecking an ex's phone. That'd go viral for sure."

"I think it's just better to cut Scott out of my life and move on."

"Trust me. Smashing the phone will make you feel better," Avital said.

Sam saw something behind her eyes. She was speaking from more than just guesswork. She looked down at the two phones on the table, saw only the instruments that had tried to ruin her life. They still could if she let them. Maybe Avital was right.

"Let's do it."

* * *

A cold wind blew over the top floor of the Bay parkade across the street from River City University. The view of the old buildings of downtown stretched all around them. The glossy tower of the Yakatori Plaza stretched upwards to glisten in the sunlight. Snow had piled in the corners of the concrete rooftop parking area. Only a few other cars were here. Sam's dad's car was parked idling, a thin tendril of exhaust drifting upwards to the sky.

"Erin, if you'll do the honours of placing the phones on the ceremonial platform," Avital said.

Erin gently put the two old phones onto the concrete meridian. Stains and graffiti provided the background.

"Sam, if you will take the ceremonial tire iron."

Sam picked up the long iron tool she'd found in the trunk of the car.

"Are you ready to begin smashing the shit out of these devices of evil?"

"I am."

"And Erin, are you ready to film Sam smashing the shit out of these devices of evil?"

"I am," Erin said, holding up her phone and pressing record.

"You may begin."

"Scott, Tommy. You are both pieces of shit and these phones represent your stupid fucking faces."

"We'll have to edit that out for YouTube."

"I hereby smash you and all memories of having dated you."

Sam held the tire iron high above her head and took a deep breath. The screen lit up, Jose's name showing as calling. Sam smashed the tire iron down over and over again, turning the phones into a broken collection of plastic and circuit boards that scattered around the concrete. With each swing she felt a weight lifted off her shoulders. Each satisfying blow pushed the memories deeper from her thoughts. Nothing could erase what had happened, but for now, the ceremony would have to be enough. She kept smashing until there was almost nothing left. She was sweating, the rage leaving her with each breath. Avital hugged her.

"I'm proud of you. This is the first step to recovery."

"It's not enough," Sam said. She started sweeping up the bits into a pile. She picked it up and carried it over to a spot in the middle of the parkade.

"What are you doing?"

"Just keep filming, Erin."

She got in the car. She pulled out and backed up to the far

end of the drive. She gunned it forward, aiming for the bits. She heard a satisfying crunch as she flattened them even more. Erin and Avital cheered, hopping in joy. She slowed the car and pulled back into a spot nearby. They both got inside.

"That was amazing, Sam," Erin said.

"What a way to celebrate the end of a horrible relationship."

"You guys want to get some bubble tea?"

Sipping on mango bubble tea while Factor 5ive music blared over the stereo, Sam felt a sense of relief. Maybe she could get over this.

"Only another month until the concert," Erin said, bobbing her head to the boy band sounds.

"I still can't believe it's happening. And the first show is here of all places."

"They probably wanted to come to a small market to work out the kinks before the tour goes national," Sam said.

"Still," Erin said. "It's going to be awesome."

"At least it's something to look forward to."

"Promise us you won't run off after them, too?" Avital said.

"Factor 5ive? They're like, what, in their thirties? That's gross," Sam said.

"You think they'll still be hot?" Erin asked.

"Depends on how much plastic surgery they've had to hide the grey hair and wrinkles," Sam said.

"I'm just glad we're all back to normal now," Avital said, giving Sam a look that meant more than she was letting on.

"Look, I'm sorry I was ditching you guys to hang out with assholes. I've learned my lesson. Can we not keep shaming me over it?"

"You don't have to be ashamed, Sam. We all make mistakes."

"Sure seems like you're more than pissed off at me over this,

Avital."

Avital looked out the window for a moment, watching the snow-covered city move by. The downtown streets were slushy and filthy, people moving from store to store avoiding the homeless begging for change. Something was bothering her.

"It's not that I was pissed off at you, Sam. It's that I saw this coming, and I didn't do enough to stop it."

"Nobody could see what they did coming."

"No, I could. See, this happened to me before."

"Oh my god, you dated Scott, too?" Erin said in shock.

"No, I mean I dated a guy who convinced me to make a video with him. He promised me it was just for us, said it would be fun, the whole nine yards of bullshit. I was sixteen. I fell for it."

"You never told me, Avital."

"I hoped I would never have to. He showed his friends. They were all laughing and staring at me, making sucking motions. I wanted to drop out and die."

"I know how you feel," Sam said.

"What did you do?" Erin asked.

"My dad brought the hammer down. He knows people and let's just say that guy and his family got what was coming to them. So I was pissed off, Sam. I saw the signs. I didn't want you to go through that, to feel it. It's something that doesn't go away. I worry all the time that what happened to you could happen. Everett looks at porn and sees me. Some guy I like or–"

"Marlon," Erin interrupted.

"Oh god, that too."

"So you're saying I'm never escaping this thing," Sam said.

CHAPTER TWENTY-TWO

"Wonderful."

"We all make mistakes. We can move on from them, right? You've got us to protect you."

Tears started flowing down Sam's cheeks. She didn't know what to say. She'd never had friends like this before. Avital patted her on the leg. Erin reached around from the backseat and gave her a hug and quick kiss on the cheek.

"Now that we know you have a tire iron, if someone tries this again, I say we kneecap them," Avital said.

Sam laughed. The light changed, and she pulled forward. They drove in silence for a while, letting the pop songs fill the space between them.

"You know, Sam, I didn't want to admit this, but Scott was hot."

Avital reached over the seat and smacked her in the arm. "Ow. What?"

"It's he who shall not be named from that band that also shall not be named going forward."

"You mean Radiant Cyanide?" Erin said, oblivious.

"Yes, that band full of assholes who belong in the sewers with all the rats. Distant past now. This is a new Sam who won't be blinded like some kind of stupid teenager. So let's just agree to protect each other from all jerks whether or not they sing rock music."

"Agreed, of course."

"Agreed," Erin said.

"Great. Now let's go to a movie!"

CHAPTER TWENTY-THREE

"...he said that? OMG," Avital shouted.

"Yeah, but then I was all, come on, that's bullshit, and he admitted he was lying." Erin's voice carried far in the empty hallway through the open door of Sam's dad's apartment.

One of them knocked. Avital called out, "Hello, Sam, we're here!"

Sam walked out from the kitchen carrying a bowl of popcorn in one hand and a massive bag of mini chocolate bars in the other. There were bottles of wine and stacks of trashy magazines piled on the coffee table.

"I hope you're ready for the best girl's night ever," Sam said.

Avital and Erin tossed their jackets in the closet. They were both dressed for comfort: yoga pants and hoodies. Somehow Avital still looked like a million bucks. They'd brought their own booze, bags of chips, and ju-jubes.

"That all depends," Avital said. "Did you get the good stuff?"

Sam placed the food on the table and walked over to the TV, grabbing a couple of DVD cases and holding them up proudly. "Of course. When I promise the best, I get the best."

Erin squealed and snatched the two movies away. "*Serendipity* and *Say Anything!* Is it just me or was John Cusack super hot back then?"

CHAPTER TWENTY-THREE

"He still is, I'd do him," Avital said.

"Ewwwwww, he's so old now!"

"I'm a sucker for those dark and mysterious guys."

"It's all planned out, girlie movies, junk food, doing each other's hair."

"Talking about old boyfriends," Erin said before stopping herself. "Well, uh…"

"It's OK. I have dated other guys," Sam said.

This was going to be everything she'd always dreamed a girls' slumber party should be, what she'd been denied having for so long because her only friend growing up had been Duckie. But first, she had something to do.

"OK, guys, I know you're all looking forward to getting plastered and ogling Lloyd Dobbler, but first I have to take care of a little housekeeping."

Sam brought a box into the kitchen and placed it down on the counter.

"What's in the box?" Erin asked.

Sam lifted the lid dramatically, then realized that neither one could see from where they were standing.

"These are the final remnants of he who shall not be named and the band that shall not be named."

She held up one of the band's publicity photos. They'd given her a stack to put up on campus and this was the only one she'd kept. She then held up a burned CD with Radiant Cyanide and a giant heart written on the shiny surface.

"You burned their CD? Why?"

"So I could play it in the car, duh. Now, of course, that's never going to happen again so I thought that since it was so much fun to smash the shit out of their phones, we could do one more symbolic gesture of destruction. Fire anyone?"

On the concrete porch outside the large glass double doors of her dad's apartment they chanted "fuck you, Scott" as Sam poured cooking oil and dropped a lit match in the box. When the photo and CD were ash, she swept up the pieces and flushed them through the garburator in the sink.

"There, that's better," she said. "Now it's time for wine!"

They laughed, they told secrets, they did each other's hair. They got drunk and read girlie magazines. They lusted over a young John Cusask. They ate way too much chocolate. It was a blast. At about one in the morning, Sam browsed through YouTube clips on the TV, pulling up old boy band videos, laughing at the terrible songs and even worse haircuts.

"OMG, remember B4-4? The weird ass triplets?" Avital shrieked.

"If you go down on me, I will go down on you," Erin sang.

"Gonna make you come tonight... over to my house!"

They all fell over laughing.

"Those guys were so gross – how did they ever get famous?"

The abomination of a video played on screen, identical twins and another guy who looked exactly like them; fake tans, frosted, gelled hair, posing in tight shirts with their lips scrunched up in perfect duck face.

"People were dumb in the 2000s if they thought that was cool. Who could have liked those plastic goofs?"

"Can-con," Sam said, "we can make shitty boy bands, too, thank you very much. But ours will be even shittier!"

Erin laughed. "At least the Moffats were kind of cute."

"EWWWWWWWWW, Erin, you paedo!"

"What! I was a little kid then! And they're actually a lot older than us now, so wouldn't that make them the paedos?"

"She might have you on a technicality there, Avital," Sam

CHAPTER TWENTY-THREE

said laughing, remembering the horrible tween band that time forgot. She found one of their videos on YouTube in an instant and started it playing.

Nature called. "BRB, guys, gotta pee," she said, rising to go to the bathroom.

"Ohhhh, find soulDecision," Erin laughed as they clicked through more videos.

Sam was washing her hands when she heard the song start. It was unmistakable. Scott's voice. Why were they watching the video?

"Guys?" No one responded.

She panicked. "That fucking song. I'm not blacking out again."

She looked in the medicine cabinet, found some cotton balls, and stuffed them in her ears. She hoped they'd muffle the sound enough to make it powerless. She took a deep breath and crept back out into the main room.

Her worst fears were confirmed. Erin and Avital were zombies, staring at the screen, watching Radiant Cyanide's video in silence. The band was just called RC now. Their new looks were plastered all over the television in an expensive looking flashy video of strobing lights and fast cuts.

"Avital? Erin?"

Their eyes were glazed over. Their mouths hung open. They were completely enraptured in the action on screen, lost in the soulful looks Scott gave to the camera with his hair blowing in the wind while Tommy and the band posed with their instruments.

"God, that thing is every music video cliché there is."

Concert footage interspersed with images of Scott singing to a model over a candlelit dinner. The YouTube view count was only in the few thousands. It hadn't caught on yet. The algorithm hadn't decided it was anything special. But from the zonked-out expressions on Avital and Erin's faces, it was doing its job perfectly.

"Avital?"

She waved her hands in front of her to no reaction.

"Erin?" She shook her by the shoulders.

They'd both checked out. Sam hit mute on the screen. Still no change. She shut off the television. They didn't budge.

She slumped down on the couch. "Maybe google has the answer."

She searched for "wake up someone under hypnosis", finding results quickly.

"Says here I need to calmly get you back to reality with soothing words and a countdown. Sounds simple enough."

She walked in front of Avital, looking her right in the eye. Her pupils were dilated. She stared off into space. The only sign she was even alive was the calm rising and falling of her chest.

"Here goes nothing. Avital, I'm going to wake you up now, it'll be a nice calm experience and you will feel totally relaxed. You'll wake up remembering that it was the RC video that did this to you and you will have a deep hatred of that band, especially Scott and Tommy. When I count to one, you will wake up. Five, four, three, two… one."

Avital didn't wake up.

"Did I do something wrong?" Sam checked over google again, browsing multiple sites this time. They all said variations on the same thing.

"Maybe Erin?"

She repeated the calming words and count down for her,

CHAPTER TWENTY-THREE

but still… total zombie.

"This is bad, this is very bad."

Then they moved, rising to their feet in unison. Erin took out her cell phone, switched it to the video function and hit record. The red light blared. She placed it upright on the TV stand. Avital took out hers and held it in her hands.

"What are you guys doing?"

They moved in close and started kissing, playfully at first, then growing more passionate. Avital filmed the whole thing in close up as her hands moved around Erin's back, sliding under her hoodie. Erin slid hers down Avital's pants.

"Oh God, no way. This is not happening." Sam pushed her way in between them, forcing them away from each other. She strained to keep them apart, but the pull was intense. She lost her grip and their faces lunged forward. Erin started kissing Sam on the side of the cheek. Avital nibbled on her opposite ear.

"Guys, come on!"

They caressed her skin, started treating her like the third member. She was crushed between them. She tried to turn away from their attack, lips meeting neck and chin. Her hands were pinned, and it was like being assaulted by two eager puppies.

The camera filmed it all.

Only one way out.

She forced them to topple on to the couch. The landing gave her a quick moment to slide out from their temporarily loosened grip. Without her in the middle, they resumed their moves on each other. She grabbed Erin by the leg and tried to tug her away, but Avital was attached to her face.

She needed something to block them. Her mind raced.

What could she use?

"A broom!"

She ran to the kitchen and grabbed one. By the time she got back, they were both in their underwear. Sam pulled them to their feet. They pressed themselves up against the wall, oblivious to the locale of their passion. She wedged the broom between their bodies. She pulled it from both sides, dragging them in to the bedroom. She twisted the shaft to get Erin inside, then back again to form a perpendicular barrier across the doorway.

The broom seemed to hold them in place. Erin was being compelled to keep going, her reach only to be stopped by the wooden handle. Sam pulled Avital's face away as gently as she could. She reached around her body and peeled her away from Erin like an orange skin. Her outstretched hands pawed at air.

"This is insane," Sam said.

She bent over and put an arm between Avital's legs, hoisting her up on her back in a firemen's carry. The girl fought her every step, but Sam managed to get her in her dad's room, tossing her on the bed. Avital immediately rose to her feet and tried to get back to Erin. Sam dove at her feet and held her tight. She was slowly being dragged to the doorway.

"I'm going to have to tie you down, aren't I?"

She toppled Avital, pulled her back to the bed. She raised her onto her shoulders again and went to her dad's dresser.

"Come on, Dad, you must have a belt or something."

She found socks. She lay Avital down on the bed and tied her to the bed frame using the thin tube socks. She thrashed and fought, but Sam had her stuck.

"Now Erin."

CHAPTER TWENTY-THREE

Erin shuffled like a zombie in the doorframe, arms out, broom handle preventing her from getting through. Sam ducked underneath the handle and secured one end of a sock to her bed frame. She grabbed Erin and pulled, the broom handle crashing to the ground as she tugged her backwards. She managed to tie her down, too.

"As long as my dad didn't buy shitty Wal-Mart brand socks, neither one of you is getting out."

She covered them both in sheets and shut the doors.

She took Avital's phone and went back to the main room to grab Erin's phone from the TV stand. She stopped each recording. When this spell wore off, they'd want to know what had happened. At least this time there was evidence. She clicked on the phones to watch the recorded videos.

* * *

"Sam, why am I tied up on your bed in my underwear?"

Sam jerked awake to the sound of Erin's voice. She slid off the couch and dashed over to her room. She opened the door, finding Erin exactly where she had left her.

"Sorry, I must have fallen asleep after watching the cellphone videos."

"What?"

"I had to try to figure out exactly what happened to turn you two into sex-crazed zombies. My working theory is that there's some kind of subliminal messaging in their music. Maybe it triggers repressed desires, or overrides inhibitions, or just makes you super horny. I don't know, I'm not a brain doctor."

She untied Erin's feet. "This was for your own good."

Erin rubbed her wrists, eying Sam with mistrust. "Where's Avital?"

"In my dad's room, she's probably waking up, too."

Erin put on her clothes and followed Sam to find Avital awake and looking confused.

"It's OK, I can explain everything," Sam said calmly as she untied her.

"What the fuck is going on?"

"It's a long story," Sam said reassuringly. "You guys went mental and started making out and then you were filming it and I had to stop–"

"You're sick, Sam," Avital said.

"What?"

"I can't believe we fell for your story."

"I just told you the story, you haven't had time to–"

"Oh, innocent me drugged by big bad rock stars made a sex tape that I regret. I had no idea what was going on."

"But that's–"

"You invite us here and roofie us? Tie us to the bed and what? Filmed us out of it? Molested us? What the hell did you do?"

"I didn't do anything," Sam said. "I was trying to stop you two from making a sex tape and–"

"To think I was feeling sorry for you after what had happened with Scott," Avital said. "I thought you'd been a victim but then you pull a stunt like this. I think P-O has a new meaning, PREDATOR one. As in, sexual predator."

"Or Perverted one!" Erin added.

"No, no, no, you've got this all wrong. I had to tie you up to stop–"

"Us from getting away, that's obvious. Geez, sicko much?"

CHAPTER TWENTY-THREE

"Come on, Avital, let's get the hell out of here."

Avital put on her clothes in a huff. "Jeez, Sam, I thought we were friends."

"No! I mean, of course we are. This isn't what happened. Not what you think, at least. Let me show you. There's a video!"

They both looked at her like they wanted to strangle her to death, their eyes growing three sizes in fury.

"Video?" they said in unison.

"You really are sick, Sam. I believed you. We both did. God, I feel so stupid," Erin said.

"I didn't take the video. It's on your phones. Both of you are in it. Just watch. It'll explain everything."

She grabbed their phones. They headed right to the door and started to put on their boots. They were going to leave. She stepped in the doorway to block their exit.

"Out of the way, Sam," Avital said.

"Please, just watch." She held up the two phones, pointing the blackened screens right at them. "Just unlock them. Check your video folder. I promise it'll explain everything."

Neither one seemed like they were about to listen but finally, Avital reached out and took her phone. She swiped with her thumb reluctantly. Erin refused to budge, but then something inside her relented and she followed suit.

They played the clips.

This has to work.

Slowly, their demeanours changed as the videos played. They'd notice the angles, from the TV stand, from Avital's hand. Neither one would have Sam doing anything more than interjecting herself in the middle.

"This doesn't prove anything," Erin said, unconvinced.

They'd see themselves kissing Sam and her desperate drive to get them into the bedroom. Erin's phone would end with an empty room. Avital's would show her being dragged into Sam's dad's bedroom and tossed onto the bed before the phone fell from her hands. From there it would only show the white ceiling until Sam came and picked it up. That was more than enough to prove her story. Right?

"All I see is two wasted girls making out and you making it a threesome," Avital said. "Is this your big proof?"

"If I was wanting to film that, then why wouldn't I bring the camera into the bedroom to capture the" – she made air quotes – "action? Why leave one phone here and the other on the floor? Think!"

"I am and I don't know," Avital retorted. "Maybe you were high or too drunk to think straight. Did you take whatever you put in our drinks, too? It clearly did a number on us."

"I didn't put anything in anyone's drinks. Look around the room. Look in my stuff. I swear it wasn't me."

"Then what fucked us up so bad that we can't remember any of this?" Avital asked.

"The RC music video on YouTube. I know this sounds crazy but I'm almost positive it has some kind of power to brainwash people. It made me and you into crazed zombie sex fiends."

Erin's mouth dropped.

Avital turned a deep shade of red.

"You're crazier than you look."

Avital pushed her way past her out of the apartment.

"This is really, really fucked up, Sam," Erin said, following her.

"No, please, listen!"

They were gone. Sam slumped down against the wall. Alone.

CHAPTER TWENTY-THREE

Miserable.

CHAPTER TWENTY-FOUR

"I understand you have concerns, doctor," he said to the man standing opposite the huge desk that cut the room in half.

"I do, sir."

"I fail to see what they could be," he said to the squirms of his employee. "The trials have been a resounding success. Uploads to our servers are at an all-time high. Sales of merchandise continues to grow. The subjects are unaware of their role and the victims unaware of their victimization. What could you find wrong with all of this?"

"I'm not privy to any of the financial aspects of this project, sir. I was referring to the fact that we still don't know what kind of long-term effects the control state can have on a subject's brain. Or what kind of long-term effects the procedure may have on the hosts either. What if people start randomly dropping dead from seizures? What if our delivery mechanisms suddenly have aneurysms on stage? What if those who've been manipulated begin to realize the–"

"It's well past time to develop a conscience, doctor. You've known what our endgame was this whole time. I didn't hear you giving any of these objections when the research was first proposed."

The man in the lab coat shifted on his feet. It was clear he had begun to have dangerous doubts. This could not be allowed.

"Perhaps it's only been since the implementation that I've begun to realize what we've unleashed here, sir. What we've done to the girls who've fallen prey to–"

"The kinds of things they've always fallen prey to, doctor. The kinds of things girls will continue to fall prey to as long as there are men with the cunning to prey on them. We've merely taken a scientific approach and monetized it in a small way. With a much greater endgame."

"Sir, I… have a daughter and–"

He stood up, knowing how this was going to have to end and regretting it. Thankfully, there were many more doctors in his employ who would be grateful for a promotion.

"Doctor, having a daughter has been the excuse of the coward for far too long. Giving in to that kind of weakness cannot be allowed, you must understand."

He smiled and put his arm around the shorter man, doing his best to put him at ease.

"But–"

"If you worry about parity, then it will please you to understand that the research is being continued to pursue control over those of the opposite sex as well."

"Really? I thought we weren't looking into that avenue. For the obvious repercussions–"

"Like you said before, doctor. You're not privy to all that is going on, nor should you be. You were simply the avenue to unlocking the controlling process. And you succeeded beautifully."

"Well, I didn't do it alone, sir. There's an entire team working in the labs and–"

"And I'm sure they'll carry on your work with renewed vigour."

"Sir?"

He used his arm to spin the man in the lab coat around so they were face to face. He jerked out his hands to the man's throat and clenched tightly. The doctor's eyes bugged out as he realized what was going on. He batted ineffectually at the hands at his throat, at the face who grimaced back at him as the life was gradually choked out by the powerful grip.

"You disappointed me, doctor. But it will please you to know that no part of you will go to waste. I understand they need more organs in Dr. Kreitzler's division."

The man gargled, his eyes pleading for his attacker to stop the death choke.

"Thank you for your service. It was very fine, yes, very fine indeed."

The spark dimmed in the eyes, the tongue lolled out, the hands went limp. He held on for a moment longer until there was no pulse and the man's lips went blue. When it was only his grip holding the body up, he let go and it collapsed to the hard floor with a sick thud.

He moved over to the desk and pressed a button on the small console. "Send in the janitor, please. Oh, and call Dr. Januz and tell her she's just been made head of the Factor 5ive project."

FOUR WEEKS LATER

CHAPTER TWENTY-FIVE

"You wanted to see me, Malone?"

"That's right, chief."

The big man in the white shirt bursting at the seams raised a palm toward Frank. "Please, I told you, call me Alex, or if you want, Mr. Grant, but I'm nobody's chief."

"Can't do that, chief, it just wouldn't be proper."

The man shook his head and chuckled. "Alright, alright, you win. You're an odd duck, Malone, but you do good work. I hear that the special assignment is going quite well. They're all really happy with the way you sit in your chair, drink coffee and watch the monitors. Like a real pro. I tell you, I might just hire a whole team of retired cops now. It's a world away from the crap I'm used to dealing with."

"That's just it, chief, that's why I wanted to see you. I want out. I want something where I can get my hands dirty."

"But Malone–"

"It's not that I don't appreciate the opportunity, I really do," Frank interrupted him. "I made a career out of these special assignments. Dictators, drug lords, hot-zones, cold-cases, the quick and the dead. The jobs nobody else could handle. As much as I like this anti-hippie factory bringing in the ratty looking dirtbags and sending out clean cut normals, I need something more. Bar brawls, shoot outs, high speed car chases, beatings... I guess I just miss the heart of being a cop."

The chief took out a folder from a drawer in his desk and opened it up, thinking over what Frank had said. "I can understand where you're coming from, Malone, you've lived a full life, done a lot of crazy things—"

"You don't know the half of it, chief, no one does... except me, of course, the members of Go-Team, maybe the boys down at the legion, a couple of dames—"

"Like I said, lots of crazy things, but you had your time on the force and now it's your chance to let the kids take over, try new things yourself. We can't all be our jobs. Eventually old man time catches up and we have to take that long walk into the sunset, you know what I mean?"

"This is what I say to old man time." Frank took out his gun and pointed it at the large clock on the wall.

"Whoa, shit, I had no idea you were packing!" The chief nervously shifted his bulk in the chair. "I'll pretend I didn't see that. Put it back in your pants and make sure it never comes on site. I'm not licensed for firearms."

Frank shrugged and put the gun back in its holster.

"What I was saying was that you can still make a difference. There's still a little action in the security game. I think I've got the perfect gig for you. Overtime."

Frank stood up and walked over to the tiny window to the chief's right. He slid up the Venetians and looked out over the downtown of River City. A sea of brick and glass, concrete and filth. A life of service, a life of sacrifice. "Look, sir, I never wanted to be a desk jockey. For years I turned down promotions, let pimply faced rookies become chiefs all to stay on patrolling the beat to keep the people that counted on me safe. I can't sit still. I hate paperwork and I've got no patience for office gossip or water cooler discussions. I need action, need it like air to breathe."

"Then I think you'll like this one, Malone. I'll even give you double time."

"A little extra scratch for my itch, eh? Tell me about it."

* * *

Friday night. The big arena downtown. Some kind of concert. Fourteen thousand screaming kids, plenty of opportunity for the bad apple to rear its ugly seed. If there was one thing Frank liked more than busting the heads of hardened criminals, it was busting the heads of young offenders. He lived to turn them back on the straight and narrow, prevent the shit from ever rolling downhill. This was finally a chance to make a real difference again.

His shift at the desk was over. He punched out and headed to the massive arena, smack dab in the middle of it all. The Yakatori plaza tower glistened in the setting sun. He'd seen that place before it was born and had been a part of its troubled history. The rest of the street, Portage Avenue, was full of what used to be his old haunts, now taken over with dying stores and offices. Crowds were moving. There was an electricity in the air. Something big was going down.

Lights flashed on the new arena, built in the ruins of a department store his parents had taken him to when he was a kid. Then it was lit up with Christmas decorations and the wonder of the season. Now, it was a great big screen

CHAPTER TWENTY-FIVE

advertising upcoming hockey games and visits from singers he'd never heard of. Change isn't always good.

Lines of kids milled about the outside, eager to see whatever mop-topped ragamuffin was the talk of the town this week. They wore things that showed more skin than was advisable in the chill night air and had hair with more angles than his protractor. They smoked and laughed and cared nothing for the future they were pissing away at shows like this.

He was let in through the security entrance, handed the same old song and dance about the headsets and given a fancy black jacket.

"What's the station this time?"

"You're going right at the stage."

"I can't sing, boss," he said.

The man with the clipboard looked at him strangely. "No, of course not. You're being given the job of keeping the girls away from the boys while they do it."

Frank furrowed his brow. "That seems a little easy."

"Then I guess you haven't seen what screaming girls can be like."

"Running away from a bomb threat? Of course I have."

"Oh god, there'd better not be one of those here tonight. Good to hear you've had that experience though. I may just need you. Now go with the crew and get set. You're the most important role tonight, uhhh, Frank, was it?"

"Malone. Yes. So you're telling me this is the top of the food chain gig. That I'm one of the biggest fish, the guy responsible for the whole kit and caboodle going smoothly."

"Not in those words but yeah."

"One mistake and the whole show would be ruined. The chief's prized pick who–"

"Just get going before the opening act starts."

"Roger that."

So the chief really had scored him a plum gig. He'd have to thank the bossman later. Maybe things were starting to look up.

* * *

"Maybe you were just a mirage. Maybe the world is full of food and sex and spectacle and we're all just hurling towards an apocalypse..."

"I hear you, Lloyd," Sam spoke to the TV. "It's all bullshit."

Sam sat on the couch, eating cookie dough ice cream straight from the container, watching *Say Anything* for the two hundredth time.

"Is that all you're going to do?" her dad asked her from the front door.

"Don't you start, too," she said.

He held up his hands in surrender. He should know better by now than to try to cheer her up.

"I was just thinking you could watch something else. There are, like, a million other movies out there."

"Don't you have a party to go to?"

He slid on his coat and pulled open the door, looking back at her, conflicted.

"You know–"

"Dad, please. I'm exhausted. Exams drained me, OK?"

"Sure but–"

"But what's even worse is that this year I've had to do all the regular activities twice."

"That's not fair."

CHAPTER TWENTY-FIVE

"I know. That's why I'm sitting here wallowing in self-pity."

"OK, but maybe try to—"

"Shhhh," she said. "It's the best part." She pointed to the screen.

He did what he always did. Gave up. He left. As the door shut, she called after him, "Have fun at the party."

It sounded more sarcastic than she'd meant but everything was shit right now. Another miserable summer holiday. She didn't have anyone to turn to either. Her old friends were dead, her new ones wouldn't talk to her. She'd tried to apologize, sent long texts to Avital and Erin but they'd never responded. Everett and Marlon had only said, "Sorry, not getting in the middle of this" as if they'd copy-pasted what they'd been told to say. When she headed down to the futon room, the gang got up and left. She'd been totally deserted.

"Fuck you, Diane," she said to the screen, but that girl who was blowing it with Lloyd just ignored her.

All the feel-good endings and comfort foods couldn't erase the fact that she was right back where she had started: alone, friendless. The end of term exams only brought heartache this season, and a summer free from schoolwork did nothing to brighten her mood.

"At least you won't desert me, Ben and Jerry." She peered into the almost empty container. "Not for a few more scoops at least."

There was hope on the horizon. A blue printed ticket tucked into the mirror on her dresser; one small chance for redemption, her ghost of Christmas future, Factor 5ive. The date for the concert they'd all bought tickets to months ago was circled on her calendar. There was no way Avital and Erin would skip it. No way she would either. They'd all be forced to sit together and Sam would put things right. She could fix this. She had to. She needed her friends back.

Two nights later, it was finally the night of the show. She repeated what she was going to say to them in the mirror over and over again as she got herself dolled up, did her hair and make-up, put on a button-up black shirt and pants.

"Guys, you know I would never roofie you, never in a million years. I love you guys, you're my best friends. I need you. I'll do whatever I have to do to fix this. You mean the world to me."

She grabbed her coat, took a deep breath and left the apartment. All she could do was hope for the best.

* * *

Frank stood with arms crossed at the front of the stage as the arena filled up with the supposed future of the country. All he saw were a bunch of young girls tarted up like whores, guys either brought along as punishment for some unknown crime or here because they were a little too artsy for their own good.

"What's the name of this little jug band here tonight?" he asked the burly bald man standing near him stage left.

The man grunted something nearly unintelligible: "Some boy band, Factory 5 alive?"

"Bunch of pretty wankers," the tall lanky Brit with the tattooed neck working stage right chimed in.

"Pretty boys, eh?" Frank scratched his chin. "Let me guess, five clean-cut youngsters singing doowop songs about love or roses or moonlight dancing. Definitely no Benny Goodmans."

"Yeah, something like that." The Brit grinned. "Brings the Birds out though."

CHAPTER TWENTY-FIVE

Frank nodded, not entirely sure what he was talking about. It was all Greek to him.

"You know Al Jolson didn't need four other guys to sing a song, neither did that rotten fish Johnny Dagon or old blue eyes himself. It's these millennials, they can't do anything for themselves. Always holding out a hand for someone to carry the work. A bunch of lazy no-goodnicks, always passing the buck."

The Brit pointed to the audience. "Yeah, but look at the action. They get a pick of the litter, mate, real choice girls."

Frank looked out over the rows of seats in front of him that stretched as far as he could see, all the way to the end boards. The great arena was hazy from smoke machines and partially lit with yellowed lights. The black floor was covered in cords leading from the stage to a control panel at the back.

"Some of the litter look a little young, limey," Frank said, seeing all ages here.

"Depends on what you like, I suppose," the man said.

"I like them to know how to write a cheque, or at least how to stuff a kielbasa."

"Maybe we can get some run off, you never know how wild some of these tarts can be."

"Just worry about keeping them away from the talent," the other man said.

Frank turned and looked at the stage, a huge platform with multiple screens, light stands, speakers, instruments, technicians frantically checking every connection and wire. It was an impressive beehive of activity.

"I'll admit this is quite a set up. Nothing like when I saw Thelonious Monk spinning in place like a top in a little club near the Rockies."

"Who?"

Frank crossed his arms over his chest. "Centre stage, right in the middle of it all, the perfect vantage point for a man with a nose for crime."

"You sure you're supposed to be here?" the big man asked.

"Don't worry, I've handled more than one kind of mob in my day. But if you think you can't handle the girls, I've got your back."

His partners for the night were a brute and the limey. Maybe not the cream of the academy, but they'd have to do. The only thing left was to wait for the show to start.

* * *

Sam passed through the security checkpoint at the entrance, looking for any signs of Avital and Erin. She paid no attention while her bag was searched for booze or cameras.

"All clear," the bored looking security guard said.

She headed down to the floor section of the arena. She looked at her printed blue ticket. "Row two, right in the middle."

They were going to have a perfect view of the stage. The show should be amazing. If they showed up…

As Sam walked up the aisle to her section, she thought she saw that old policeman again standing at the base of the stage. He was wearing a security guard shirt, scanning the crowd and talking to two other guys in the same shirts.

Couldn't be him.

She shook the notion from her head. The guy at the stage was indeed old, but there was no way he'd be here, too. Why would anyone hire him?

CHAPTER TWENTY-FIVE

You're seeing things.
She found their seats.
Empty.
Maybe she was just the first to arrive. She sat in the middle seat and waited. She checked her phone for messages. Nothing.

"So you did come."

Avital's voice jerked her from the screen. Sam turned to see her and Erin approaching up the aisle. They were stepping over the chairs from the third row. Avital looked pissed, but Erin didn't. Was that a good sign? "Uh, hi guys, nice to see you?"

"Is it?" Avital spat harshly.

"Of course, you guys are my best friends."

"We bought these tickets before you did what you did. No refunds. I'm not about to miss this show, but I don't have to like being here with you."

"Look, I'm–"

"I'm certainly not going to sit beside you." Avital took a chair away from her.

"We're seats six, seven–"

"I'll sit in the middle," Erin said.

Sam slid over and Erin dropped in next to her. Avital slid one over, too.

"How's it going, Sam?" Erin asked.

"Shitty, of course. I miss you guys."

Avital scoffed, but Sam ignored her. "I've texted you this but let me say again that I'm so sorry about what happened. But you have to believe me, I had nothing to do with it. I would never slip you guys a roofie, not in a million years. I don't even know where you'd get a roofie or even what they look

223

like. Is it a pill? A liquid? Some kind of powder? I mean, I…"

She could see Avital losing interest. Erin's eyes pleaded with her to get to the point.

"I'm rambling. That's not what I was trying to talk about. Just think for a second logically. If I was going to roofie you, wouldn't I have tried to hide it? Like maybe not tell you about the video? Not leave you tied up? Done something? I gave you guys the phones, I showed you the evidence. I did all I could to keep you from doing what happened to me. That scene could have been way worse. Who knows how far it might have gone had I not stopped it? Then you'd be on that German site and–"

"Right, cos we're both such fucking uncontrollable lesbos that we couldn't stop going to town on each other for the camera." Avital shook her head, rolling her eyes, giving her the full dramatic business.

"I didn't say that. I have no idea what triggers it or how, but you have to believe that it was the song, not something I did. The music has some kind of subliminal hypnosis mind control shit going on. It's the only explanation for you two, what happened to me with Scott and Tommy. There could be others. Oh God, maybe anyone who hears the song. I–"

"If you think that I'm going to buy that some kind of magical mind control rock song turned me into a lesbo and you into a cock whore, then you're further gone than I thought."

Erin looked sympathetic, but Avital was steaming.

"But–"

"But nothing, we're done talking, Sam. If Erin wants to listen to your shit, then it's a free country." Avital turned away in her seat. She started playing with her phone, ignoring them both.

CHAPTER TWENTY-FIVE

"Erin, you believe me, right?"

Erin looked over at Avital with a pained expression, before taking a deep breath. "I do."

"You do?" Sam and Avital said in unison.

"I know that it all sounds so insane, but I know you're telling the truth. Something happened. To me. I haven't told you yet, Avital, I was so embarrassed. I still am. I can't understand how but–"

"Told me what?"

"I was curious. Sam sounded so honest. But mind control? That stuff's science fiction, right? So I decided to watch the band who shall not be named's YouTube video again. I wrote it down. I set up another camera. I had to make sure." She took a deep breath, wiping a tear that dripped down her cheek. "I blacked out."

"You blacked out?" Avital dropped her phone to her lap.

The rows of seats around them were fast filling up with people. Show time quickly approached. Erin motioned for them to lean in and hear what she had to say more privately.

"I woke up later in bed. Naked. I was…"

"What?" Sam asked. "If those assholes did something to you, too, I swear to God I'll–"

"I wasn't wearing anything… and there were things around me… You know, private things, that a girl uses sometimes, when she's feeling a certain way."

"Ohmygod, dildos?" Avital practically shrieked, drawing looks from the girls next to them.

"Shhhhh," Erin said. "Yes, but that's not the worst part." She took another deep breath, struggling to find the words. "The camera I'd put up showed the whole thing. I'd used my cell to, uhhh… make some videos… you know the self kind?"

"And they somehow ended up on that German site, right?" Sam asked, dreading the answer.

"I don't know how. I'd never even heard of it. I never signed up for an account. How did I have access? God. It was there. He found it."

"Everett?"

Erin dropped her hands into her face. "He messaged me. I'm so fucking embarrassed. If he told Marlon, I'm—"

"You see, Avital, I was right," Sam said. A wave of vindication washed over her. This was the biggest I told you so moment in her life but acting like a jerk at this tentative time wouldn't help.

"We both know Erin would never do that on her own. I was nowhere nearby. The only explanation is either she roofied herself or the song has some kind of power."

The lights dimmed around them. The concert was starting. A video appeared on screen showing highlights of Factor 5ive's career. Avital crossed her arms. "Look, I'm not sure I'm ready to admit that some shitty rock song can turn girls into mindless zombies."

The music hit and the guys were on stage. Spotlights illuminated each one. Everyone stood up screaming, the shrill cries of fourteen thousand girls deafening.

"Girl, if you're home tonight…" the guys sang. All issues were instantly tossed aside, and despite themselves, Sam, Erin, and Avital were on their feet screaming right alongside the others. "I wanna pick you up…"

"Ohmyfuckinggod!" Erin shouted.

"And take you out…"

"Ahhhhhhhhh," they shouted, jumping for joy to hear the band's biggest hit.

CHAPTER TWENTY-FIVE

"We'll have a real good time…"

The room erupted like a volcano, ear drums shattered as the waves of high-pitched squeals blended into a sound of fury lifting the building six inches off its foundation.

* * *

"What in hell is going on?"

An ocean of girls rose to their feet and shrieked like banshees, their cries piercing his brain like daggers. Frank held his hands to his ears, trying to stop the horrible noise from shattering his mind. The brute tapped him on the shoulder, handing him some ear plugs, mouthing something unintelligible and pointing to his own ears.

"Just what the doctor ordered."

Frank stuffed the yellow foam inside his withered ears. He could immediately hear himself think again. The screams were muffled, as if he was underwater. The music behind him sounded like the shit they play in the mall.

This he could handle.

But then the rush started. The girls stood and pushed forward against the railing, trying to reach out and touch the band. The guards held them back, every man doing his best against the horde who wanted to tear apart the five guys on stage. Frank turned to see what the fuss was all about.

"I don't get it."

They looked like five normal guys to him, maybe dressed more like pimps than he thought necessary, but not a long hair among 'em. White, brown, Asian, they seemed to cover all the bases. Dark hair, light hair, nice teeth, good bone structure, looked just like the faces you see on billboards looking for call centre workers.

"I'll never understand these kids…" he said.

He gave up on the youth of today and went back to focusing on keeping the girls away from the talent. To his left, a girl tried to hop the railing. She was surprisingly fast for something so small. She hadn't taken more than three steps before Frank grabbed her arm. She tried to bat him away, shrieking at the top of her lungs, eyes never leaving the boys up top. One of the brutes grabbed her and hoisted her over his shoulder, carried her to the far end of the stage and out of sight.

"One down, thirteen thousand, nine hundred and ninety-nine to go…"

* * *

"This is awesome!" Erin seemed to scream, but Sam couldn't hear a thing coming out of her mouth.

"This is awesome!" she shouted back.

They jumped up and down, arms out, trying to reach the band. Just a few short years ago, these were the five hottest guys in the world. Now? A little older, thicker, greyer, wiser, mature looking. Still the best of all the boy bands.

She didn't know who to keep her eyes on. There was Joey the bleached blond Adonis, Sam's teenage crush, the unofficial leader of the group. On stage, he crooned a soft ballad, bending over the mic soulfully. Sam felt a part of her go limp.

What a dream.

Of course, he wasn't alone up there. There was middle eastern Nazim, dark-haired muscle head Freddy, vaguely

CHAPTER TWENTY-FIVE

Hispanic smooth-skinned Theo, and Anthony, the lone black member. Some called them carefully manufactured to appeal to the widest possible range of girls, Sam called them amazing.

They all danced along to the song in a perfectly timed series of steps and twirls that drove their respective fans wild. Each took his turn with a verse of the song, but you couldn't hear anything apart from the wild screams.

It looked like they'd finished the number; they stopped moving, standing with their arms outstretched, breathing heavily. It was too loud to tell. Girls were in tears all around them. Sam was lost in one thought: how amazing this all was.

They broke into their super hit, *Girl, We Were Meant 2 B* and all hell broke loose. The screams somehow found a new plateau. Sam thought her head was going to explode. She covered her ears, desperate to keep the sound out, but it was no use. The piercing wail stabbed through the thin skin of her hands. She shut her eyes and felt tears welling up behind closed lids. This had to stop. All dogs in a three mile radius must be howling.

A tap on her shoulder. She opened her eyes to see the old security guard reaching forward over the railing. There was something small and yellow in his hands. He motioned to his ears then to hers.

Earplugs?

She graciously took them and shoved them inside her ears. Instantly the noise was drowned out. The old man pointed to one of the other guards holding a struggling girl over his head, then pointed to his own ears then to her. He seemed to be trying to tell her that he had gotten the earplugs from that guy, either that or if she wasn't careful, he'd get that guy to toss her out. Who could tell with this much noise?

She mouthed thank you.

He noticed someone trying to hop the rails and leapt after her. With the earplugs in, she could hear her own thoughts again. The noise was muffled, still loud, but tolerable. She could at least hear what the guys were singing now.

"Girl, we were meant to be,
 you and me,
 it was destiny,
 together for eternity."

Joey's voice sounded a little tuneless, but maybe it was just age. It had been a decade since they were superstars after all. Now that she could focus, she noticed that each guy seemed just off. Their picture perfect looks dissolved to reveal a few more grey hairs, faint wrinkles hidden behind manicured brows and features, slight paunches, fake tans, thinning hair. Somehow, the earplugs did more than just muffle the noise, they'd shattered part of the illusion that these guys had put up.

Sam watched them move clumsily to the beats. They couldn't shimmy or slide like they used to. Their voices alternately cracked or sounded gravelly. They seemed to read from teleprompters at their feet. The backups did most of the hard work, the other singers covered for the slip ups. They sweat through their shirts, were breathing heavily. They started to remind her more of her dad than a schoolgirl crush. How had she not noticed before?

Despite that, the concert never let up, the screams refused to die down, but Sam's enthusiasm was diminished with each passing song. Eventually, the band started humming and Joey

CHAPTER TWENTY-FIVE

took the mic. "Ladies and gentlemen, it's been a pleasure being here in River City tonight."

He was met with anguished screams from a crowd realizing the night was coming to an end.

"We've just about got to go, but we promise we'll be back soon. You've been a beautiful audience."

The wails became a desperate cry to make them stay just a little longer.

"Right now, we'd like to take a few special ladies on stage to tell them just how much they mean to us."

The place erupted with a sonic boom. Every girl and some of the guys in the arena began leaping in the air for their chance. Avital and Erin went nuts, crying out for selection. The members of Factor 5ive played coy, scanning the audience for their picks. From behind the earplugs, it all seemed very rehearsed, but damn it if Sam didn't scream and jump herself.

Joey caught Sam eye to eye and pointed at her.

Is this for real?

She turned to Erin and screamed. A burly security guard reached for her and helped her out of the crowd to the stage. As she climbed up, she noticed Avital and Erin picked to come as well. The three of them, up here on stage with Factor 5ive!

Is this a dream?

More girls were chosen, two for each member. Joey had three, he was the leader after all. Erin, Avital and Sam jumped in jubilation as he went down on one knee in front of them.

The lights went out. A huge spotlight shone down on them as he sang out, "Girl, you are my everything."

Then another spotlight shone on Nazim and his two girls. He sang, "My sun, my moon, my stars."

Next a light on Freddy and his ladies as he sang, "Destined

to be together."

Another light on Theo and his admirers. He crooned, "We're the perfect match, so..."

Finally, a spotlight on Anthony with his girls as he sang, "Say that you'll be mine."

Is this happening? Are we really on stage?

She looked out into the arena and saw nothing but a wave of screaming girls, an entire room of outstretched arms and crying faces, all jealous of her.

This is happening. I am on stage!

Avital and Erin were in some kind of trance, enraptured, barely able to move. As Sam looked around, all the girls up on stage with her seemed to be caught in the spell of their crushes, like deer in headlights. Like zombies.

Joey touched her chin and pulled her to look at him, winking as he sang. His touch was soft and she wanted to melt. He held his hand over his heart.

"We can make it happen,
　if you just give us a chance...
　Tell me that you're ready,
　for a little sweet romance."

That did it. She gave in to the guy she'd dreamed about for years. Her defences melted away in his blue eyes. She felt her heart fluttering. She wanted to swoon, but managed to keep her footing. The song floated by like a dream. She watched each member of the band serenade his girls. One of them fainted. Tears rolled down Avital and Erin's faces. They quivered in happiness, unable to move. This was the culmination of all their collective teenage dreams. It was almost too much.

I will remember this for the rest of my life.

She wished it could go on forever, but every song had to end eventually. Factor 5ive led their girls to the front and they all bowed for the audience. The piercing, pleading cries of a jealous and adoring audience washed back over them. Then, a roadie in a black jacket led them all off stage. Just like that, the greatest concert of all time was over.

CHAPTER TWENTY-SIX

"Five, five, five, five, five, five!"

The sound of fourteen thousand screaming fans echoed in the white hallway painted with the logo of the River City Jets. Sam and the other girls were corralled through the backstage area, the maze-like underbelly of the arena. Her head was spinning. She had a hard time orienting herself. The roadies didn't slow down to let them sight-see. The cheering never let up, an unreal keening from beyond.

She was having trouble feeling her fingers and toes as they were herded like sheep, then deposited in some kind of dressing room. A couple of leather couches were positioned around a coffee table. A buffet spread was set up on a large bar at the other end. It was eerily quiet; the sounds of the cheering did not penetrate through the thick concrete walls. A pair of double wide full length mirrors hung on one wall, a classy art print of River City on the other. Doors into another smaller room were shut.

Avital and Erin stood looking shell-shocked. They weren't blinking. The girls were all grouped together in their stage pairings. No one spoke. No one moved. Sam's focus drifted, her thoughts jumbled together. The lights seemed to pulse to the echoes of the distant chanting that reverberated in her head like a heartbeat.

"What a concert, am I right?" Sam said to blank stares.

Had she said anything? It felt like she'd spoken but no sound came out of her mouth. Her eyes were heavy. She wanted to lay down and fall asleep, but she fought the impulse. She needed to know what was going on.

"Avital? Erin?" This time she heard her voice. Slightly slurred, muffled from the earplugs, but definitely there. She'd felt the vibrations in her throat.

Her friends didn't seem to have heard her. Were they just too star-struck from having been chosen to be here? "Guys?"

She moved her hand towards their zoned-out faces. It seemed to move on time delay, skipping like an old CD-ROM game playing on an underpowered computer, snapping through the air in front of their faces. No reaction.

It's like they're zombies.

The door opened. Factor 5ive came in, towels over their shoulders, sweat glistening on their spray tanned brows. Away from the spotlights and stage atmosphere, she could see even more of the subtle ravages of time on their faces; crow's feet, grey hairs, skin pulled a little too tight, the subtle lines of recent surgeries.

"What a night," Joey said.

"Am I glad that's over," Theo agreed.

"Fucking right," Freddy spat, heading straight to the bar and pouring himself a drink.

They didn't even acknowledge the girls, like they were just a part of the decor.

What is going on here?

Sam started to speak but stopped herself. Better to play it

cool and act exactly like the others. She had to see where this was going. She had a hunch it wasn't any place good.

"I'd say this was a pretty good dress rehearsal for the tour, eh, boys?" Joey said proudly.

"There were some lighting cue problems stage right, and I don't think my mic was turned up all the way," Nazim countered.

"Easy fixes. Bring 'em up next sound test."

"At least we get two days off now," Anthony said, his mouth full of tiny cocktail weenies from the catering tray.

"Where are we next?" Freddy asked between pulls of whiskey.

"The fuck would I know," Joey said. "I just get on the bus and get off the bus, same as you."

"Oh, fearless leader doesn't have it all in his little black book?" Freddy countered.

"Shut up, Freddy, I'm not going through that shit again."

"Come on, guys," Nazim interjected, "no one needs to lose his cool. We just finished the first show of what's going to be one hell of a tour. We should be happy they still love us."

"Yeah, man," Theo said. "Besides, we got other matters to attend to." He pointed to the line of girls.

They all turned to look at them. Ten eyes staring at Sam and the others as if they were nothing more than meat. The girls were oblivious, like statues in the park.

"We must have really done a number on them, boys," Joey said, smiling. His teeth stretched his skin to a leathery lizard-like smile. "They're completely stunned at our celebrity."

"I've seen girls faint before, but never freeze up like this."

"He said this would happen. He said people would be so happy to see us back that they'd lose their minds."

CHAPTER TWENTY-SIX

Freddy took a shot and walked up to Avital. "Look at this one." He walked around her like he was inspecting a prized thoroughbred, examining her body in great detail. "And they said River City didn't have any real talent. Fucking fine."

Joey grabbed his shoulder. "Dude, stick with the ones you picked on stage, she's mine."

"I would've picked her, but you beat me to it."

"Sorry if I have a quicker eye for talent than you do. You can have one of my other ones if you want."

Freddy looked over Erin leeringly. He snapped his fingers in her face.

"You think something's wrong with this one?" He poked her. "Hello? Girlie?" He shook his head in frustration and turned to Sam. She did her best to appear as out of it as the others as he walked around her. He slapped her butt and waited. It took everything she had not to flinch or turn around and punch him. He looked her right in the eye. His breath reeked of alcohol as he grabbed her with both hands like he was checking melons at the supermarket. When he spotted the mole above her eye, he pivoted and walked away. "I'll just stick with my own."

"Suit yourself," Joey said.

An invisible pulse passed through them. The five guys all froze. A cocktail weenie fell from Anthony's mouth, landing half chewed on the concrete floor. Their pupils seemed to expand and fill their whole eyes. They became rigid, listening to some unseen sound.

What?

Theo and Anthony wordlessly took their four girls into an adjacent room. Nazim headed over to a couch with his and sat them down side by side. Freddy pulled out a camera from a bag on the table. It wasn't a cellphone or crappy little consumer model, this was an expensive professional job. He removed a tripod from another bag and he set it up next to Nazim's couch.

Nazim took the bags from him and mechanically folded them into neat squares, placing them on the table. Freddy mounted the camera to the tripod then turned it to face the couch. The two girls hadn't moved an inch. He turned on the camera, the red light blinking on top.

Sam almost gasped.

She stood in total shock as the two girls turned to each other and began passionately kissing. Nazim maneuvered the camera around them, getting close ups as the girls attacked each other with force.

Stop this!

Her tongue refused to move from the roof of her mouth. She tried to lunge forward and pull away the camera, but her legs were fused to the floor. They'd become a part of the cement. She stared down at her feet. The motion took what felt like an hour. When she looked back up, the two girls were undressed on the couch.

Wake up. Don't do this. Don't let them.

Nazim loosened the camera from the tripod and turned to Freddy. One of his girls dropped down to her knees and started undoing his pants. He took out his phone and began recording her. The other girl quickly joined in.

I won't let this happen.

She tried to reach out. She tried to scream, tried desperately to move even a finger.

Joey approached Sam, Erin, and Avital. His movements jittered as her mind rebelled against whatever it was holding her in place.

Not you. Not like this.

Sam was trapped again. Just like with Scott and the others. Frozen, held by some mysterious force. Only this time, she was aware of what was going on. Her eyes darted around the room to see Freddy taking advantage of his girls, with Nazim alternating filming the scene and the one of his others thrashing on the gargantuan couch.

Nazim crouched down to get a better angle. She spotted something at the back of his skull, just near the hair line. Stitches. A scar? Had he always had that? What was it from? Neck surgery? That seemed like the kind of detail she'd have known about back in her obsessive days. Unless he'd had it in the years since.

No. It was fresh. The stitching was still visible. But why was that important? Why were her eyes drawn to that? *Scott. Tommy.*

Who?

Was this her mind's attempt to avoid seeing what was really going on, what they were doing to those clearly brainwashed girls. An unimportant detail. No. Important. The scar. The scar. Why is the scar so important?

Brainwashed. Hypnotized. Drugged. All of them.

Only them?

Was the whole crowd under the spell? Whose spell? How?

Fight it, Sam.

There were three of them and only one of her. Her body wouldn't move. How could she stop this when she couldn't even lift a finger?

Joey reached under Avital's shirt. He lifted her up from under the waist and carried her over to the other couch. He laid her down and began unbuttoning his pants.

Erin! Wake up. We have to stop Joey.

Erin didn't budge.

Joey was going to take advantage of Avital. He had his phone in his hands. Nazim pivoted to capture the scene. Avital lay completely passive.

The song. It must have been the song they brought us up on stage to sing to. Just like Scott's band. What is the connection between the two groups?

If she could only move, she could get all the evidence she needed. Brainwashed girls. Nonconsensual filming. Assault. It was all right here. Somehow, Factor 5ive had the same control laced into their music that Radiant Cyanide did.

I have to move. I have to move.

She wasn't scared of them. Hours of training in multiple attacker combat should be more than enough to take out a washed-up boy band.

"S-t-o-" The words slurred silently from her mouth as her tongue was finally pried free. She could feel her fingers again, was just about to step forwards when the door burst open.

"Stop!"

She froze. She didn't dare turn to see who it was. The man's footsteps approached, clunking on the concrete floor. She nearly lost her balance when he came into view.

Simon Karlsson. He waved his hand in the air and Joey stopped half a foot above Avital. Nazim massaged his temples. Anthony jerked in shock at the two girls kneeling in front of him.

"Fucking shit!"

"Oh, my head."

"Play time is over, I'm afraid."

CHAPTER TWENTY-SIX

"Mr. Karlsson," Joey said. "When... why?"

"You should be happy to know that your metrics are through the roof. Tonight's show will solidify your international comeback. You are back, my friends. With my help, you will take this trial run all over the world. Think of what you will accomplish."

"Couldn't you at least have knocked?"

Karlsson examined Avital laying out of it on the couch, the two women kneeling obediently at Anthony's feet as he hurriedly stuffed himself back in his pants. Nazim put the camera back on the bar near the meat tray. He showed no emotion. "I see the second part of the trial was a success as well."

"Could we at least have gotten a chance to finish? This is prime River City steak," Joey said over the passed-out Avital.

"River City was just the testing ground. Your predecessors have already primed the territory. You have much bigger places to conquer. Many more subjects, you can be assured. These ones are unimportant."

"We're not fucking kids anymore Mr. K," Joey countered. "You might be our manager, but we can do what we want to who we want."

"You lack vision."

"I'm seeing pretty clearly that we've got some choice subjects, as you call them. I prefer groupies, but whatever. They're all pretty willing if you ask me. Starstruck and ready to fuck. Just the way we like 'em."

Hypnotized, you motherfuckers. Not a single one of us is consenting to any of this.

"Unlike you I see more than just what lays in front of me. It is true you have proven the efficacy of the controller mechanism on a group scale. But there are more methods of control than simply what we've gifted to you."

"Karlsson, you need us. You said it yourself when you organized this reunion. We tick all the boxes. Us. The guys who sing and dance up there and have legions of girls screaming, begging to come backstage and do what these ones were about to. Now at least let us enjoy it before you go giving us all this great and powerful manager of stars business. You could even have seconds if you want. Firsts with one of those two," Joey said, waving his hand towards Erin and Sam.

Simon Karlsson turned to regard the two of them. Oh God, was he considering the offer? Was he going to try something now? The man looked like he was twice her age. His serpentine features made her want to throw up. A sparkle of recognition flashed in his eyes as he saw Sam.

"Interesting," he said. "I will have to mention to the team that one of the original subjects has turned up again. They may wish to explore what this means." He turned back to Joey. "I have no interest in your offer. I only expect you to follow my orders."

"Get bent," Anthony said.

Karlsson sighed. "I can put you all back where I found you. It can easily be done. Janitors and nobodies living away from the fame and fortune; no money, no girls, nothing. Would you be liking this? To be returned to the fecal matter that I pulled you from? It is a simple thing."

"You couldn't. You said it yourself. Metrics through the roof. About to be on top again. People would ask questions," Joey countered.

"Would they?" Karlsson smirked. "Does anyone still ask where 98 Degrees are? Or O-town? Menudo? How about Westlife, Boyzone, LFO, Dream Street, All-4-One or 2-gether?" He pointed menacingly. "I created you and I can destroy you. An accident. A scandal. You've generously provided some material, you know."

Nazim looked at the camera, saw the tripod in front of the two girls on the other couch and put two and two together.

"Jesus." Nazim grabbed the camera and held it up as if he was going to smash it.

"Simply one mechanism," Simon said.

"Shit, my phone," Anthony said, scrolling through his videos. "What the hell, man?"

"Delete it," Joey said. "He's got nothing if—"

Simon held his hand up again. This time Sam could see that it clasped an amulet from underneath his shirt, a sparkling purple amethyst, glowing in the light. Sam's eyes grew three sizes at the revelation.

Is that what I think it is? A heartstone? Are they motherfucking golems?

Nazim stopped, gently placing the camera back on the table. Anthony put his phone back in his pocket. Joey stared ahead blankly.

He's controlling them. He's the one.

Karlsson put the amulet back in his shirt.

"Good to see you listen to reason, very fine indeed. Although it's not like you have any choice in the matter, do you?"

Joey snapped back to reality. Anthony and Nazim came to stand beside him. The door opened to the other room. Theo and Freddy emerged, their clothes disheveled, eyes having trouble adjusting to the difference in light.

"You'll never guess what those two girls let us do to them,"

Theo said.

Sam could see through the door before it slowly shut. She wanted to punch them both in the face. The poor girls were laying naked on the large bed. They'd been more than violated.

What a bunch of degenerates. Just how aware are they in this whole thing?

Simon patted the gem in his shirt. "Excellent. Now that we are all present, I must unfortunately be the bearer of bad news. A certain sheik from the URA has heard of your triumphant comeback. He has commissioned you to play for his daughter's birthday with a most generous payment. We must fly out tonight. Immediately. There can be no more time for any of your after-show antics. The plane is leaving in one hour."

"A sheik's daughter, eh?" Joey said.

"I can assure you there will be many potential subjects at this party. The possibilities I am imagining will be most interesting."

"I never have been to the desert," Anthony said.

"Compared to a billionaire's girl, this bitch really is nothing special." Joey spat on Avital's chest derisively.

"Hey, Mr. Karlsson," Theo asked. "Don't sheiks usually have, like, harems?"

"Dude, this isn't the eighteen hundreds," Nazim said.

"All of your questions will be answered shortly," Simon said. "Please, we must be leaving, come, come."

"What about the next date?" Joey asked.

"Easily reached. Oh, and on the plane, I can play for you the demo for the new single you will be recording when we can be back at the studio next week."

"Oh god, more work?"

CHAPTER TWENTY-SIX

"Now, now," Simon said. "Think of the perks."

The group left the room, leaving Sam and the girls alone. Everyone had passed out. Erin swayed in place, snoring on her feet. The others dozed on the couches in various states of undress. She felt violated all over again even though nothing had happened to her this time. Instead, she'd seen more victims who were totally unaware of what had gone on.

"Erin? Avital?" she said, her words flowing normally now. Was that a symptom of being away from the band? Away from Simon? She wondered how he'd administered that kind of control over Factor 5ive. It was the same level she had with Joshua when holding his heartstone. But the boy band weren't golems. Neither were Scott and the guys from RC. What had Karlsson done to them to make them that way?

At least now she had a target. She knew who the head honcho of this sick operation really was. Would bringing down Karlsson and his twisted empire put everyone back to normal? Or was she going to also have to find a way to deal with a golem boy band and a bunch of wannabe rockers? Maybe destroying the heartstone would free them. Lots to figure out, lots to do. She had to get a plan together.

Karlsson said they'd be back in town to record a new single. That's my chance.

She was going to make Simon Karlsson pay for all the girls in this room and who knew how many others. But she couldn't do it alone. Right now she had to figure out how to get out of here. The only problem was she wasn't even sure where here was.

CHAPTER TWENTY-SEVEN

"If any of you are awake, now would be a good time to show it."

None of the girls reacted. Sam went over to the meat tray and grabbed a slice of salami. She opened the door to the private bedroom and saw that the two girls hadn't budged.

"There's free meat here, girls."

The door to the dressing room opened. Sam froze. Was Karlsson back?

Instead, security guards marched in. Two huge brutes and an old man.

"Man, must've been one hell of a party," one said, looking past Sam to the two naked girls.

"Wish I could shut my wife up like that," the other laughed.

"Hey, they were drugged, OK?" Sam said.

"Relax, girlie," the dark-haired man said. "We see this all the time. Chicks fall all over themselves for guys in a band."

"It's not like that—"

They ignored her and went into the other room and brought out the girls with blankets wrapped around them and their clothes in a bag, The poor wrecked victims moved with glazed over eyes as the men escorted them out, leering at the exposed

CHAPTER TWENTY-SEVEN

skin that flashed beneath the blankets.

"We'll send a couple more men, Gramps," one said to the old man.

"Pretty nice spread here," the old man said as he stuffed his face with kielbasa from the meat tray. "Were you ladies having some kind of polish sausage party?"

"It wasn't a party, more like a–"

"Drug fuelled hippie orgy?"

"Not by choice."

Now that she got a better look at him, she realized that it was the same weathered, aged man she had seen on the floor, the one who had given her the ear plugs, the same old cop who had saved her from Duckie a year ago. How many times was she going to run into this guy?

"Something like that shouldn't be anyone's choice," the man said. "How come you're the only one upright and partaking?"

"Ear plugs, I think," Sam said. "Thanks for those by the way."

"I can't stand seeing someone forced to listen to what they pass as music these days. Even if they did pay for a ticket."

"Believe me, if I'd known what was going to happen, I would have stayed home."

"Good girl."

The old man kept eating, shovelling more food into his face than Sam thought his stomach could hold. He watched her, smiling politely, not budging.

"So, what happens now?" she asked him after a moment of silence.

"After my lunch break? I figure it's a school night, right? So all you ladies go home and pretend this whole thing never happened."

"I'm not going to let them forget it," Sam said. "Those

assholes shouldn't get away with what they did."

More guards came in and started helping the two girls on the couch.

"Man, those guys partied hard," one said.

"Time to get a move on," the other said to the passed-out girls. They didn't budge so he hoisted one up on his shoulder and carried her out. The other was more gentle, but took the sleeping girl in his arms out the door.

"Do I have to smack some respect into every guy's head?" Sam asked. "None of those jerks has any compassion for these girls."

"You're probably right," the old man said. "But you can't change a jerk's opinion by doing something only jerks would do."

"Nobody here was in their right mind."

"Except for you."

"Right."

"You should always be careful who you let yourself be in your wrong mind around. Drug addicts, politicians, commies, hippies… Stay straight and nobody can take advantage of you."

The man had almost eaten all of the meat on the tray. She couldn't believe someone so thin and old could pack away so many cold cuts. With a last handful of ham, he wiped his hands on his jacket and turned to the still out of it Avital and Erin.

"Alright, time to go, let's move it along before someone tries to charge me for that buffet."

"These are my friends here," she said.

"What exactly happened to them?" Frank asked as he waved his hands in front of their faces.

"Too much excitement."

"Too much of something."

"It's hard to explain, I think there's a bit of brainwashing in it if you ask me."

"Bohemians," Frank snorted. "A little singing and dancing and you lose all your sense."

"I'm not sure if I can get them to my car on my own. I'm in the parkade down the street."

The old man scratched his chin. "I'm only supposed to take you out the back way, but I'd be some kind of cop if I turned down a citizen in distress." He slung one of Erin's arms over his shoulder.

"So it is you," Sam blurted out. "You are the cop who shot Duckie!"

"Was. Retired now." He looked pained as he stared wistfully off in the distance. "And shot who? A duck? Can't even remember the last time I went out hunting, I usually only shot bad guys."

"That's just it, he was a bad guy. He was trying to, well… you shot him before he could do anything worse."

Sam took Avital's arm, and they walked down the stark white hall, past busy crews packing up the stage show and the returning guards who had booted out the other girls. "Can't say as I remember the specifics. I've shot a lot of people in my day."

The weight of Avital dragged on Sam's shoulders. "Strange house, operating table, the guy who fell apart?"

"Great Gatsby, the patchwork man! I remember it. One of the strangest cases I'd ever busted up." He eyed her again. "You look grown up."

"University, moved out, you know how it goes."

"Like fun I do," he said as he kicked the back door open with his foot. The metal door went flying, revealing the moonlit night in the arena's back loading area. Trucks were backed up to a concrete loading dock. Men moved boxes and cases into the cabs. A guard waved them over to another door at the far side with a bright red exit sign flashing overhead. Frank led the way. She followed, Avital's dead weight beginning to weigh on her.

"I'm not sure I ever got to thank you properly for saving my life," Sam said through short breaths.

"It was my cop's duty, kid, to serve the public trust. Sometimes that means filling a bad guy full of lead."

"He wasn't bad, just confused."

"That's how it starts. They're confused as to what's right and wrong. First a little petty theft, then the flim-flam game, then murder, extortion, kidnapping... er, making patchwork men."

They reached the door. Frank smiled to the guard, a bearded man as wide as he was tall with a surly look on his face and tribal tattoos peeking up from his collar. "Gonna help these ones to their cars, Jimbo, a little too much sauce if you get my meaning. Be back in a jiffy."

"What do I care, Gramps?" He let them pass out into the side street adjacent to the arena. It was dark, streetlights and vehicle headlights the only illumination. A line of cars drove by as they exited the parkade.

"So, you retired then?" Sam asked.

"Forced to. The fat-cats downtown think I'm too old."

"How old are you?"

"That's classified."

"But you're a security guard now?"

"They prefer the term public safety technician," he said.

CHAPTER TWENTY-SEVEN

She led them into the parkade. Her arms were beginning to tire. She pointed to the elevator. "I'm on four." They loaded the girls inside and Sam took a brief respite from holding Avital up, leaning her against the walls as they rose silently on metal cables. "You work concerts then?"

"Overtime. Spend the days at some lab downtown."

The elevator opened and Sam picked Avital back up, leading Frank and Erin over to her car. He helped her get them both in the backseat and buckled them up. "Thanks again, mister," she said. "That's twice you've helped me out tonight."

"Maybe you can save my life sometime, kid. Now you get those two girls some coffee and tell them to lay off the heavy stuff before they die of consumption."

* * *

"They did what?"

"It's all true, every disgusting detail."

Avital paced back and forth in Sam's apartment, fuming. She looked for something to kick. Sam tossed her a pillow from the couch. She revved back and hoofed it halfway across the room.

"What did they do to me?" Erin asked.

"Nothing, thankfully. Joey and Anthony fought over Avital, but he was interrupted before he could really do much."

It was morning now. The two of them had finally come out of their strange trance. They'd fallen asleep almost as soon as Sam had gotten them in her car, and she'd kept watch over them all night to make sure neither tried to make another video.

"Then I drove you guys home and drank too much coffee

so I could play zombie nursemaid."

"So they just left me standing there? And they both wanted Avital?"

"Trust me. You got off easy. Some of the other girls were taken to a back room. Let's just say it could have been way worse."

Avital turned her anger to Sam. "So, you expect us to believe that all the girls brought up on stage were hypnotized by Factor 5ive, taken backstage, and made to perform sex acts for them on video?"

"I was there."

"Then why didn't it affect you?" She crossed her arms over her chest.

"Frank gave me ear plugs," Sam said.

"Right. The geezer security guard who helped you get us home."

Sam nodded.

"And during all of this sexual assault going on, you just stood and watched?"

"I didn't know what to do. It would have been five on one."

"You said you were some kind of ninja though."

"Hapkido. And I'm not a black belt. I was going to try when it looked like Joey was going to rape Avital. Then Karlsson came in and stopped the whole thing, so I didn't have to."

"I'm sure the girls they took to the other room are grateful for that."

"What did you want me to do, Avital? The whole scene was totally fucked up."

"How is it that you keep ending up in all of these" – she made air quotes – "fucked up situations?"

Sam didn't know if it was the coffee or Avital's refusal to

CHAPTER TWENTY-SEVEN

forgive her that was giving her a splitting headache. She rubbed her temples, trying to figure out how to get through to her friend.

Erin touched her shoulder. "I believe her, Avital."

"Again?"

"There's too much evidence. You have to see that. First the video by the band that shall not be named, now Factor 5ive. There's something big going on here."

"Right. This hotshot manager, what did you say his name was?"

"Simon Karlsson. He's using music to take advantage of young girls. He's a real sicko."

"What do we do about it?"

"We figure out how to expose his whole operation."

* * *

The more Sam dug around online, the less she liked. Simon Karlsson was a ghost. For someone who supposedly managed so many big acts, he had no personal web presence, no website, no discussion of his methods, no interviews in Rolling Stone. Simon Cowell he was not. Karlsson appeared to eschew the glory, was never in the press bragging about the success of his charges. If she had not heard his name, and seen him in person, there was little to tell her that he was even alive at all.

Google, for once, was not her friend.

"What about the German porn site?" she said as she browsed.

It wasn't that hard to find, porn never is, but it wanted her to sign up for a membership.

"Oh god, is this going to spam the shit out of my email with more porn?"

She thought long and hard about whether or not she was going to sign up.

"It's the only way…"

She created a burner email and PayPal account and secured a one month log in to "Das Porn Hub." Once through the paywall, she was met with banner ads claiming it was the internet's biggest all amateur porn site. Looping thumbnails of videos of girls in every possible position flashed all over her screen.

"OK, so porn sites are fucking disgusting."

She'd seen her share of dicks, but this was ridiculous. Every single free space on the page was filled with some kind of dick: moving GIFs of growing dicks, photos of girls looking at massive dicks, ads for how to increase the size of a dick.

"For something supposedly catering to straight men, it's sure obsessed with penises."

The site had a search bar, and a listing of the categories of the different videos.

"I'm going to need a dictionary for some of these."

Some were obvious, others obtuse, others confusing; any messed-up fantasy a guy or girl could have was here. Sam needed to see what was up here from River City. Was there anything from backstage? She tried searching 'college,' then 'university.'

"There's thousands of videos. I am not going through them all."

She tried River City, but found no hits.

"They'd never be that obvious."

She clicked on the 'oral' category. Hundreds more videos. Glancing over the thumbnails, she was sure she spotted one of the girls from backstage at the concert. She opened the video and sure enough, there were the two poor hypnotized girls going to town on what had to be Freddy.

"That's the proof," she said confidently. "This is the site benefiting from the videos made under sonic mind control. Now to figure out the people in charge of it."

The upload a video button on the page took her to a standard form; name of the video, type, are the participants over eighteen, nothing but simple checkboxes. There was no other information.

"There has to be something here."

She browsed around the different parts of the site looking for anything; a mailing address, tax information number, a company name, but all that happened was she was bombarded with more and more GIFs of dicks.

Das Porn Hub was bare of any identifying markers.

"The longer I stay here, the more my computer is gonna fill up with pop up ads and spyware. The last thing I need is a fucking German porn virus."

She shut down her browser.

"This is getting me nowhere. I need to confront Simon directly."

There was only one person that could help her get close to him, and he was quite possibly the last person she ever wanted to see again.

Scott.

CHAPTER TWENTY-EIGHT

Why do I have to keep coming back to this piece of shit house?

Sam stood on the walkway, gathering up her courage. The rundown little white house with its ratty chain gate, garbage covered grass and peeling paint faced her impassively. An old pizza flyer blew past her, skidding along the snow on its mission of exploration.

She took a deep breath, trying to put out the fleeting images of what had happened to her here out of her mind. She had to come back. There was no other way to reach Scott. She'd smashed his phone. They weren't playing their usual gigs on Friday nights anymore. The others had quit their day jobs. This was the only place she knew they'd be.

Partying, of course. But would they be alone?

Sam checked the plugs in her ears. She wanted to be ready in case they were practicing. They'd given her some kind of immunity with the YouTube video and at the Factor 5ive concert, so she had to hope they'd work here, too.

"No sense standing out here in the cold all night."

A feeling of deja vu washed over her as she knocked on the door. Each reverberation of her knuckles was like the pounding of Jose's drum kit as they played the songs that had knocked her out before. Visions of waking up next to Scott and Tommy popped in her mind. Twice. There would be no third time. She was here on a mission and wasn't leaving until she had what she was after.

Knock, knock.

As expected, no one responded.

She turned the knob. The door was open and the cracked old wood creaked as it swung inside slowly. She looked behind her to see Avital, Erin, Marlon, and Everett in the car waiting. This time she wasn't coming alone. She'd brought backup. They'd probably only get in the way if this turned physical, but at least they could call the cops or be her getaway if things spiralled out of control.

She made the hand signal telling them to give her ten minutes before coming to get her, as per what they'd discussed.

"Keep the car running," she mouthed. As if they could even see her face from the poorly lit front step.

The only weapons they carried were their anger and rolls of quarters stuck into socks. Sam hoped that they wouldn't have to resort to those, but they were a simple tool that hurt like hell when swung at the right spots. They'd practiced on pillows. Avital was a natural.

"OK, jerks, I'm coming for you," she said quietly.

She wanted Simon Karlsson. Scott and Tommy could help. If not, she'd be back to square one. But at least she could make them feel some pain for what they'd done to her. She waved back to the girls in the car one final time and went inside.

* * *

"Is she sure she knows what she's doing?" Marlon asked Erin back inside the running car.

"She does take kung fu or something, so I guess she can handle herself."

Avital looked at the tube socks filled with quarters on the seat next to her that were their only weapons. "I hope so, I just had my nails done."

* * *

Sam crept inside. The house was quiet, as immaculately clean as an Ikea catalogue. It was like a DVD skipping, a scene playing on repeat. She knew what was going to happen before she even entered the living room.

They're going to be waiting for me.

There they were, exactly as she had suspected, Jose on drums, Tommy, Vic on guitar, Ben on bass. Staring off into space, as if in a trance.

"Hi, guys," she said softly, knowing they wouldn't respond.

Finally, she could see the truth in this. With her mind clear the similarities to Joshua were striking. They were in what she termed a 'Golem Trance,' a state where their actions were dictated by whoever held the heartstone, the amulet that gave its owner the ability to use his or her thoughts to make the golem do whatever they wanted.

Deja vu.

What she didn't know was whether or not the guys were always golems or if they'd had something done to them during the Karlsson makeover.

No. It was him. They never showed any signs before.

The scars, on the base of the hairline near the back of the

CHAPTER TWENTY-EIGHT

neck. Scott had one. She'd seen them on a few of the Factor 5ive guys, too. She had to know.

She walked around the static members of RC and confirmed it. Tommy, Ben, Vic, Jose. They all had the same marks. Faint stitching closing some kind of wound that seemed like it should have healed fully by now.

She turned to the bedroom. Scott. She knew where he'd be. She pushed into the cramped room. Scott was at the desk writing away furiously in his own trance state. She looked over his shoulder to see his words, neat scribbles about love and happiness and respecting your woman.

What a crock.

She slowly reached for his scar.

"Scott, we need to talk," she said.

The scar was a raised bump. As if it was holding something inside the skin. It was hard and cold to the touch, about two inches long, slightly ovular.

She dug into his desk as he worked, looking for something sharp. She found a small pair of wire cutters. She maneuvered them towards his neck.

Easy.

He stood up abruptly and took his notebook towards the other room.

"Not now," Sam said and grabbed him by the arm.

He brushed her away like a mosquito and walked out. Shocked at how easily he'd pushed her aside, she followed him into the main room with the wire cutters.

He sat on a bar stool, the band ready behind him, their instruments set up, in hand. They stared at her blankly in their fancy shirts.

"Scott, I need you to answer a few questions."

He ignored her. Jose clacked the drum sticks three times before the group went off into a bouncy intro.

"Stop," she shouted, but she was drowned out by the music. Scott started singing:

"You came to me with problems,
　didn't know what to do,
　You needed more than answers,
　I had the key for you."

Tommy and Vic played catchy twang guitar. Ben plucked at the bass rhythmically. The sound was muffled by Sam's earplugs.

"I want Karlsson," she said. "He did something to you. I need to know what it was."

Scott looked at her with cold, dead eyes as he sang. The room seemed to vibrate. She could feel the soundwaves emanating from the amps on the floor sliding along the hardwoods, slowly wrapping themselves around her leg, slinking up her body like invisible snakes. They had form and structure, like creeping tentacles. Around her stomach, over her arms, inside her shirt. Her skin rose with goose pimples. She could feel her legs sinking into the floor, her eyes becoming heavy.

No. Not like this. Not again.

"You know where this is going," the voice of David Bowie from the poster on the wall said to her. "Just let it happen. It's much easier that way."

She ignored Bowie.

"There's no way I'm waking up in that bed again."

CHAPTER TWENTY-EIGHT

"We can make it happen,
 just take my hand and come,
 I'll take you on a ride and
 we'll have so much fun."

The ethereal tendrils of sound slithered around her cheeks, began burrowing into her face like worms. They forcefully pried apart her lips. Her eyes grew heavy. She could barely keep them open.

"Yes, yes, relent," Bowie said.

"Fuck that noise," she shouted. Using the last of her strength, she lunged forward and grabbed the plugs of their amps. She yanked them out of the wall so hard that she took the outlet clean off, ripping out wiring in a great shred of drywall.

The sound died instantly.

The band played on with empty guitars, the flat sound of the strings strumming to Jose's deadened drums and Ben's silent bass. Scott sang with a diminished voice. He sounded hoarse and lifeless. The enveloping mist evaporated in a flash. She was free from the pull.

"We'll go where no one's gone before,
 to a universe of love."

Had they always sounded this bad?

Whatever sway the music held was gone. Instead of an up-and-coming new band of dangerous and sexy rock stars, they were painted wannabes in nice shirts. The band played on but she felt the power in her limbs again, could blink away the grogginess.

She rose to her feet.

"Simon Karlsson. I want him. You're going to help."

They responded with the lifeless sounds of dead instruments.

"He's the boss, right?"

They still ignored her.

Sam threw the bunch of cords and chunk of the wall at Jose's drum kit, the only thing that still sounded halfway normal. She knocked the entire kit over, cymbals crashing to the floor. Jose's sticks waved over empty air.

"I'm not fucking around here. I want to know how he's doing this."

Nobody spoke. Even David Bowie had gone quiet.

She marched up to Tommy and pulled hard on his guitar neck, wrenching him out of place, snapping the clasp. She swung it wildly into the wall, smashing clean through the poster of David Bowie, and the drywall into the bedroom beyond. She grabbed Vic's, tried to do the same, but he came toppling over with it. She put her foot on his chest and slid the guitar off his neck. She threw it at the window. It crashed right through to the outside.

She turned and reached for Ben's bass neck. The distraction almost cost her. She nearly missed Scott's lunge. He'd moved much faster than she'd anticipated he could, reaching for her body with outstretched hands. She thrust out her palm and hit him right in the nose, knocking him off balance. Blood snaked down from smashed nostrils but he didn't stop coming. He smacked his shoulder into her stomach, knocking the wind out of her.

She was pushed to one knee just as the rest of the band leapt into action. Ben swung his bass, just missing the top of her head by a fraction of a inch as she dropped down. Tommy

CHAPTER TWENTY-EIGHT

leapt out with a flying kick that she barely pushed aside with an inside out block. She'd saved her face but the blow sent a shooting pain through her arm.

Jose grabbed a cymbal from the floor and threw it forward like a frisbee. Somehow, luck was on her side as the backswing from Ben's wild bass swing knocked it off course.

Now it was real. They were alive again, in a different kind of golem trance. One of action. Joshua had experienced them, too.

Fucking hell.

She rolled to the side as Tommy kicked again. She grabbed a barstool from beside the couch and swung it at Scott's face. It shattered in a million pieces off his dead look. His eyes rolled back in his head as he fell over. He looked to be out cold.

Four to go.

Ben swung again with his bass. Sam stepped inside the blow, grabbing his wrist and pushing at his shoulder joint, sending him toppling backward. Tommy kicked, his shoe glancing against Sam's head, sending stars shooting through the edges of her vision. She staggered backward, rolling over her shoulder. She saw them coming and rose with her arms aloft to block more kicks.

Jose joined in, the two of them kicking frantically at her. She could only turtle up. There were too many of them. Master Park's criticism rang through her rattled mind. Remember the lesson, use them against each other.

You can't stay here and take these shots.

She swung out her elbows, hitting both attackers square in their nuts. Their eyes bulged out as the ultimate man pain broke through whatever spell held them. That was her opportunity.

She leapt up and grabbed Tommy by the shoulder, swinging over him, kicking right at Vic's face. Her shoe shattered his jaw, knocking him down to the couch like a sack of flour.

Three left.

With Tommy held in front of her as a kind of shield, Ben and Jose tried to grab at her. She twisted around with them, using Tommy as a blocker. He reached behind, trying to grab her hands. She jerked down on Tommy's traps, squeezing and pulling back, toppling him backwards. His head whiplashed down and hit the ground with a sick thud. His eyes glazed over but he wasn't out.

She threw two quick straight punches at Jose and Ben, hitting each in their outside eyes. Neither one flinched. Ben grabbed her shoulder, Jose her hair. Jose yanked her head around while Ben slugged her in the midsection. She desperately grabbed Jose's hands, twisting down briskly and snapping his wrist. In class that move would drop an opponent, but not him. He just let go of her hair and swiped at her with his now broken hand.

Still holding her shoulder, Ben swung at her head wildly. She chop blocked out with a ridge hand, a move that put almost as much pain on the blocker if done wrong. He was unfazed, and she felt a reverberation run through her shoulder.

"Shit," she muttered.

The two of them exploded back to action. Ben pulled her forward by the shoulder. She let the momentum carry her, sliding quickly in with a headbutt, slamming the ridge of her head right on his nose. She felt cartilage explode. She kneed him right in the midsection, bending him over, then grabbed the back of his head and slammed his face down on her knee again, this time putting him out for good.

That just left Jose and he had one useless hand. He didn't make a sound, showed no distress, wasn't even breathing hard. There was no way they should have had this much pain tolerance if they weren't golems. Or on bath salts.

She feinted a forward lunge and tricked Jose into bringing his hands up to block high. She then busted out a spinning sweep kick, a technique she had yet to really master, but the adrenaline and circumstance worked in her favour; she swiped his legs right out from underneath him. He fell hard, head hitting the coffee table corner with a sick wet crunch. He lay flat with his head at an awkward angle.

"Whoops," she said, cringing. "I hope I didn't break his neck."

They were all out. She found the dropped wire cutters and moved to Scott's prone body.

She grabbed him by the collar and dragged him over to the easy chair. His face was a mess, tiny cuts bleeding down in a crimson mask. It felt good to see him hurt, too.

She took out his wallet from his back pocket. Inside was the business card, a simple white block with bold black lettering, with an address and phone number for Karlsson.

She flipped him over and dug the edge of the wire cutters into the back of his neck.

"Here goes nothing," she said and snapped the stitch. Then the next one and the next one after that until they were all gone. A thin line of blood began seeping out of the never healed cut. She slid her finger inside, felt the hard surface of a stone. The loose tissue slid over her skin as she pushed her fingers further inside his neck, finding the edges of the rock. Blood poured out faster, coating her hand, dripping to the floor. She found the sides. Slid her fingers around and pulled. The stone was stuck. There was something holding it in.

"I really hope you can feel this right now," she said.

She pushed the wire cutters into the wound, slid them through until she found what was holding the stone in. The cold metal was coated with slowly oozing blood. She closed the cutters over the spot and snipped it. The gem popped out in a splash of blood, landing on the floor with a wet plop.

It was a tiny red ruby. Not much bigger than a thumbnail. It glittered in the blood-soaked light.

Scott's neck oozed thick red gore at an alarming rate. She grabbed her hand and held it over the wound. Something stirred in him. Perhaps the spell was wearing off without the stone, or perhaps he was just about to come to and attack her again.

He looked at her with confused eyes, blood dripping off his lashes. "Sam? What are you doing here?"

"You have to answer a few questions, Scott."

He looked around the room groggily, saw all of the damage and his knocked-out band mates.

"Holy shit, Sam, you really are a Yoko."

She blanched. The stone twinkled, reflecting her impassive face. So he wasn't under the spell of Karlsson. At least not all the way. He was just an asshole.

"Holy shit, Sam," Avital gasped behind her.

She turned to see Avital, Erin, Marlon, and Everett, mouths agape at the mess she had caused. Bodies lay everywhere, blood covering both the walls and Sam. Scott was leaking a concerning amount of gore. The four other unconscious or worse band members were strewn about the room.

"I guess you didn't need our help after all," Erin said with her sock full of quarters in hand.

Sam held up the business card with bloody fingers. "I have what I was after."

"Did you really beat the shit out of them all?" Avital asked.

"They didn't want to cooperate."

"Is that guy dead?" Marlon asked.

"Possibly."

Erin's eyes bugged out as she saw the wire cutters in Sam's hand and the injury to Scott.

"Remind me not to get you pissed off like ever," Everett said, looking over the carnage with newfound respect.

"Help me find some towels for him. I don't want him to bleed out."

She lay Scott back down and moved over to Tommy, flipping him over and taking the cutters to his neck.

"What the hell are you doing to them?" Avital asked in shock.

"Saving them. I think."

She started snipping.

CHAPTER TWENTY-NINE

The Durchschlafen building rose deep in the heart of River City's downtown revitalization district, a building so modern that Sam would have assumed it was some high powered law firm or mega corporation's head office. It had no sign out front, no markings to tell her what it was or wasn't. It was only the business card that gave her the name. As far as anyone knew, this was just another high-rise in River City, as much a part of the scenery as the Yakatori plaza a few blocks away. There was no indication of anything nefarious going on, no billowing clouds of smoke, no smell of brimstone, no armed guards, just a line of the people who went in and out, looking like any other office worker downtown.

Sam walked right in through the front doors. It was a lobby like any other; elevators, security doors, a desk out front manned by a bored looking security guard. She walked in like she owned the place and went right to the building directory hanging on the wall under glass. The words were spelled out in white block letters. The listing for the eighth floor was innocuous, "SK Management." She hadn't really expected Golem Inc., but still…

CHAPTER TWENTY-NINE

Here goes nothing.

She rode the elevator up, watching the numbers change and feeling a growing adrenaline in her. What was she going to walk out to? Waiting guards? Drawn weapons? A cackling Karlsson ready to take her in to a secret lab to perform the same experiment on her that he'd done to Scott and the others?

She fingered the bag of blood-crusted gems in her hand. She was going to stop this, even if she wasn't entirely sure how just yet.

The number eight lit up. The elevator doors slid open impassively. An office door at the end of the hall. She exited onto the eighth floor and walked straight through it to meet a familiar face. "You!" she said. It was the old cop. Again! This was his plum gig? Could she get any luckier?

"Me?" he repeated. "Is it? I've been wondering where I went."

"No, you're right here, this is perfect!"

"I know! Now I don't have to go looking for my lunch."

"No, I mean, I need to get in here and you work here!"

"You want in? Do you have an appointment?"

She looked around the simple lobby. Nothing more than the security desk, a few magazines on a small table between two chairs and a set of closed automatic glass doors. She walked right up to them and stood in front, but they did not respond. "I need to see Mr. Karlsson, I've got business with him."

She waved her hands at the doors, but they refused to budge.

"Who?" Frank asked with furrowed brows.

"Simon Karlsson, he works here."

"Sorry, kid, they don't give me any names. They just use cards," he said.

"What?"

"I sit here and watch people scan themselves in. It's boring, trust me. There are no meetings, no appointments, nothing."

She approached the desk, covered in screens showing empty hallways. "So you don't know what's going on back there?"

He sipped from a white Styrofoam coffee cup. "As far as I can tell, they take a bunch of dirty hippies and turn them normal, the lord's work if I do say so myself."

She put her hands on the desk and leaned in, lowering her voice, looking to see if there were any listening devices present. "What would you say if I told you they were creating monsters with the power to brainwash young girls into performing non-consensual sexual acts on camera?"

He put down his coffee. "I'd say you've got one hell of an imagination, kid."

"It's true, I swear." She leaned back upright. "And Karlsson is at the head of it all."

Frank frowned. "I don't know what bus from crazy town you got off, but I haven't seen anything like that around here."

"Well, what have you seen?"

"I told you, hippies go in, norms come out. They run some tests on 'em. Like the old army physicals, I guess. There's also a lunchroom. It's all pretty kosher back there."

"That can't be right, this is where my ex was turned into a hypnotizing space cadet. Also, an asshole. But he may very well have been that before and I just couldn't see it."

He took another sip from his coffee. "Tell you what, kid, I'll do some digging around, see what I can see then I'll let you know if anything crackpot is going on."

She looked through the glass doors, but all she saw was an empty hallway. She tried to figure out which screen showed that hallway from his console. "Can't I just go inside? I know what I'd be looking for and–"

"Hell no," he interrupted. "I've been charged with protecting that door and for now, that's what I'm gonna do. Until I see some proof, I'm not gonna go busting in accusing the good people in there of creating serial rapists."

"But this is really important!" Sam pleaded.

Frank shook his head. "We all think what we want is, kid, doesn't mean the big bad world is gonna give it to us."

Sam eyed the door, eyed the old man, tried to think if she could get past him, through the door and inside before being taken down. He was so old. She could probably take him. Then she spotted a tazer at his belt. She'd heard more than one news report of those things knocking people down for good. She was in no mood to test the theory. An image of a mad dash and a leap through a doorway, fighting through an army of golems to the desk of Simon flashed through her head. No matter how she worked it out, it always ended with her beaten down and broken, betraying the only chance at having an ally on the inside.

Not much of a plan, Sam.

There was no point in blowing her revenge now in some hot-headed crusade. But there was another way. She could take Frank's help and get some actual evidence that could bring down Karlsson. Together they could expose the horrible truth to the world. The old guy looked at her, his hand twitching, like maybe he was expecting her to make a break for it. She just smiled innocently. "So, if you do find something?"

"You'll be the first one I tell," he said.

It would have to do. Vengeance could wait for a few more days.

* * *

Frank watched the girl leave, relieved he didn't have a situation on his hands. He never liked hitting a woman, especially a young one, but if it was the only way to do his job, then he would. The taser at his belt was more of a show piece, not something he'd actually use on someone. Back in his day they didn't need a pocket electric chair to take a punk down, they used good old-fashioned gumption. The bossman had told him it was standard issue now, so he did what he was told. No sense getting busted down to an even shittier desk job…

"The stories these kids tell," he said to himself as he put his legs up on the desk and took out his worn copy of *Doc Savage*. He absently read over the yellowed pages, killing time. The girl's words kept nagging in his head.

"She was convinced that something bad was going on back there," he said. "So sure of herself. But then crazy ones always are."

It was strange that he kept bumping into her. Never in normal circumstances either. Mall fights, patchwork men, real psycho stuff; stitched-up bodies falling apart, operating tables in track housing, strange doctor kids with bondage fetishes, robberies; it all seemed to get weirder and weirder. He never was given an explanation that satisfied him about all that had gone on the past few years. Maybe she was on to something.

He thought about hippies and norms, punk kids going inside freaks and coming out respectable. When had he ever heard of something like that happening before? This new generation had been going down the shitter a long time, it was only when there was a war on that they straightened up and flew right.

CHAPTER TWENTY-NINE

Why now? The more he thought about it, the more suspicious it was.

"Those dirty ass flower kids ought to be out protesting something, getting high, having a love in, not coming here for re-education and a haircut. It's just so unlike them."

He had convinced himself now. He looked through the glass doors to the benign quiet hallway. There was definitely something wrong happening back there and he was going to find out what.

* * *

Saturday night. Frank took an extra shift, trading with the weekend guy for a chance to be here when the place was dead. Hockey Night in Canada could wait, he had some sleuthing to do.

"Thanks, Miguel," he said to the overnight guard. "I'll take it from here. You just get home to your breakfast burritos and wife."

"I keep telling you, Malone, I'm not Mexican!"

"It's OK, I'm a cosmopolitan guy, some would even say a real man of the world. I don't care if you are here illegally, I won't spill the beans."

"I moved here from Windsor!"

"Right," Frank said, tapping himself on the nose. "Windsor. Si, señor."

Miguel tossed his hands up in the air and walked away. Frank waved goodbye to his Hispanic co-worker and took his usual spot behind the desk, the illusion of normalcy despite the detective bones vibrating inside his body. He could smell something back there and it wasn't coffee.

No sense in waiting all night.

He stood up and stretched, making a point to say out loud, "I could really use some coffee." He locked the front door, putting up a sign that read "Back in ten minutes" on the window.

"That should keep anyone away while I take care of business."

His scan card got him through the glass doors, the soft whir of machines doing the job of a man letting him inside where the action happened. It was quiet. The place was dead. As far as he knew, no one came in on weekends. The white halls were sparkling and bare, the offices empty. The only sounds were his own footsteps.

"Now if I were making a brainwashing sex pervert, where would I do it?"

The weekend card allowed access to more of the site than his weekday one. He pushed into an office at random. He walked behind the desk, looking over a normal selection of family photos and Post-it notes. He pulled open the desk drawer and shuffled around inside for something nefarious.

"Just a bunch of stationery."

He tossed pens and paperclips out on the floor.

"Maybe a false compartment."

He tugged on the bottom of the drawer. It didn't want to budge so he jammed a pen inside and pried it off. The whole thing broke into four pieces.

"Nothing. This is just a desk."

He tried the pictures on the wall, pulling them off, looking for a safe or secret panel, but again nothing. He tossed the glass frames over his head to shatter on the floor. He pulled up the carpet, but it wasn't hiding anything underneath either,

CHAPTER TWENTY-NINE

so tearing it up was another waste of his time.

"Well, this room was a bust," Frank mumbled, leaving the place a trashed disaster.

He moved on to another and still another office, but all he found was an old one-dollar bill stuffed inside someone's desk chair, hardly the sign of evil.

"Maybe the hippie reconditioning room."

He walked around the corner of the hall to where he'd seen the testing before. He let himself in. The room wasn't anything special, a flat table with a white spongy mattress covered in thin tissue paper, a whiteboard un-illuminated, a small desk; all clean as a whistle. For some reason, though, it reminded him of that house in the suburbs, the one with the crazy kid playing doctor. There were no machines in here, but there was another door. This one wouldn't open for his key.

"A wise guy, eh?"

Frank shoulder checked the door, but only managed to dislocate his joint. He had to stop and pop it back in. He tried kicking, but the thing was too solid.

"God damn it," he grumbled.

Then he had a crazy idea. He took out the taser and zapped the control panel. Blue streaks of light shot from his hand and fried the machinery like an egg. Steam shot up, the smell of charring circuits filling his nostrils.

Baddabing!

The door opened about a foot, he could work with that. He wedged himself through the crack, cursing all those late-night donuts as he held his breath and squeezed inside.

"Now we're talking," he said as he entered a taxidermist's dream theatre. One entire wall was covered in jars. They were all shapes and sizes, with a strange thick green liquid inside. He couldn't quite see the contents through the murky water, but whatever it was had to be bad. A skeletal model of a person stood looking at him with dead eyes near a table of surgical instruments. A large silver machine on wheels was parked in the corner next to a huge computer console, like something from the good old days when the bigger they were, the better. He tapped a few buttons but the thing stayed black. On one wall there was a display case filled with a plush purple velvet fabric bedding. Precious stones glittered as they lay in contented luxury on the softness.

"A jeweller?" Frank said, confused.

The room was trying to tell him something, but he didn't speak the language. He needed a translator for these secrets. He plopped down in the computer chair to think. What was he missing in here? The answer was right in front of his face: the wall of jars. He took one down, trying to peer inside. The damn thing was too viscous. He shook it, but all that did was create a few bubbles. There was no lid that he could see, no way in to whatever was desperate to stay hidden.

"Only one way to find out," he said and spiked the jar like a football. The glass shattered, spraying thick green slime everywhere. Something fell out. It took him a moment to realize what he was looking at, it seemed so crazy to even think of it. But there it was, as clear as the eye could see, one half of a human brain, glistening in the light, ooze sliding off its greyish sponge-like surface.

"Well, there's your answer and it's direct from crazy town."

He looked around at the mess of the room; the door propped open partway, glass and gore on the floor. He fingered the one-dollar bill in his pocket and a thought occurred to him.

CHAPTER TWENTY-NINE

"Shit, I'd better get the janitor in here."

CHAPTER THIRTY

T-Minus thirty minutes till endgame.

Sam sat in her car in a parkade down the street. She was dressed all in black. She fingered a ski mask in her hands nervously.

"Well, Sam, are you ready for what could be the biggest fight of your life?"

Simon Karlsson was going to be at the recording studio, working with Factor 5ive on a new single. He'd be exposed, vulnerable. If she could get him alone, she could get his heartstone away, prevent him from doing any more damage with his brainwashing/porn golem cult. Then, she and Frank would expose what he'd told her that he found in that mysterious room back at the Durchschlafen building this afternoon.

"Half brains in jars, fancy gemstones, more strange machines and massive computers than an IBM garage sale."

"Just make sure they don't know you know so that we can show the press."

"Where am I supposed to put a loose brain? In my pocket?"

"You can figure it out, Frank," she'd said. "We can't risk them finding out they're discovered."

CHAPTER THIRTY

"I'll put it in my lunchbox," he'd said helpfully.

She hoped he'd cleaned the place up and kept his discovery secret. They'd look like lunatics if they brought the press down to find a room cleared out and full of nothing.

She texted Avital on her phone. "You guys ready for operation distraction?"

The response came back with an image of a thumbs up.

"OK, five minutes."

"This is your chance. Karlsson is always on the go, so if there's ever going to be a time to take him out, it's now. You can do this. You've got help. You're not alone."

She spoke into the rearview mirror of her car, trying to amp herself up for what was coming. She was a bundle of nerves. The adrenaline was already flowing. She had the wire cutters in her pocket, the gang had their socks full of quarters. This was just a recording studio. Nobody there would expect them to pull something like this.

"Trust the training," she said. "You took out Scott and the guys. You can take out a bunch of pushing middle age boy band geezers."

She'd fought golems before and won, but the experience had always been hell. This time felt different. This felt like the culmination of something bigger. She hadn't dared tell Avital, Erin, Marlon, and Everett what they were potentially walking into. If the plan worked, they'd never have to face what she feared. She didn't want them getting hurt. If she had Simon's heartstone controller, then they wouldn't have to be.

"Get in. Get the stone. Stop Simon. That's it."

This was it. She stared at the phone in her hands, just waiting for the five-minute cue.

Ping!

"It's on."

* * *

Avital pushed open the doors to the Big Shiny Tunes recording studio. It was a flat block of a building near the old warehouse district. The signage was subdued, the windows blacked out. There was nothing to tell them that it was even occupied except for the chained in parking lot at the right side with a limo parked across two spaces.

"Just follow my lead, guys," she said to the others.

The small lobby was tastefully painted in dark reds and blacks, with posters of famous bands that had used the place over the years. Crash Test Dummies, The Watchmen, Johnny Dagon, Burton Cummings, even Tom Cochrane. Press clippings under frames, gold records, even a mounted autographed guitar from Randy Bachman lined the walls. A few leather chairs rested around a circular table covered in *Rolling Stone* and *Entertainment Weekly* magazines.

A lone security guard sat at a desk reading a copy of the *River City Free Press*. He looked up in shock as the four of them walked in.

"Uh, hey, this isn't a public building, guys."

"Oh, we're not the public," Avital said. "We're the leaders of the Factor 5ive fan club here for an official interview and photo shoot. We made this appointment weeks ago. They're expecting us."

Avital pointed to Marlon who held up a digital camera, then to Everett who held up a pad of paper and a pen.

The guard didn't seem convinced. "Nobody told me about this. As far as I know, this session is top secret and—"

CHAPTER THIRTY

"Exactly. How else would we know about it unless we were *in* the know?"

He put down his newspaper. "See that red light?" He pointed to a large circular light over the door to the studio proper. "That means a session is in progress. You walk in there and you could throw them all off. I could get in shit."

"So it's all happening on the other side of the door?" Avital asked breathlessly. "Oh, this is so exciting." She leaned over the desk seductively. "Surely there's an appointment book down there, right? I made the meeting with Simon Karlsson's office myself and–"

"With Mr. Karlsson? Oh geez, I–"

THWACK.

The man's eyes rolled back in his head. He turned slowly to Erin before collapsing to the ground, knocking the paper to the floor as he sprawled on the carpet.

Avital turned to see Erin holding the sock of quarters, staring at the unconscious man on the floor.

"Why'd you hit him? He was about to let us in!"

"It was taking too long," Erin said. "Besides, I really wanted to know what it was like to hit someone with these things."

"Have you girls always been crazy?" Everett asked. "Or has it just been since we've been hanging out with Sam?"

"What do we do with him?" Marlon asked as he leaned down to check on the man. "He's out cold." A trickle of blood leaked from a small cut near the guard's temple.

"Tie him up and gag him," Avital said. "We can't have him alerting anyone."

"Yup," Everett said. "Definitely crazy."

* * *

Sam checked both ways as she crossed the street. She darted to the fence and leapt up, her hands grasping the cold links through thin gloves. She was up and over in no time, landing in a crouched position near the side of the limo. She was panting. Waiting to see if anyone saw her. She crawled over to the employee entrance, staying low. She reached up and tugged on the door. It clicked open. She ducked inside.

* * *

The internal lobby and sitting room were empty. A massive meat tray lay on a large table in the centre. Two couches were pushed up against the wall. Potted plants filled the corners of the room. More posters and gold records lined the wall. A huge glass wall showed the recording space where the members of Factor 5ive worked on their parts. They were dressed casually, with headphones on, staring over papers with lyrics.

Another door led to the engineering booth. This one had tinted windows and an imposing steel handle.

"What do we do now?" Everett asked.

"Eat!" Marlon said, grabbing some cold cuts.

"No, we go and keep the band busy," Avital said. "That's the plan. Block the door, do whatever it takes so Sam can do what she has to with that Karlsson guy."

"He's in the booth?" Marlon asked with his mouth full.

"Yup. So we go in there." She pointed to the recording room.

* * *

"Mister Karlsson, we're ready for another take."

CHAPTER THIRTY

"Very fine, yes, very fine."

Simon pressed the intercom button.

"OK, boys, it's all set up. We take it from the top."

"OH MY GOD, I can't believe it's really you!"

Simon stared in shock as four people barged into the recording space. Two women and two men. They rushed up and began snapping photos, chattering wildly, disrupting the whole session. The band was taken aback, looking to him through the window for help.

"What the hell are those kids doing in there?" he asked the engineer.

"How the hell would I know? They just came out of nowhere!"

"Well, send them back there. We have a hit to record."

"Right away, sir." The engineer pressed another intercom button. "Security!" he called out.

There was no answer.

"Security's not responding, sir."

"Fire him later. Now get in there and stop those kids."

The engineer rose from his desk and ran out of the booth.

* * *

Sam pressed herself up against the wall and watched the engineer dart out of the booth and into the recording space. He was shouting something at the gang who were playing their part perfectly. Factor 5ive was distracted. Simon would be alone.

"This is it."

She crept alongside the wall and stopped at the door to the booth. She couldn't see inside. What would he be doing?

Watching through the wall? She had to hope she would take him by surprise. She pushed her way in.

He was looking at his phone. The sounds of the situation in the recording room were muted. It was dark inside. He seemed totally unaware of her presence. She raised her hands, reaching towards his neck. She could see the golden chain just below the collar of his shirt. Two feet away. This was going to work.

"Did you honestly think you were going to just walk in here and disrupt all that I've built? What, apprehend me, put me away? That I am so defenceless that you, a simple nothing girl, could do this?"

"Well, yeah, kind of," she said, freezing in place, suddenly realizing how poorly thought out her plan may have actually been.

Karlsson spun in his chair and stood up. He was a good foot taller than her, wiry, more intimidating than she remembered.

"Girls like you always think you can change the world, that you are special, that you will win in the end against the big bad wolf. This is the folly of your generation. You do not understand that you rage against a futility."

His dark eyes gleamed in the light of the computer console. He flashed a serpent-like grin as he took a step towards her. She found herself backing up. This room was too cramped to fight in. She'd played right into his strengths. She needed more room.

"I understand that you're turning people into golems. That you're using them to hypnotize girls to make porn."

"To make money."

"It's mind control."

"Is it?" He stepped towards her, and she backed away again.

CHAPTER THIRTY

"Or is it perhaps that many girls are more willing than you think? All they need is the right release of inhibition. Do they not fawn over celebrities? Bend over for the rock star at the drop of a hat? Mick Jagger, David Bowie, Steven Tyler, Robert Plant, Miles Davis, Leonard Cohen, John Mayer, Chris Martin, Tommy Lee, Bret Michaels... should I continue name dropping?"

"No, I get it."

"Do you really think that they all had to coerce the women they slept with over the years? Of course not. They were just in a time that did not shame these acts."

"That was probably all the drugs."

"Women become moist for men such as these at merely a glance. I simply offer a glance that cannot be resisted."

"Then you film them for a porn site."

"Really?" Simon said mockingly. "I do no such thing. What transpires between two adults in the privacy of their bedrooms, whatever acts of deviancy they chose to perform, is of no concern to me. Neither is it if those acts end up on the internet. We do live in a very exhibitionist culture after all. Who are we to say what's wrong?"

"But those girls were under mind control! There's no choice involved, they were coerced!"

"So you say. And I'm sure you would like to believe this, but the evidence doesn't support it."

He flipped his phone around to show her what he'd been looking at. It was her. The video with Scott and Tommy. She was being passed back and forth like a basketball, moaning in grainy, tinned sound.

She hit the door. It fell open behind her. She tumbled backwards to land hard on the floor. He walked towards her, brandishing the phone like a talisman against her rage. She crawled away, unable to face the horror of what had happened to her.

"You see? Where is the lie? Where is the coercion? You were enjoying this."

"No. No, I wasn't. Not in a million years. Not like that. Not–"

"Look. Listen. This is who you really are. The music simply released it."

"NO!"

"I am a manager of popular entertainers, nothing more. You are angry and regretful over your own personal encounters with such entertainers. You have come to understand that you are nothing more than a common whore who–"

"No!" She lunged to her feet and dove at him, trying to shut him up, desperate to knock the phone out of his hand. She grabbed his wrist and tried to bend it against the joint. He was much stronger than he looked. He pushed the screen closer to her, forcing her to see it all. She shut her eyes, tried to fight against his overpowering strength.

"See how you crave their manhoods. How you begged for–"

Then it was all so obvious.

She kneed him as hard as she could in the balls.

He coughed, his grip relaxed. He dropped the phone. He moaned and slowly fell to his knees. She looked at the phone on the floor, facing up, the video staring right back at her.

"That wasn't me. You all took something away that I can't get back. You exposed something I never wanted. And I won't let you do it to anyone else."

She stomped down hard on the phone, shattering it cleanly in a flash of sparks. The video died in a splash of circuits and

CHAPTER THIRTY

chips. She felt a wave of relief wash over her. She knew it wasn't gone, but she'd moved past it now. She hoped.

She turned to the bent-over Simon, looking down at the hunched and moaning figure and seeing nothing but a predator. She reached for the chain around his neck.

"Thank you, boys, for coming."

Simon looked over to the door behind them. Sam turned to see Joey, Nazim, Freddy, Theo, and Anthony pushing through the door from the recording room to enter the sitting area one after the other. They formed a line facing her, five formerly pretty boys with greying gelled hair and expensive collared shirts.

"I trust you will deal with her in the manner she deserves."

The band had the dead-eyed look of being under the spell of a heartstone. Sam noticed that Karlsson's hand was up under his shirt. He had to be holding onto the gem. If she could only get it, she could break his control over them and stop this before it got worse.

She saw her friends in the recording room, bound with cable, looking plaintively towards her. Avital mouthed something that seemed like, "I'm sorry." The engineer stood shell-shocked, unable to process what was going on.

Simon slowly rose up. "I think our website could use a new video, perhaps five on one, or gang bang, or however it is you young people refer to it. I'm sure you will enjoy it in your own way. If not, you will at least never forget the experience."

He smiled.

She lunged for the shirt, was only a foot away when something stopped her in mid flight.

"Do make sure it's painful," Simon said and left the room.

Joey held her by the shoulder, squeezing so tight she was

losing feeling in her fingers. The others were slowly closing the circle, surrounding her. She'd be up shit creek if she didn't act fast. She held up her hands in submission, hoping to throw them off guard. "Look, fellas, we don't have to do this. If you just let me go now, no one has to get hurt."

They said nothing. They were no longer in control.

"Suit yourself," Sam said.

She thrust out her hand, fingers bent in a blade, hitting Joey square in the throat. She heard the crack of windpipe, his hands flew up to his neck and he made a sick gargling sound, desperately trying to breathe.

This was her chance.

She grabbed him by the collar and rolled back, tossing him over her head into Theo. The two of them went crashing down in a heap. She rolled through to her feet in one smooth motion. Anthony kicked at her, surprisingly fast. She leaned back. The foot just missed her face. He spun with the momentum, throwing out a back-fist, but she blocked with both hands, catching him at the elbow. She thrust forward at the joint, snapping his arm the wrong way with a loud crack.

Anthony's arm dropped, made useless in an instant.

Nazim lunged and Sam jabbed out, hitting him in the nose, stunning him. Freddy leapt over and grabbed her in a headlock, trying to force her down to the ground. She dropped her centre of gravity, basing out, and stepped behind his legs, turning her body to cause him to fall over her. She landed on him and pushed away with both hands on his face, breaking the grip. In class, you'd roll back into an arm-bar and lock the joint, but here, Nazim was trying to punch her in the face, so instead, she bent Freddy's wrist back until it snapped. He should have screamed, but he was mute.

CHAPTER THIRTY

She took a shot to the side of the head from one of Nazim's punches, faster than she had expected. Stars danced in her eyes as she staggered back. Joey, choking, bumped into her. She slipped over his foot, hitting the hard floor as she tried to brace herself.

Theo reached out and grabbed her left foot. She kicked down at his head, but he wouldn't let go. Again and again, as hard as she could. His face swelled up, blood pouring from where she stomped with all that she had, but he still held tight.

Nazim pounced, pinning her down, his heavy body laying on top of hers. She couldn't squirm out, they were too strong, there were too many of them. Freddy slapped her with his limp wrist, not realizing how ineffectual it was.

She heard Joey cough. She saw him jab something into his neck. He had cut the skin in his throat below where she had crushed his windpipe. He was breathing like a cancer patient. His pulped voice box growled something unintelligible, gore sliding down his neck.

Freddy grabbed her behind the back, pinning her arms at her sides. Joey and Nazim slapped and hit her over and over again. Her vision was going dark. She'd been so close. She just wasn't strong enough for five on one in the end. More blows rained down, and then she passed out.

CHAPTER THIRTY-ONE

Sam came to, slowly. Her head was pounding, her vision blurry. She saw what looked like a hotdog staring her in the face. *That's odd...*

Then she awoke fully and panicked. Factor 5ive stood around her, pants around their ankles. Nazim held a camera in his hand filming as they made ready to demean her. Nothing had happened yet, so she could only have been out for a second. She was propped up on the couch, a huge golden record for the Crash Test Dummies *Mmmm, Mmmm, Mmmm, Mmmm* glittering above her head.

Her arms were tied together behind her back with some kind of fluffy handcuffs. She tried pulling, but was stuck fast. Joey's throat hole bubbled a sick sound as he looked at her with dead eyes.

She saw the faces of her friends watching horrified beyond the circle of men surrounding her. They were struggling to free themselves from the cords holding them tight. Avital was shouting something to the engineer, who simply stared wide mouthed.

Erin yelled something, too. Finally, the man nodded and turned to go help them out.

She didn't know if they'd make it in time. Factor 5ive

pounded away furiously, their hands working at an impossible pace. It was only a matter of time, she had to break the handcuffs herself.

"Wake up. Stop. Please."

Nothing.

She was wide awake now. This one wouldn't be so easy to put out of her mind. Cognizant, present, forced. The horror she felt seeing her video flashed back in her mind. That was like watching someone else's movie – there was a distance between reality and memory.

"Stop."

Erin must have felt the same way. What about the shame and humiliation that all those other girls would feel if they knew? Were they already feeling it? How many were there? How many more would there be?

She pulled harder at the handcuffs. She could feel the fuzzy elastic stretching. They weren't police issue, just sex toys. Whose?

Pulling. With all her strength. They strained under the pressure. Five middle-aged men surrounding her. The studio. Knowing Karlsson was still out there. It was too much.

I won't let them.

"I said stop."

She pulled as hard as she could, not just for herself, but for all the other girls out there who'd been exploited like her and Erin. For the ones who had no choice and the ones who made the wrong one. She strained against a world that let a generation of women be abused for another generation of voyeurs. She clenched to stop the cycle of abuse in one small way. For everyone who never wanted something private made public, who was forced to confront the judgement of others, for anyone suffering from the fear that a mistake or past decision would one day return to haunt them. She pulled, twisted and tugged as hard as the five pigs around her. The bonds snapped in a great shower of pink fuzz and rubber. Sam yelled in anger, reaching out for her oppressors' most sensitive areas.

* * *

Marlon sat in a chair, stacking meat onto bread, muttering to himself, refusing to look away from the food. Everett checked the knot on the cords that held the unconscious members of Factor 5ive tight. The engineer wrapped paper towels around the bloody gashes at the backs of their necks.

"That was incredible, Sam," Erin said. "I've never seen anyone move like that. What you did to them. You–"

"I only did what I had to."

"Well, they won't be pulling anything like that ever again," Avital said dismissively.

Sam clutched the small bag in her hand, feeling the stones rolling around inside. "They won't be pulling anything for a long time."

"What now?" Erin asked.

"Karlsson got away," Sam said. "I have to stop him."

"Someone has to be here for the police though, right?" Erin asked. "They're going to have a lot of questions."

"You have Nazim's phone. Everett got some on his, too. There's probably even security cam footage here somewhere," Sam said.

"And you're on all of it," Avital said. "The cops are going to want to talk to you."

CHAPTER THIRTY-ONE

"I just need time. Stall them."

"What if they press charges?" Everett asked. "You beat the shit out of them."

"They won't. The video will show them trying to…"

Avital patted her on the shoulder. "I'm sorry it took me so long to believe you about all of this."

"I understand," Sam said. "It is pretty insane."

"But it's not over."

"No, it's not."

"Then go finish it."

Sam nodded and grabbed the bag of stones pulled from the necks of Factor 5ive.

"Oh Sam, the P in P-O? It stands for Powerful one."

She hugged Avital and Erin quickly and left.

CHAPTER THIRTY-TWO

Frank watched the tall, angular man he now knew to be Simon Karlsson float through the sliding doors into the hallways beyond.

"Funny, he doesn't look like some kind of mentalist pornographer, but then, who really does nowadays?"

The man's clothes were a little rumpled, but he was otherwise unmarked. He wondered if everything had worked out with the girl's plan.

A tinny ping drifted up from his pocket. He pulled out the cheap plastic cellphone he'd been finally forced to buy and saw a message from SAMANTHA.

"He there?"

Frank tapped the letters on the screen, his leathery fingers having a hell of a time getting anything to come out in English.

"Whooville?"

"Karlsson. He got away."

"I justified sawblade himself."

"On my way. Don't let him leave."

"10:40."

He replaced the phone where it could do no harm and checked the screens. Karlsson had disappeared into one of

CHAPTER THIRTY-TWO

the offices. As far as Frank knew, there was no other way out, so he'd know if the man was going anywhere. All he could do now was wait for the girl.

"There's something about that kid I like," he said as he sipped from a coffee cup.

She always seemed to be right in the middle of the crazy and bat-shit stuff that went on in this city. The kinds of things most people didn't even believe were possible. It reminded him of what he was like back in the day. Heck, what he was like now, too. She could be the great-granddaughter he never had, or at least someone to carry on his work when he was ready to finally take that ride into the sunset.

Keep it together, old man, you're too involved to ever retire from this stuff.

Camera three showed him someone riding the elevator up. She wore all black. Her clothes were torn, and she had bruises and bloodstains on her face. Her eyes were determined. She clenched a bag in one hand. He shut off the recording of the security cameras.

"Here we go," he said.

He rose, leaving his taser on the desk. He walked over to the sliding door. He looked away and bent down just enough to allow his passkey to trigger the electronics that opened it. He counted to one hundred staring at his shoes until he felt a slight breeze blow by him. The deed done, he walked back over to the desk, now empty of taser, and sat back down. He watched the screens and saw the black form rushing down the hallway. She moved from one monitor to another. At least she was inside now and there'd be no evidence of what she was going to do. All he had to do was make the call.

* * *

"Yes, it seems like the controlling mechanism still has a few bugs in it."

The voice on the other end of the phone had a million questions, but there wasn't time to answer them all.

"A girl. Yes, a lone girl. She resisted the device. No, I'm not sure how. But she has experience with the process. I understand that shouldn't be possible, but it's true. She traced it to me. No, I don't think she has any idea of the scope of the operation. Of course, I'm doing what I can to stop her. Yes, I understand the severity. Yes. Yes. Very fine. It will be taken care of."

Simon Karlsson hung up the phone. For the first time in a long time, he felt worried. Sure, he was rich and powerful, with deep connections to a secret society with grandiose plans already set in motion, but he had just been confronted by a person who shouldn't exist.

"Doctor Januz will have to go back to the drawing board," he muttered as he moved through the halls. "What good is control if it can be broken?"

He checked his phone again. Still no message from the boys from Factor 5ive. A twinge of worry crossed his mind. Surely they could handle a lone girl?

"Perhaps we could have the good doctor study her to figure out how she resisted the mechanism," he said as he entered the laboratory room. The door seemed to struggle opening. The panel looked like it had short circuited. He'd have to call the technicians in here to get that fixed.

He sent a text to the guys. "Bring the girl here. I have a new use for her."

CHAPTER THIRTY-TWO

Nobody would miss a lone girl. They disappear all the time. They could dissect her and that would solve two problems at the same time.

He stood admiring the wall of brains, preserved in the viscous formula. Each one was a key to a new kind of humanity. Each one held their own secrets. Each one would offer them so much.

He played with the stone dangling from the chain at his neck. The heartstone linked to those inserted into the base of the skulls of each member of his bands. With this he had complete control over them simply by touch and thought. It was so simple. Think and they do. They didn't even need to be golems.

"Your research taught us much, Necromancers. But you were all so short-sighted. Control is power. And we will use it properly."

Black magic, dark science; some might call it evil. Simon called it inevitable. With phase one mostly a success, phase two would begin soon. From there, the future was theirs.

He grinned, imagining the world they would create.

"Soon," he said. "So very soon."

It would be glorious.

* * *

"Security!" a shocked looking girl in a power suit shouted as Sam rounded the corner. In a flash of contact, Sam smacked her in the temple, knocking her out. It was amazing what one could do when one knew the right pressure point attacks. The girl was breathing normally, and Sam dragged her limp form back into the photocopy room.

She rushed into the hall. She peered into each office window looking for Karlsson. He was here somewhere. She saw people sitting at desks, men and women in lab coats working in medical rooms, then, finally she found the door to the examination room.

The lab beyond it that Frank had described was exactly as it sounded, a nightmare melange of brain jars and sterilized equipment, with machines lining the walls. She could see Karlsson inside, his faint blond hair slicked back, tiny round glasses, crisp Italian suit. He stood admiring the jars, oblivious to her watching gaze.

Frank's keycard, that she had so deftly taken from his belt as she ran past, didn't open this door. So she did what he'd told her, tasered the hell out of the control panel. It burst into an explosion of sparks and burnt wiring, opening partway, and she pushed her way in through the half-opened space.

"I see you are again full of surprises."

Karlsson turned nonchalantly, like seeing someone all dressed in black forcing their way into his mad scientist lab was the most normal thing in the world.

"You," she said, pointing an accusatory finger at him. "Your time is up. I'm bringing you in."

"If you are believing this, then you are as senile as the old man."

"We've got you dead to rights. How do you think you're going to explain this place? The videos? Everything!"

"I won't have to."

"As soon as the cops get here you sure as hell will."

"All they will find is one intruder and one confused old man. Both subdued, of course."

"Subdue this," Sam said and lunged with the taser aimed

CHAPTER THIRTY-TWO

right at his chest. She hit him square and pulled the small trigger. Nothing happened. She shook it and tried it again.

"Shit, it must have been shorted out on the door."

He looked down at the tiny black plastic toy, then back to her, eye to eye. There was something sinister in his iris she hadn't noticed, a hint of green that wasn't quite right. "If you are most finished, I believe you've yet to meet my private security team."

She turned to see five shadows standing on the other side of the half-opened door. One reached in and ripped the entire door clean off its hinges. She gasped as the men stepped into the lab. They were hairless, covered in some kind of thick sludge, and moved with robotic jerkiness.

"Scott! Tommy. Vic. Ben. Jose? I thought–"

"You thought you'd what? Cured them?"

Simon reached into his shirt and held up his heartstone. His eyes glowed maniacally. Sam dumped the bag of stones on the floor and stomped on them, shattered the fragile gems into dust.

"Oh, I'm afraid that won't work," Simon said. "These aren't your old friends. Not anymore."

"What did you do to them?"

"Improved them."

"Wait, are these golems?"

Simon nodded. "And I'm in full control."

* * *

Frank watched the clock. Five minutes was up. Time to call in the boys in blue. He grabbed his cellphone and swiped his finger along the screen. The stupid thing wouldn't open. Over and over again. It wasn't detecting his thumb.

"What a piece of crap," he said.

He lay it down on the console and reached for the land line. A huge hand fell on his as he touched the receiver. He looked up to see a glistening wet, completely bald man staring at him. Behind him were two more. They were naked, smooth and hairless, heavily muscled. They stared at him stone faced.

"Uh, guys, you forget to get dressed or something?"

The lead man lunged at him.

* * *

"Scott, Tommy," Sam said, backing away. "Are you in there?"

"There is nothing to reason with, girl," Simon said. "These creations share little with those you knew. Except the desire to do my will."

Karlsson was so confident. He stood holding the gemstone as if he'd already won. Sam backed away from the horrible naked forms of golems made in the image of the guys from Radiant Cyanide. She knew it couldn't be them. They had no tattoos, but the likenesses were uncanny. Whatever sick things Simon was up to here were beyond even what she'd thought. She had to stop him. There was only one way.

"I think you will make a wonderful golem, too, girl," Simon said. "I can think of many uses for one such as you. I–"

She jerked around and charged him. His eyes grew three sizes in shock. He backpedalled, slipped on the floor and stumbled. She grabbed the gem, wrenched it free, shattering the chain. Simon cried out and tried to take it from her hands. She elbowed him in the nose and rolled over her shoulder. She came up in the other corner of the room, brandishing the

CHAPTER THIRTY-TWO

stone.

Simon held his shattered face, blood pouring out between his fingers. "Give me the stone," he shouted.

"Take it," she said.

"Assuredly."

He stepped forward but was held in place. He looked over his shoulder at the Scott lookalike golem gripping him with one hand.

* * *

BLAM.

The naked man didn't even flinch with a three-inch hole in his bare chest. That hadn't happened before whenever Frank had been forced to use old faithful, Big Bertha.

"Jesus, kid, what are you on?"

No blood poured from the wound. The man simply stepped forward. Frank backpedalled. He threw a magazine, then threw a chair. Nothing stopped the thing. The other two followed. He took aim.

"No more warning shots, I guess."

He was set to pop the man's head like a zit when he suddenly stopped in his tracks. The light seemed to fade from his eyes, and he collapsed to the floor. Frank cautiously stepped forward. They all looked dead.

"I guess whatever it was wore off, eh?"

He kicked them gently in the side. They didn't budge. He re-holstered the gun he wasn't supposed to be bringing to this gig.

"Just goes to show that you should always come to work prepared."

He checked the screens, looking for any sign of Sam. He pressed a few buttons until he found the one for the laboratory. What he saw made him almost flinch.

"Good god, girl, what did you do?"

He rose from the desk and went through the sliding doors.

* * *

The room was covered in blood. Simon lay in a heap on the ground, his features pulped. The copies of Scott and the others were torn and ripped into pieces. Her hair was matted with red. Her face was a crimson mask. She panted from exhaustion with her hands at her sides, holding the gemstone so hard that her fingers had gone numb.

"Great Gatsby, girl, this place looks like an abattoir," Frank said behind her.

"I had to stop him. It was the only way."

"Looks like you turned him into chilli sauce, kid. There's not enough to scrape up with an ice cream scoop."

She let the stone fall. It had happened so fast. One moment the gem had been in her hands, the next the golems were tearing Karlsson to pieces. Then they'd turned on each other until there was nothing remotely human left. The stone had reacted to something primal within her. She hadn't even realized what she was doing.

"I couldn't control them," she said. "It was like… an animal instinct."

"There's no way in hell I can get this cleaned up before the cops get here."

She looked at the stone on the floor, covered in blood, glowing faintly. What had been different about this one? Why had she lost control?

"That little thing is the source of it."

"You're not in your right mind, kid," Frank said. "Shell-shock."

"No, I think I understand now. You can't reason with this. You can't ignore it. You have to fight it."

"You did, and you won. Now let's figure out our story."

Sam took her phone out and dialed the police. "People need to know," she said.

"And they will. But there's going to be a lot of questions here you can't answer."

She could only whisper, "It was too evil…"

"I hear you, but I'm not so sure the boys in blue will."

That snapped her out of it. "They're going to think I killed these… So many people."

Frank sighed. He gently patted Sam on the shoulder, soaking his hand in blood. "There's only one way out of this for you."

"Jail?"

"Kid, you have your whole life ahead of you. I'm old. They tell me I'm past my prime and almost done. You get out of here, I'll take the rap for this."

"You?" she asked, confused.

"I can sell this one. They'll give me insanity. Or maybe they'll believe me, who the hell knows? With my record of service, they just might go easy."

"But your career? All the good work you did… they'll just forget it all."

"Most of it was top secret anyway. But as long as you remember what happened, that's all that matters."

She hugged him, soaking him in more blood. He put his

hand on her shoulder in as close to a fatherly gesture as he was able.

"Why?"

"I've had a good life. You go out and do something with yours."

"I don't know what to say..."

"Just say that you won't stop fighting whatever it was that created that." He pointed to the wall of brains. "I have a feeling this place was only the tip of the iceberg."

She'd covered his clothes in gore. She tried to wipe a bit of brain off his sleeve. "I've made a real mess of things," she said.

"Story of my life. Now you get the hell out of here before my old co-workers show up."

She nodded and ran off down the hallway.

* * *

Frank watched Sam leave and took a deep breath. He looked around the room and tried to piece together his story from the body parts and human entrails all over the floor.

"The party got a little out of hand, officers," he said.

He returned to the main room, eyeing the nude bodies laying in a pile. "Really fucking out of hand."

He sat down at his desk and put his feet up, waiting for the police to come.

CHAPTER THIRTY-THREE

"And that's why you ran from the, let me see my notes here, Big Shiny Tunes Recording Studio instead of waiting for the police to show up?"

"I had to get out of there," Sam said to the two detectives sitting on the couch in her dad's apartment taking notes.

"You should never leave the scene of a crime before—"

"What Detective Hooper means is that while you really should have waited, considering what those guys were trying to do to you, it's understandable that you'd want to leave. Your friends stayed, so everything worked out."

The detective with the shaved head furrowed his brow at the woman who cut him off. She was dressed in slacks and a dark purple button-up shirt under her black jacket. Her dark hair caught the light, and she gave off a feeling of warmth with her brown eyes and slightly downturned mouth.

"Detective Tockett is right," the man said reluctantly. "You had cause."

There was something going on between the two of them that Sam wasn't picking up on, but then she was a little distracted. The television was on mute, showing the news stories of the day. The Factor 5ive arrest was all over the place. The band had made international headlines for their attempted group assault on a local River City girl. The press was having a field day talking about the sordid details and what had been turned up on their phones.

"So, are we done now?" Sam asked. "I'm pretty wiped after all of this... insanity and just want to crash."

Detective Tockett looked to Detective Hooper for any objection, but the man just folded his notebook over and nodded slightly.

"I think that's enough for now," he said.

The woman stood up. "Thanks for your help, Miss Abraham. I'll have the trauma team contact you in the morning to help you deal with what happened. They can answer any questions or direct you to services or counselling you might need."

"I think I'm good actually, ma'am," Sam said. "Maybe for the first time in a while."

The woman seemed skeptical as Sam escorted them to the door of the apartment. "It couldn't hurt to talk to someone," she said. "Sometimes these things have a way of sneaking back up on us when we least expect them to."

"I've got my friends," Sam said. "And I've got a tub of double chocolate brownie fudge in the freezer."

"I'm not so sure that–"

Detective Tockett held her hand out and stopped Detective Hooper in mid thought. "Both good supports, but everyone needs more sometimes. Consider it?"

"Deal," Sam said.

She waved goodbye and shut the door of the apartment. She went back to the television and sat down on the couch. She turned up the volume again.

"Our other top story tonight concerns a security guard who

CHAPTER THIRTY-THREE

is being accused of the murder of Factor 5ive's band manager, Simon Karlsson, in addition to at least five unknown others in a downtown office earlier this evening."

Footage of Frank being dragged away flashed on screen. "They're monsters, I tell you. Brain transplanted sex cultists working for–"

His words were cut off as he was taken away in handcuffs.

"The downtown office building was a central hub in the local branch of the international concussion research program. On site, the brains of former NFL, CFL, NHL and professional rugby players are being studied in a cross border, multi-year–"

Sam hit mute and changed the channel.

"Goddamn it. Even dead, Karlsson has an out."

The CBC, CTV, Global, CNN, the BBC. The story was everywhere. Frank's face plastered all over. She felt awful for him. He'd taken all the blame and without any of the rewards. Sure, she'd done her part to end the madness, but he was going to be locked away for the rest of his life.

"He volunteered," she said. "There's nothing you can do for him. No one would believe you even if you told the truth."

She changed the channel again and again, looking for anything to get her mind off this nightmare.

"Here we go, the sports network," she said, stopping. "Nothing here could possibly talk about Factor 5ive or Karlsson."

It was showing footage from the NHL draft. A man in a suit was speaking into a microphone as reporters snapped away. The banner of the River City Jets hung behind the speaker. She turned up the volume again.

"–solid skater, great shot, good hockey sense, should be a real asset."

The image shifted to grainy footage from local games. A player making moves, scoring goals, hitting others. The jerseys looked familiar.

"Wait," she said. "Is that the John A team?"

Stock footage of River City, archival shots of famous Jet players, then the image returned to a wider shot. There were other people at the table with the speaker at the podium. It cut to a shot in the crowd, Rick Hansen, sitting nervously with an awkward smile as the man spoke.

"A hometown story is special. There's a connection with the fans that goes above the norm. It keeps the spirit strong within the community. And that's why the River City Jets are proud to announce that we've decided to draft University of Manitoba freshman Rick Hansen."

Rick leapt to his feet, smiling. He hugged his dad next to him. The camera followed him as he moved to the podium and slid on his jersey. He was given a team hat that he pulled over his gleaming dark hair.

"I'm looking forward to doing my best to make the team and contributing what I can. It's a dream come true to play for the hometown and I hope I won't disappoint the fans."

A reporter off camera shouted out a question barely audible. The team general manager pushed next to Rick and spoke into the microphone.

"We're confident that Rick has made fundamental improvements in his game and the lack of drafting status last year was simply an oversight made by…"

The words faded out when Sam spotted the owner of the River City Jets, sitting on the other side of the general manager. He was nodding along as the man spoke. His hair was black instead of blond, but he had the same angular features, the

CHAPTER THIRTY-THREE

same prominent cheek bones, the same aristocratic air; he was the spitting image of Simon Karlsson.

"What the hell is going on?" Sam said as words from pundits spoke over the footage.

"...an entry level deal with the goal of him reporting immediately to the team for the coming season."

"...seeing what the kid's made of."

"...a real blue chipper!"

"Gamble or publicity stunt?"

"...averaged two points a game in league play..."

"...questions surrounding the signing..."

The man watched silently. There was a slight bulge in his shirt, a golden chain around his neck. It couldn't be...

Pundits, players, fans, random people on the street; everyone had something to say. She didn't hear any of them, she could only see that whatever it was she'd thought she'd stopped, was only the tip of the iceberg. Karlsson had a twin brother, or maybe they were golems, too. He was somehow involved with the River City Jets. Her old boyfriend Rick was walking into something he had no idea about. How far did this thing go? Who was really pulling the strings?

There was only one way to find out. Samantha Abraham was going to become a hockey fan.

TO BE CONTINUED

About the Author

Author, filmmaker, martial artist, collector, gamer, dad; Winnipeg based I.D. Russell has been crafting a shared universe of books and films for the past decade and a half. Beginning with the feature films *The Killing Death* and *Cybernetic Showdown* and continuing with the *High School Hell* and *Revengist* book series, his crazy comedy/horror/action stories have found an international audience. *Rock 'N Roll Nightmare* is the first book in the *River City Hell* Series and the latest project expanding the world of River City Police Officer Frank Malone and University student Samantha Abraham. The next six books in the series have been written, so plenty more is on the way!

Check out *The Killing Death* and *Cybernetic Showdown* now streaming on Amazon Prime, Tubi, Vimeo, and Gumroad. Visit the YouTube pages *Ringo Jones Productions* and *Jeremy Sockman Movie Reviews* for additional content or click to www.ringojones.com to stay up to date on all upcoming work!

Follow on Facebook, Twitter, Instagram, and YouTube!

You can connect with me on:
- http://ringojones.com
- https://twitter.com/IDRussellAuthor
- https://www.facebook.com/IDRUSSELLAUTHOR
- https://www.instagram.com/idrussellauthor
- https://www.patreon.com/ringojones

Subscribe to my newsletter:
- http://ringojones.com

Also by I.D. Russell

The story of Frank and Samantha expands in:

Heart of Stone (High School Hell Book 1)
It's bad enough being the most unpopular girl in school, but when a strange new exchange student shows up, Samantha Abraham discovers she may be in love with a golem.

It was love at first sight for Sam when Joshua, the dark and mysterious foreign student from Eastern Europe, walked in to class. He's dreamy, great at hockey, and she's landed the chance to be his tutor. But the more time she spends with him, the more he seems to harbour a sinister secret. It's starting to look like he's a criminal, but he might also be a monster . . .

With the help of her over-zealous, secretly- crushing BFF Duckie, and with the popular girl bullies nipping at her heels, Sam must go up against a bunch of weird science, and a hellish high school social life, before she has a remote chance of a first kiss . . . or of surviving the Halloween dance.

Heart of Clay (High School Hell Book 2)

Samantha Abraham has the power to magically control her boyfriend's every action, but now someone wants that power—and wants him dead.

After the fallout from Heart of Stone, Sam has learned the truth: that her boyfriend, Joshua, was created in a lab by a mysterious scientist known only as The Professor. A magical ruby gives her the power to control him by thought. It seems like the perfect relationship, until a gauntlet of assassins show up in River City with murder on their minds.

On a quest for the truth that takes her to Toronto and into the den of her enemies, can Sam, Duckie, and hockey-hunk Rick save Joshua's life before it all goes to hell?

Heart of Flesh (High School Hell Book 3)

Samantha Abraham lost everything when she lost Joshua—but the fight for the ruby, and what it means, isn't over yet.

Sam is back in River City and the events of Heart of Clay have left her raw. If deranged necromancers were bad, you'd think Debbie and her slugs would be small potatoes, but Sam's life has gone straight back to hell in her senior year. Even with her high level hapkido skills, and a budding relationship with hockey hunk Rick Hansen, nothing seems to fill the gaping hole that Joshua and Duckie's disappearances have left . . .

But just as suddenly as he vanished, Joshua reappears with grave tidings, and Sam must decide what lengths she'll go to prevent her life—and her boyfriend's body—from falling apart.

The Killing Death

He was ready to retire but then a madman started leaving victims in pieces. Can this aging cop solve one last crime before a killer finishes his deranged pizza?

When an unhinged pizzeria owner stumbles on an ancient Egyptian ritual, he begins a spree of brutal killings that leave a city in shock. It's up to veteran detective Frank Malone and his rookie partner to piece together the clues and catch the murderer. One problem, this isn't just a simple case of catch the bad guy, it could resurrect long dead spirits of evil.

With Egyptian magic, action, gore, and an insane ending you won't believe, this comedy/horror book is a wild good time!

Under Blood Lake

Somewhere in the darkness below the surface of Lake Winnipeg, the Deep Ones are waiting.

He thought it was just a simple weekend trip to put his brother's affairs in order and lay him to rest, but when River City's toughest cop shows up in the sleepy harbour town of Lakeshore, he unwittingly steps right into a community suffering under an ancient curse. Someone is pulling the strings and suddenly he's got bigger fish to fry. Off duty, without a weapon and under orders to stay on vacation, can Frank survive when he faces up to creatures more inhuman than real?

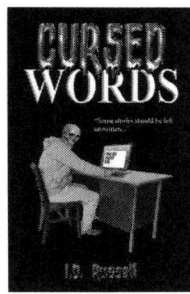

Cursed Words

Some stories should be left unwritten...

Fifty years ago the Van Lundgren estate was the sight of unspeakable acts of evil. The truth has been long buried and forgotten. Now, the house is re-opening as a bed and breakfast and twelve souls show up for the weekend. But some crimes transcend time and when a raging thunderstorm traps them inside, the guests start dropping one by one. Soon the survivors are going to learn that some horrors can never truly be locked away.

Trapped in a nightmare, there's only one truth...

Sticks and Stones may break your bones but Cursed Words can KILL YOU!

Drug Wars Part 1: Lethal Dosage

Yellow Sunshine. More addictive than opium, more potent than cocaine, more dangerous than heroin. It ruins lives, destroys communities, and threatens the very country itself. It will take the River City police force everything they have to fight the scourge from street to bloody street.

Someone's dealing the worst drug the city has ever seen. THE REVENGIST is on the case with a brand new partner and a list of broken lives he's going to avenge. But to find the source of the poison, they'll have to go so far undercover that they might never make it out alive.

Drug Wars Part 2: Blood Money

MechaMountie. The secret CSIS project in cybernetics set to revolutionize the world of law enforcement. Stronger than ten gorillas with a brain faster than twenty IBM computers, the robot is laying down the law in a city under siege!

After the death of Eddie Camponelli, River City is in chaos. Rival gangs are shooting up the streets, attempting to gain control of the drug trade. The police are powerless until the government sends in their top secret weapon.

Now THE REVENGIST is in for the fight of his life to prove that no robot can do his job better than he can. He's going to show that he's still got it, even if it kills him!

Drug Wars Part 3: Iron Curtain

Ninja. The silent assassins. Using ancient martial arts techniques passed down through the secret orders of hired killers, they stalk by night and murder without a trace. Now they've come to River City and it's not to sightsee!

He might have killed the world's biggest drug supplier in Carlos Mendoza, but that only made the real bad guys mad. Now they're after him with everything they've got. In an all out battle for the future of Canada that spans the globe, THE REVENGIST is in a fight for more than just his life!

The explosive finale to the Drug Wars trilogy!

Go-Team # 1: Bitter Rivals / African Assault

The old Go-Team is gone, long live the All-New Go-Team. Led by Jessica "Doll-face" Dawes; they're sent in to infiltrate a tiny African nation in the throes of a bloody civil war. Their mission: to try to preserve the peace in the face of a brutal warlord.

But are the supreme sniper Brutal-Suzy and the kung fu assassin Hunglo enough to take on the American's better equipped, highly public, no-so-secret commando team: Uncle Sam Squad?

It's a battle between Bitter Rivals for the right to save Baangolo in an African Assault full of action, suspense, and... spring break?

Manufactured by Amazon.ca
Bolton, ON